The Crypt of the Ancients

The Crypt Trilogy: Book Two

Bill Thompson

Published by
Ascendente Books
Dallas, Texas

Books by Bill Thompson

Brian Sadler Archaeological Mystery Series
THE BETHLEHEM SCROLL
ANCIENT: A SEARCH FOR THE LOST CITY
OF THE MAYAS
THE STRANGEST THING
THE BONES IN THE PIT
ORDER OF SUCCESSION
THE BLACK CROSS
TEMPLE

Apocalyptic Fiction
THE OUTCASTS

The Crypt Trilogy
THE RELIC OF THE KING
THE CRYPT OF THE ANCIENTS
GHOST TRAIN

The Bayou Hauntings
CALLIE

Middle Grade Fiction
THE LEGEND OF GUNNERS COVE

DEDICATION

This book is dedicated to three loyal and faithful friends
who sit in my office by my side every single day
for months as I write.

Sometimes they're nice and quiet,
as well behaved as you could ever ask.
Sometimes they make so much noise I can't work.
Mostly that's when the postman comes around.

I love and appreciate you, Katie, Brother and Sister – three
four-legged kids who make our lives happier and more
meaningful.

CHAPTER ONE

The state of Chiapas, Mexico
Present Day

The rebel who stood in the front of the bus wearing a ski mask and holding a machete terrified the tourists. What had been nothing special twice today was different this time. The masked man had come on board first, glaring with dark, fierce eyes at a group of intellectuals who had paid to visit archaeological sites. A second man stood at the bottom of the stairs in the open doorway of the bus, his finger on the trigger of a Kalashnikov rifle.

This all started as just another routine checkpoint along Highway 199, the road to Palenque. Zapatista rebels occupied much of Chiapas, Mexico's southernmost state. Roadblocks were designed more to irritate the local police than to intimidate the populace. Masked men with automatic rifles had stopped the driver and thirteen passengers on the modern private bus twice already this morning. When the rebels boarded the bus, they saw a Mexican driver and thirteen foreigners on an archaeology mission and accepted a few pesos for their cause. They left and the group continued toward the ancient Mayan city of

Palenque. Each time it had taken only minutes from start to finish. This time it was different.

As far as the tour participants knew, only three people on the bus were fluent in Spanish. The driver spoke no English. Two others, a local guide and the archaeologist who'd been hired to accompany the group, spoke both English and Spanish. When the rebel boarded, he'd said something to the driver, who muttered a coarse vulgarity in response and looked away. Suddenly the man spoke again. Everyone heard him, including those who didn't speak his language. There was no mistaking his intention. He spoke in a cold, harsh tone and his eyes blazed furiously. When he stopped talking, the driver spat on the floor near the man, turned off the engine, removed the key and handed it over. From his seat immediately behind the driver's, the archaeologist heard the exchange of words. He observed the driver's defiance and heard him curse at the rebel. Then came the clipped words of the man with the knife. "Turn off the bus and give me the keys, you fool. This isn't about you, but I'll kill you if you cross me again."

Hoping to diffuse this situation quickly, Dr. Mark Linebarger, the archaeologist, jumped in and spoke calmly in Spanish. "We have no issue with the Zapatistas. I'm guiding this group of Americans on an archaeology tour. How about we donate a hundred pesos to your efforts and wish you success? Then we can get on to Palenque before the sun is too hot!"

The people on the bus would never forget the horrifying scene that happened in the next ten seconds. Everyone had read this situation incorrectly. This wasn't another routine Zapatista roadblock at all. It was anything but.

The driver handed over his keys, figured this was a hijacking and decided he wasn't going to let it happen. He'd be fired if his employers lost a brand-new tour bus, so he made a snap decision. While the archaeologist talked to the masked man, the driver slowly moved his left hand down alongside his seat. He'd stuck his old .22 pistol in a pouch just in case of something like this. You never knew what could happen in rural Mexico, and it paid to be ready. He was ready, but not for what happened. Unfortunately for the driver, things went wrong in an instant.

As Dr. Linebarger watched helplessly in what seemed to him like slow motion, the driver brought the pistol up in a sweeping move. He had it across the steering wheel and almost aimed at the masked intruder when the man noticed it.

A single swoosh of the rebel's two-foot-long machete cleanly severed the driver's head. It hit the floor with a noticeable thump that every single one of the stunned passengers heard clearly. Held in place by a seat belt, the driver's body remained upright. The hand holding his gun fell limply to his side and dropped the pistol. It landed on the floor near the head.

Then the screams began.

CHAPTER TWO

Half an hour earlier this busload of archaeology enthusiasts was motoring down a two-lane paved highway on the way to the Mayan ruins at Palenque. Two days ago they'd all met in Villahermosa, Tabasco. They'd spent two nights at a rustic hotel and visited nearby ruins at Comalcalco and La Venta. This morning after breakfast they boarded the bus that would carry them to other archaeological sites over the next several days.

Ten passengers had paid around three thousand dollars each to Crestmark, a Durango, Colorado-based company that specialized in archaeological adventures for armchair explorers. Over the years, the quality of these tours had earned the company a sterling reputation; nowadays their groups often included academics and professionals in the fields of archaeology and anthropology. Today's was no exception. In addition to Mark Linebarger, the trip's hired archaeologist, there were three professors, a surgeon, the retired director of the Texas Archaeology Society, a PhD candidate in archaeology and several amateurs. Everyone wanted to visit the ruins. It was a diverse group, but these tours thrived on diversity. It kept things interesting.

The paying customers consisted of seven men and three women seeing ruins in the southern states of Tabasco and Chiapas. Over ten days they would visit five important sites. In addition to the ten, there were three others who were on staff. Ted Pettigrew, the tour director, was a man in his thirties from Durango who led the group's activities and kept things running smoothly. Mark Linebarger, a renowned professor of archaeology from the University of Toronto, was paid to come along and enhance the experience for the guests. And there was Julio. He was a native of Villahermosa who spoke fluent Spanish, English and Mayan. Julio fulfilled the government's rule that a local Mexican guide be along when they visited the ruins. The fourteenth person on the bus was Manuel, the driver from Mexico City who had picked up his passengers in Villahermosa.

When they returned from the Olmec ruins at La Venta yesterday afternoon, they had a welcoming reception and dinner. These receptions were always interesting and fun – everyone stood, gave names, occupations and said why he or she was on the trip. Later over cocktails and dinner, several people paired up with new friends and got to know the people they'd be spending ten days with. Although most of the group were singles in their thirties, there were two couples – Warren and Mary Spence and Win Phillips and Alison Barton. The Spences were in their seventies. Win and Alison weren't married – they had only been dating a few months.

After breakfast they had boarded the bus for a three-hour trip to the beautiful ruins at Palenque. Tonight they would stay at the Palacio Hotel, built in the 1600s as a conquistador's hacienda. In only two hours they had already been stopped twice at makeshift rebel checkpoints.

Zapatistas controlled a good deal of this occasionally volatile Mexican state. Angry at the federal government for years, the group wanted the state of Chiapas to secede from Mexico. The officials responded by ignoring their occasionally disruptive behavior.

Some passengers grumbled about more delays as the bus had once again slowed to a crawl, then stopped for the third time. At the last two stops, the rebels had blocked the highway with rusty green tanks they'd stolen from armories, but there were no vehicles this time. Two masked men stood in the middle of the road, one with an automatic rifle and the other holding a machete. The bus driver erred on the side of caution and stopped. He wouldn't have run them down anyway; the rebels were a nuisance, but everyone in Chiapas knew they were basically harmless.

"Why don't the police come out here and stop this nonsense?" Mary Spence asked impatiently.

The guide Julio responded cheerfully, "It won't take long. These are my people, protesting a lack of concern by the federal government. They mean us no harm."

Those words couldn't have been further from the truth.

CHAPTER THREE

"Oh my God!"

"He's going to kill us all!"

"Stop him! Stop him, somebody!"

These were the terrified, unbelieving, piercing screams of people whose lives were transformed in seconds.

There was pandemonium as the horrified passengers watched blood first spurt, then dribble from the headless body strapped in the driver's seat. The sickly smells of vomit and involuntary human excrement spread as quickly as the panic. Mary Spence, recently retired and sitting beside her husband, Warren, fell into the aisle in a dead faint. He leaned into the aisle to help her.

Ted was the leader of the group and a vice president at Crestmark, the tour company. He sat in the right front seat and struggled to avoid throwing up. The man with the machete stood directly in front of him, so close Ted could have touched him. The driver's body was two feet away. He thought it strange that he felt more responsibility than fear. He'd never been remotely close to danger, but he was in charge of this group. He had to be strong for the others. His mind raced to create a plan. Presuming the passengers had any time left for planning. There was no telling what this madman wanted or what he'd do next.

The rebel stepped around the head on the floor and spoke to the archaeologist. *"Decirles que dejen de gritar."*
Tell them to stop screaming.

"What'd he say? What does he want?" Ted hoped for something, anything that would thrust him out of this horror and back into reality.

"He says make them stop screaming."

Ted stood, faced the group, and held open palms before him to calm them. His voice trembled as he struggled for words that would calm them.

"Everyone, listen to me. We have to stop the noise. What we've seen is horrific, but he's telling us to be quiet. This is crazy. It's impossible to imagine. If we're going to survive, we need to do what he says, and do it right now. We can figure this out later. For now, please be quiet. We don't want more trouble."

As best they could, the passengers complied. Gasping sobs of anguish and fear continued, but the bus got dramatically quieter. The only voice was Doc Spence soothing his wife, who had recovered from her fainting spell.

Using the archaeologist as his interpreter, the masked man told the passengers to hand over their cell phones. He knew each of these gringos had one, and his accomplice gathered them into a bag and brought them to the front of the bus.

The man in charge handed the machete to his partner and took his gun instead. "Diego, get rid of the phones," he barked in Spanish. He gave more instructions, and then Diego left. He went into some nearby bushes, stayed a couple of minutes, and returned empty-handed.

Then everyone heard an engine start and saw two men drive away in a pickup that had been hidden in the jungle.

"What are they doing?" Ted quietly asked the archaeologist.

"He told Diego to have the pickup driver go to the meeting point and wait –"

"Silencio!" The man swung his rifle around and shouted again. *"Silencio!"*

Mark stopped mid-sentence and shook his head. There would be time to talk later. Hopefully.

Ted stood and said, "If it's money you want –"

"SILENCIO!" The man punched Ted so hard in the face it knocked him backward into his seat. The passengers watched in horror, gasping as the group leader they'd known less than forty-eight hours nursed his wounded jaw.

Their captor talked to Mark in rapid Spanish. Julio, the local guide who sat behind Ted, lowered his head as he listened. This horrifying episode wasn't coming to an end. The nightmare had just begun.

CHAPTER FOUR

At the cocktail party and introductory briefing in Villahermosa two nights ago, everyone laughed during introductions when a man in his forties with a pleasant British accent spoke. He said he was Gavin Michaels, a Brit turned American citizen who'd lived in Rosemary Beach, Florida for years. He was the author of more than twenty archaeological mysteries.

"Who knows? Each of you may be in my next book!" he said with a grin. A few people nodded to each other – they'd recognized the author's name.

Paul Silver's turn was next. He told the group he was an American from New York, living temporarily in Villahermosa and working as a consultant for the Mexican state oil company, Pemex. He said he was particularly interested in the Olmec culture they'd seen at La Venta today. Paul was a handsome guy in his thirties with striking European features. His olive complexion gave him a perpetual tan. Hailey Knox was the only unattached female in the group. As she listened to him, she decided she wanted to know more.

When it was her turn, Hailey told the group she was twenty-seven, working on a PhD in archaeology with an emphasis on Egyptology at UMC, the University of Marin

County, and she lived in Napa, California. "I know some of you are fluent in Spanish," she joked, "and I'm fluent too – but in hieroglyphs! I know, I know – it may not be too helpful here in Mexico, but if we find a room full of glyphs, I'm your gal to interpret them! And maybe we *will* find hieroglyphs here!" Those last words were in a conspiratorial whisper. She laughed and several others did too.

The next morning she went through the breakfast buffet and headed directly to the table where Paul sat with a young couple, Win and Alison. Hailey had met them last evening over cocktails.

"May I join you?"

They all responded cordially; Paul pulled out a chair next to him, thinking how sexy this lady looked. He'd noticed her last night at the intro party, but this morning she looked absolutely bewitching. She wore a tight-fitting cotton shirt with long sleeves rolled up, a pair of shorts that accentuated her curves perfectly, and her legs looked like they went on forever.

Unaccustomed to these feelings, Paul snapped back to reality. He prided himself on always being in control, especially when it involved emotions. For years he hadn't allowed himself to become close to anyone. Sex was one thing, but for him sex didn't involve a relationship and it wasn't intimate. It was a single, solitary moment of release.

Aren't you getting a little ahead of yourself? He smiled at the thought. *I'm already thinking about sex and I don't even know who she is.*

There was something about Hailey Knox that was different. She was captivating. He'd have to be careful – he always was. In Paul Silver's life there was no room for mistakes … or commitments, for that matter. But still …

14

As they ate breakfast, Paul asked Hailey what she meant about hieroglyphs in Mexico. Did she really believe that they might be here somewhere?

"Actually, yes." Her answer surprised Win and Alison but not Paul. She said she'd come here to research a theory about Egyptians having visited the area in pharaonic times. "If they came, it stands to reason they recorded their visits. They were prolific with glyphs both in Egypt and in neighboring countries they seized. Why not here?"

"Really?" Paul replied, wondering if she was working on the same ideas he was. "Egyptians in Mesoamerica? Isn't that a stretch?"

"I don't think it is. Remember all those Olmec heads we saw at La Venta yesterday? The Olmec people undeniably had seen Africans – right? They didn't dream up the facial characteristics that are shown on those statues."

"Obviously. But Egyptians don't look like that ..." He was pushing to get more information, to see if she knew what he did.

"I have a theory that's also the subject of my thesis. I don't want to bore you – my friends say I get a little tedious when I start in on things I love – but if anyone's interested, get with me this week and I'll tell you more!" She flashed a big smile and went back to her breakfast.

Paul was absolutely interested. A beautiful woman with an unusual theory. He was beginning to think Hailey might cause this trip to be more entertaining than he'd expected. And her theory – Egyptians in Mexico – was precisely why he was here as well. He never thought he'd run across someone else on this tour that thought Egyptians might have come to Mesoamerica. Maybe this was a fortuitous coincidence.

Everyone finished breakfast and boarded the coach for the several-hour trip to Palenque. Hailey deliberately waited until Paul climbed on board. He picked a window seat and noticed she was standing in the aisle right behind him.

"Care for some company? I want to know more about why you came on this trip and about that falcon amulet you're wearing!"

"Sure!" *What the hell. It wouldn't hurt to see what she was all about. He wanted to hear her Egypt-Mexico theory anyway. As far as the amulet went – he'd lie about that. She'd never know it was a flash drive.*

She smiled as she settled in for the bus ride. *I'm not going to drop the rest of my theory on him just yet. Better to break my ideas to him slowly so he doesn't think I'm a loony. I can't even publish my conclusions in my thesis – they'd laugh me out of the doctoral program for the stuff I've found out about Atlantis!*

CHAPTER FIVE

Although almost everything Paul had said when it was his turn to talk last evening was a lie, the part about his burning interest in the Olmec culture was true. He particularly wanted to see the ruins at La Venta and to pick Mark Linebarger's brain. The Toronto archaeologist was recognized worldwide for his knowledge of the Olmecs, and he'd published six books about the mysterious people and their statues with such unusual physical characteristics.

The Olmecs were known for their carvings of huge stone heads. Some of these colossal stones were twelve feet tall, and all bore distinctively African facial features. Although no one knew for certain, most people believed that people of African descent must have visited Mesoamerica long ago. There would have been no other way for the jungle-dwelling Olmecs to know African people even existed.

There was something else Paul wanted to explore, something he'd come across purely by accident in his research. It would require a side trip to a rarely visited site far down the Usumacinta River. For over a year he had been investigating a possible connection between the Olmec people and the Mayan city of Piedras Negras. Paul was onto something that might link them in a very strange way. Something very important might have been hidden in the jungle city, brought by visitors from a faraway land, a people whom the Olmecs used as models for their African heads.

It would have been simple for Paul to have gone to Toronto, met with Mark Linebarger in person, traveled to Mexico on a private jet to visit La Venta, then hired a guide to go to Piedras Negras. He had the means to do whatever he wanted, and his real occupation left him plenty of flexibility in his schedule. Paul had chosen anonymity in his quest to find an Olmec-Africa-Mayan connection. If his theory could be proved, it would be a major historical discovery and would shock those who wouldn't accept anything outside what they could touch and feel. He had to be careful not to attract attention to himself, so he joined an archaeological tour and lied about who he was. The man who called himself Paul Silver didn't want publicity. The less people who even knew he existed, the better.

The primary reason Paul was on this tour was a journal. He'd come across it accidentally and paid almost nothing for it. He went to Salt Lake City to research the Spanish connection to Mayans who may have intermarried with the conquistadors. While he was there, he noticed an ad in the local paper about an archaeologist's estate sale, and he attended. When he realized the man had been part of the Brigham Young University team in Piedras Negras from 1997 to 2001, he became much more interested in the things that were being auctioned. In the few minutes before the sale started, he pawed through stacks of boxes, ignoring everything else. He wanted to know where the man's notes were. He came across a large box of handwritten journals, gave it a quick look, and took it home for ten dollars. He'd been the only bidder.

A professor named Isaiah Taylor wrote the journals. He was a young and therefore minor member of the BYU team. Paul learned on Google that he'd contracted jungle fever during the 2001 season and died at age twenty-seven a few weeks after coming home to Utah. His parents had put his belongings in a storage unit and paid the rent for years until they decided it was time to let them go. That day's auction was the result of that decision.

Isaiah Taylor didn't have a PhD. Obviously his superiors thought his journals less important than those of the senior members. The important people's notes were in BYU's archives, not in a cardboard box at an estate sale. No one seemed to care what Isaiah Taylor thought.

Paul spent hours reading page after page of boring entries. What kept him going were the occasional snippets that provided a fascinating look into Piedras Negras, one of the most important trading posts in the ancient Mesoamerican world.

Taylor had been a meticulous note-taker. He dutifully recorded everything he and the team saw and did over the fourteen-week 2001 season. Paul skimmed the details about potsherds, crude weapons, eating utensils and bones. He persevered in hopes something interesting would turn up – something that could corroborate a theory he had about the Olmec and Mayan civilizations. From Taylor's notes he learned that the Mayan name for Piedras Negras was Yokib – the "entrance" – because of a massive three-hundred-foot-wide "bottomless" sinkhole. They believed it led to Xibalba, the spirit world below.

Buried halfway through the last journal of the series was the entry that got Paul's adrenalin flowing.

Being this deeply in the jungle, we have endured pests of all sizes, from huge snakes curled snugly around

tree branches three feet from our heads to "no-see-ums,"
tiny gnats that buzz and bite the dickens out of one's
exposed skin. It was a welcome break today when my boss,
Janet Strickland, discovered the entrance to a cave twenty-
two feet below ground level, in the east wall of the sinkhole.
Dr. Houston (the team's director) sent Dr. Strickland and
me down to see what was there. My first impression was it
felt gloriously cool and damp – very inviting given the
oppressive, muggy heat we've experienced.

We found a cavern 7.5 feet high, 10 feet wide and
42 feet long. (Here he drew a sketch of the rectangular
room.) *The walls are rough stone. There is a fire pit in the*
middle, with ash and remnants of wood. In the rear wall is
a hole about 4 feet in diameter that appears to be a tunnel
extending into the wall itself. We don't have time or the
equipment with us to explore it today. Our season is almost
over, so it will be added to next year's agenda, Dr.
Strickland says.

I carefully inspected the walls and floor of this
room and found only one thing – but it was a curious one. I
saw a three-inch ushabti on the sandy floor near the tunnel
at the back. (Here he included a crude drawing of it.) *I have*
never heard of this type of funerary object other than in
ancient Egypt. I showed the piece in situ to Dr. Strickland,
who dismissed it immediately as irrelevant. Her exact
words were, "Don't spend time trying to figure out how an
Egyptian ushabti ended up in a cave at Piedras Negras.
You'll tarnish your reputation – a reputation you don't even
have yet – trying to justify something that couldn't possibly
have come from Egypt thousands of years ago. This thing
was obviously planted here in recent times."

It just doesn't make sense why someone in the
twentieth century would drop an Egyptian ushabti in a

remote cave so deep in the jungle it's unlikely anyone will ever see it. I wish I could pursue whether the object could somehow have ended up here in ancient times, but that's neither the purpose of our expedition nor the way to achieve tenure at BYU. Don't rock the boat, especially with Dr. Strickland looking over my shoulder. So I'm taking her advice. I'm dropping both the idea and the figurine. I'm tossing it into the tunnel for someone else to discover. Who knows – one day another archaeologist may determine it's the key to discovering ancient trade routes between Mesoamerica and Africa!

Taylor's journal was written in 2001, in what was supposed to be the fourth of five dig seasons at Piedras Negras for BYU. It turned out to be their last – Isaiah Taylor never saw Piedras Negras again, nor did any of the others. Even today no one has explained why the five-year project was abruptly terminated a year before its scheduled end. The dean of the archaeology department claimed the sudden withdrawal was due to bandits, political unrest in the area and the like, but those things had been going on for years. They were relatively minor, nothing new, and on the surface they shouldn't have caused a major university to abandon a fully funded expedition a year early. Was there something else?

Paul was captivated. For some time he'd knocked around a crazy theory, and now the notes of a minor archaeologist named Isaiah Taylor might just help prove it true.

He began planning his trip to southern Mexico. First he'd visit the Olmec capital of La Venta on the Gulf of Mexico, then the ruins at Piedras Negras. According to the infrequent visitors, the jungle had now reclaimed the city explored by BYU fifteen years ago. It was a lost city once again. Getting there would be difficult and potentially dangerous these days, but he would do it somehow. For enough money, someone would take him to the ruins.

And so he was here today as just another participant on a Crestmark archaeology trip. His cover as a consultant for Pemex was perfect; it provided just enough information to appear legitimate, but not enough for anyone to check him out. His plan had been to break away from the tour for a day or two when they got to Frontera Corozal. The group itinerary was to visit the ruins at Yaxchilan. He'd hire a boat and go to Piedras Negras instead.

Now everything had changed. They were prisoners, kidnapped by rebels. The others would consider themselves fortunate Paul Silver was along today before this journey was over.

CHAPTER SIX

Since Paul spoke fluent Spanish, he understood the rebels. They hadn't said where they were going, but they mentioned several hours of driving. Once the bus left the main highway and pulled onto a rutted side road, Paul had a good idea where they were headed. So did Ted and Mark. The road only went one place – a tiny village that was on their itinerary for later in the week. This road dead-ended at the river town of Frontera Corozal. If ransom was the goal of their captors, they'd probably either be taken across the Usumacinta River into Guatemala or along the river somewhere, maybe to Yaxchilan. The river went on for miles to the north, but after the ruins at Yaxchilan, there was nothing to see for hours and hours except jungle. In the opposite direction there was no habitation at all for more than fifty miles.

Hailey was glad she had been next to Paul when the hijacking happened. She was terrified but struggled not to let him see her fear. On the other hand, Paul was calm. That eased her mind. He seemed like a good guy and a smart individual.

There's safety in numbers, she thought to herself. *Even though I just met him, Paul's the only person I know on this entire bus.*

Scared, she clutched his arm and nestled up as the bus drove mile after mile in the darkness. He couldn't really respond to her closeness; he was preoccupied just like everyone else. They'd all been violently thrust into a situation none had experienced before – except Paul. Everyone was lost in a million thoughts, a million fears, a million what-ifs. They could be dead in seconds, just like the driver. They had nothing but the here and now.

As he played scenarios in his mind, Paul became aware of a pleasant sensation. Hailey smelled really good. In better circumstances he might have enjoyed the attention of this beautiful young vixen. Even Paul, who avoided commitments, might have allowed himself a weeklong fling. Now those thoughts were replaced by the horror of what they'd already experienced.

Immediately after the hijacking, Paul had switched silently into a persona who hadn't seen the light of day for a long, long time – a person who could respond to the kidnappings and brutal murder. As he sat next to Hailey, her arm locked around his, Paul Silver slipped into the background. His psyche transformed into that of an assassin once called Juan Carlos Sebastian – a man Paul once had been. A man accustomed to danger.

CHAPTER SEVEN

In the 1930s an unassuming man named Edgar Cayce was hypnotized in hopes he could regain the speech he'd lost after a severe case of laryngitis. It turned out he was a clairvoyant; his friends began recording his hypnotic sessions, which they termed "readings," during which he responded to questions. Initially he used his newfound powers to help heal people from illnesses – he was so successful that Cayce has been called the Father of Holistic Medicine.

As the years passed, his trances began to include far more unusual subjects. He talked at length about the origin of the universe, how the pyramids of Egypt were built and the activities of a race of aliens from the star Arcturus who existed in a different dimension. For this and other reasons Cayce was the subject of considerable controversy during his lifetime and afterwards. A devout Christian, he was frequently upset himself by the bizarre things he uttered during his trances. At one point he considered stopping entirely when he felt his supernatural readings were becoming at odds with the Bible he so faithfully read. And yet, skeptics pointed out, he *didn't* stop. He continued spewing out fantastic tales about Atlantis, aliens and "stargates" that were pathways through the universe.

Convinced by associates that his work was beneficial, he kept going. In fact, his volume of trance sessions vastly increased. At the time of his death more than ten thousand readings had been recorded. Those transcripts exist today.

Paul had never heard of this mystic who prophesied during hypnotic trances, but as he researched the ancient history of Mesoamerica, he saw Cayce's name appear over and over in a very unusual context.

During some of his sessions, Cayce stated that the people of Atlantis, aware of the imminent destruction of their civilization, sent emissaries to create Halls of Records where the knowledge of the ages would be deposited. Three libraries, which Cayce claimed were established twelve thousand years ago, have never been found. According to Cayce's hypnotic visions, the first was in an underground cavern near the Sphinx at Giza, Egypt. Another was close to the Caribbean island of Bimini that, according to Cayce, was near where Atlantis itself used to be.

According to the psychic, the third Hall of Records has been hidden since 10,000 BC in Piedras Negras, Guatemala.

Suddenly the ramblings of this long-deceased mystic became much more interesting. Paul was open-minded about Atlantis. Several ancient volcanic eruptions destroyed cities, any one of which might have been the model for Plato's Atlantis. Maybe a technologically advanced civilization existed tens of thousands of years ago – maybe not. Now he wanted to explore the lost city of Piedras Negras even more.

———

Some experts doubt there was interaction between the Olmec and Mayan peoples, but Paul was convinced it was both real and widespread. Their timelines overlapped, their cities and temples were relatively near each other – in some cases less than a hundred miles apart – and their trade routes crisscrossed.

As he studied the origins of the Mayan people, Paul quickly realized there were vast differences of opinion. Several nineteenth-century scholars theorized the Maya descended from Toltecs, who themselves were descendants of a superior race called Atlanteans. That culture imparted technological, astronomical and horticultural secrets.

It was a fact that the name Maya itself was Egyptian. In the eighteenth dynasty – 3500 years ago – a particular high priest of Amun served first under pharaoh Amenhotep III then his son Amenhotep IV, who was later called Akhenaten. That high priest's name appeared on statues and stelae. His name was Maya.

Paul had reached his conclusions logically. The huge stone heads at La Venta were unmistakably African. If the Olmecs had seen these Africans, could there have been others – such as Egyptians – too? Could the Mayans also have benefitted from Egyptian influence? How else did a tribe of Mesoamerican indigenous people suddenly begin to create gigantic stone structures, temples, tombs and royal dwellings that sat atop hundred-foot buildings? Was Edgar Cayce right? Did the Atlanteans visit Piedras Negras and establish a hidden library there? Did their advanced civilization influence Mesoamerican cultures?

Paul's trip to southern Mexico was to have been the first step in finding answers to these questions.

CHAPTER EIGHT

Egypt
1323 BC

Amenhotep IV, the father of Tutankhamun, converted to monotheism five years into his reign as pharaoh. He forced the Egyptian populace to worship only the sun god Aten and changed his own name to Akhenaten, "devoted to Aten." The pantheon of gods the people had loved was represented as various human and animal figures in art and culture. They had protected everyone for millennia, but suddenly everything changed. No one could worship the old gods anymore. It was forbidden.

At the time Amenhotep had his change of heart, Maya was high priest of Amun, the most senior religious person in the country. He refused to go along with the pharaoh's command and was summarily dismissed. He'd been famous – like the king himself Maya's name appeared on stelae and temples throughout the land. Now slaves chiseled it away, ordered by the pharaoh to obliterate Maya's memory. It was a greatly embarrassing, humiliating event, and Maya hated Akhenaten for it.

After twelve years the pharaoh died at last. He was laid to rest in Akhenaten, the new city he'd built as capital of Egypt. His son Tutankhaten became pharaoh, to the delight of the religious community. Although the new king was a monotheist too – his name ended in "Aten" just like his father's – things could finally change. The old ways could be reinstated because the leaders had a special power over the new king. He was a child – a boy only nine years old.

The pharaoh had two advisors, both very powerful men. General Horemheb would lead the military and maintain political stability between Egypt and its allies. Ay was vizier, a sort of prime minister who acted in place of the child as ruler of the people. Ay was truly the power behind the throne and he was also the closest friend of the deposed high priest Maya.

Ay and Maya returned things to the way they had been before Amenhotep's conversion to monotheism. The boy-king became Tutankhamun, losing his "Aten" connection, and Maya was reinstated as high priest with even more power and prestige than before. He oversaw the reconversion of the people to polytheism, and times were good.

The priests were back to business as usual but many, including Maya, detested the child-king and his father for what they had done. Tut may have pretended to embrace the old gods, but he'd ascended the throne as a believer in the sun god just like his evil father. Deep in his heart Maya nurtured the hatred and vowed this pharaoh would pay for the sins of his father. Since these heretics had forced Aten upon the people, he would ensure that the child pharaoh would never ascend to heaven. He'd be doomed to spend eternity in the underworld.

Finally the glorious day came. The king had died nine days before at age eighteen. Today he lay on a slab as the senior priests performed the embalming ritual. They removed the viscera. Four organs would be saved, each in its own canopic jar with a god's head on top. For protection. The chief priest smiled at the thought. This boy, like his father, had worshipped Aten. And now, *for protection,* the pharaoh's organs would be put in jars adorned with heads of the gods he and his father had rejected.

We'll see about protection, Maya thought as his fingers worked through putrid, stinking viscera in the body cavity. Large jars of natron sat around the body. As the last step the salty paste was smeared throughout to soak up moisture and speed the embalming process. Natron smelled almost as awful as the decaying organs themselves; the priests wore linen masks soaked in unguents over their noses and mouths to get through it.

As chief priest, Maya had to ensure the correct organ was placed in its corresponding canopic jar. Those would be placed in the sarcophagus next to the body, to accompany him to paradise. One priest bowed his head and presented Tut's lungs, which Maya solemnly put in the jar with the lid of the baboon-god Hapi. Another offered the stomach – it went into the jackal-headed god's jar. A human-headed god was on the lid of the vase with the king's liver. Last were the intestines, placed in the jar crowned by a falcon. Maya then sealed each and placed them aside.

The priests began spreading the natron. No one noticed Maya reach inside the pharaoh's chest and remove something. He wrapped it in a cloth and slipped it into a cloth bag nearby.

Finally they were finished. "I now place the scarab in the chest," he announced solemnly. He palmed the tiny scarab and leaned over to place it inside the cavity. He replaced the rib cage and the ceremony was finished. No one saw what he had done and no one checked the cavity to ensure the scarab was there. They began wrapping the body in linen for his trip to the afterlife.

The scarab went into the cloth bag too. Maya's work was finished. This heretical pharaoh was going to hell.

———

Maya kept a little vase with the Supreme God Amun's head on the lid hidden in his house. How fitting that a part of Tutankhaten, the boy-king who worshipped only a single god, was now in a jar capped by Amun, chief of the deities he and his father had shunned.

Maya refused to call the dead pharaoh by his newer name, Tutankhamun. He always used the Aten birth name. The king had been dead three months – no one had expected him to die after only ten years as pharaoh, although Maya had prayed fervently for it each day. It was an answer from the gods when the child was gone at last.

The new pharaoh was Maya's closest friend. The vizier Ay, the man who had served as advisor to the boy-king and engineered the return of the country to polytheism, was king now. If not for Ay, Maya would not be high priest today. Ay was not in the bloodline of Tutankhamun; he ascended to the throne by marrying Tut's young widow. It was fortuitous for Maya, who was now set for life in Egypt's highest non-royalty position.

Maya had only one problem – his Amun vase held two things that would doom Tut to hell. If the people ever found out, he and his friend Ay would be executed. Something had to be done with the jar.

Only Ay and Maya knew the secret. Tut had been buried with all the usual pomp and pageantry. His earthly body – most of it – was hidden away in the Valley of the Kings, where it would lie undisturbed for thousands of years.

CHAPTER NINE

Maya sat on the floor next to Ay's throne. The king handed him an ancient piece of parchment with faded drawings and arcane script.

The pharaoh whispered, "This map was given to Narmer, first pharaoh of Upper Egypt, more than two thousand years ago. The people we call the Ancients – the Atlanteans – sailed to a land across a great ocean and created a library there to hold part of their knowledge and records. They called it the Crypt of the Ancients. It is marked here." Ay pointed to a particular spot on the map.

An educated man, Maya knew the legend of the Ancients. Its premise was simple – Egyptians learned their skills in art, medicine, architecture and construction from the Atlanteans. Knowing they faced cataclysmic destruction soon, these peaceful, advanced strangers eagerly taught others what they knew. The first time the Ancients came to this land was ten thousand years ago, long before the Egyptian civilization itself. They built a subterranean library and deposited thousands of scrolls, instruments and tools. Egypt was sufficiently far from Atlantis to survive the eventual destruction of its civilization.

By the time the cataclysm occurred, many Atlanteans had relocated to what was now Europe and Asia, integrating into the primitive indigenous populations and becoming intellectual leaders, teachers and guides. Their knowledge allowed the development of sophisticated civilizations in today's China, Mexico, Central America, India, Egypt, and Turkey.

The people learned how to transport hundred-ton stones many miles, raise them into the air and construct massive pyramids using mysterious technologies of which the general population was totally unaware. While Egyptians were learning how to build pyramids so were the Olmecs, Mayans, Toltecs, Incas and Aztecs, half a world away. One civilization taught all of them – the people of Atlantis. Or so went the legend of the Ancients.

Tomorrow the high priest would begin a journey. He would take the jar to the place on the map, across the legendary great sea. He would find the library – the Crypt of the Ancients.

Ay hugged his friend and wished him well. They would never see each other again. Maya had only a vague idea where he was going and no idea how long it would take. When he arrived in the place where he was destined to hide his secret jar, the gods would tell him.

Maya left Egypt with nearly fifty men. There were horse soldiers, charioteers, common laborers, a chef and a farrier to ensure the welfare of the horses. Artisans and craftsmen, teachers, a master architect and a man who was crew chief for the construction of a pyramid came too. They traveled for weeks, crossing the great western desert to the land of the Libu, now called Libya. Phoenicians were there – seafaring men who were expanding their trade routes all over northwest Africa. Maya was prepared to pay dearly for their nautical expertise. He traveled incognito for safety and the secrecy of his important mission. He was the highest religious figure in mighty Egypt, but he carried the credentials of a wealthy merchant.

They came to a Berber port on the western Mediterranean that was bustling with Phoenicians from the east. There were boats everywhere, and Maya wasted no time putting out word he was interested in hiring a boat. He was directed to the harbor, where ship owners did business in a multitude of taverns and cafés along the docks. People who wanted to hire a boat went from table to table, assessing the captains, the size and capability of their vessels, and the cost of the journey.

At noon Maya took a break from the morning's fruitless interviewing, walked to a nearby café and ordered a meal. He sat outside near the water and watched a finely dressed, prosperous-looking man approach his table. An hour later the search was over. Maya had found what he wanted – a Phoenician captain and crew. The captain said he'd made the trip to the land across the western ocean once before. That was a plus for Maya. He paid the captain half his fee. A few days later he hired a crew of local African men, who began loading provisions for the long journey.

The man Maya hired was a wealthy ship-owner and captain named Paltibaal, which in Phoenician meant "my refuge is the god Baal." The Egyptians considered Baal a pagan deity, but he was god of sun and storms, and his sister was goddess of the sea. Maya decided an extra dose of prayers to Phoenician gods couldn't hurt. It might even help protect them from stormy seas.

The ship sailed in fine weather through the narrow straits that the Greeks would later call the Pillars of Hercules and into the great sea. Once land was far behind them, the captain followed the roughly drawn Atlantean map towards territory many days' travel to the west.

On his other trip Paltibaal had landed in what was today called Massachusetts. He traveled as far as he could up a river and camped at a spot later named Dighton Rock near the modern town of Berkeley. His men drew pictures and wrote words in Phoenician. Two thousand years later experts would argue whether the petroglyphs carved on Dighton Rock were ancient Hebrew or Latin, if indigenous people had drawn them, or if they were simply a hoax. Reverend Cotton Mather mentioned the rock in a book in 1690, referring to its inscriptions as curiosities. No one ever learned what the mysterious petroglyphs really were. No one would ever know the Phoenician Paltibaal and his crew had carved the drawings and words thirteen centuries before Christ.

The ship was tossed in rough seas as they traveled southwest toward the equator. Following the map, they passed near one of the tiny islands that was now part of the Bahamas chain. They sailed in light winds through the Gulf of Mexico.

Six weeks after the voyage began, they spied the land drawn on the ancient map. Maya gave thanks to the gods for safe travel as they sailed into a secluded lagoon that was now called Michoacan in the Mexican state of Tabasco. When the captain saw Indians, he presumed they were the same race as those he'd encountered previously. He couldn't have been more wrong – these were Olmecs. Originally farmers, today they were an advanced civilization structured into a class hierarchy and were already making ornaments and jewelry from jade and obsidian. They had extensive trade routes; although they had never seen Phoenicians or Egyptians, they welcomed the strangers whom they thought were here to engage in commerce. The Olmec leaders were particularly fascinated with Paltibaal's African crew. They had never seen men with such prominent features. They ordered artists to sketch them. Later they'd carve their likenesses in stone to memorialize these unusual men.

Within a few days Maya and his crew had established a camp on the shores of the Gulf of Mexico at a place where the Olmec ruins of La Venta lie today. There were nearly a hundred people, including the Phoenician boat captain and his African crew. Maya's own men waited patiently to learn why they'd come here, but he said nothing.

One morning when they rose, they saw Paltibaal's mighty ship far in the distance. The god Amun had spoken to the high priest, assuring him this was where he should hide the vase, so here they would stay. Maya had sent the vessel back, keeping twenty of the African laborers to help establish a colony. These men were basically slaves, beholden to whoever paid them. They adapted to Maya's leadership and in turn he treated them as fairly as his Egyptian servants. None of those who remained would ever see their homelands again.

Maya explained to his men why they had to stay – to fulfill a secret mission entrusted to them by the pharaoh of Egypt. Even he himself would never return. The men were comforted by this news. There was no question they would obey. They were accustomed to following orders, but the fact that the highest priest in their land was staying too made them understand they were part of something important – a secret mission ordered by their pharaoh and accomplished by Maya.

CHAPTER TEN

The state of Chiapas, Mexico
Present day

As the bus rolled down the highway, Ted reached across the aisle, tapped Mark and said, "We need to feed everyone. Ask him if I can pass out the lunches."

The masked gunman replied, "Do it quickly. Give me and my man a lunch also."

Ted and Mark took box lunches from the overhead storage areas. They went down the aisle, giving lunch and a bottle of water to each passenger. When he got to Gavin Michaels's seat, Ted whispered something. Without a glance at the author's face, Ted moved on down the aisle. Finally he returned to his seat as Gavin started to write a note.

There were settlements – tiny communities – along the road they were traveling. Most were a few shacks, a mangy dog or two, some cows or goats and maybe a horse for transportation. Sometimes you'd see a couple of rickety tables and a few chairs, the local version of a restaurant with authentic down-home cooking.

Gavin opened the window.

"What are you doing?" Dick Mansfield grumbled from the seat behind him. "You're going to let out the air-conditioning!"

"One sec," he whispered.

In a few minutes a cluster of shacks appeared. Locals were standing just off the highway, holding up fruit for sale, in hopes the fancy tour bus would stop and make their day. They could sell more to the people on one bus than they'd otherwise make in a week, but most of the buses were on their way to one ruin or another. They almost never stopped.

Gavin tossed something out the window. It landed on the ground near a little girl in a tattered brown dress as the bus sped on down the highway.

He shut the window and hoped Ted's plan would work.

CHAPTER ELEVEN

Ted had to let the outside world know they'd been hijacked. Someone had to write a note; it couldn't be him because he was in the first row, right next to the kidnappers. Someone else had to do it.

When he'd been allowed to walk down the aisle, Ted asked Gavin to toss a note out the window the next time they saw people on the road. "Put some money inside," he suggested. "Maybe that'll make them feel obligated to help us." He also gave Gavin a phone number.

Gavin's note was in English. Spanish would have been better, but his Spanish was limited to a few words, none of which could convey the predicament they were in. He was succinct but got the message across.

We have been kidnapped by rebels who cut our driver's head off. There are two kidnappers on the bus and thirteen of us. We don't know where we are being taken or why. Call this number and tell them to call the police. Please help us.

He wrote down the phone number Ted had given him. It was the direct line for Ted's boss back in Colorado.

He pulled a rubber band from his backpack. He put the note around a tube of lip balm, wrapped a US twenty-dollar bill on the outside, secured it with the rubber band,

and opened his window. Soon the bus slowed for a set of speed bumps in a settlement. There were people selling things beside the road – he tossed the note toward them.

There was no way he'd know if it was successful or not until … unless … the police showed up somewhere down the road. It was a real long shot since they didn't even know where they were headed.

None of the people selling fruit and vegetables paid any attention to the little bundle tied with a rubber band that was lying in the grass. Litter was a constant thing in this country. Everybody threw stuff all over the place. Obviously a rich person on the bus had decided to throw his trash out the window.

For hours, the little Mexican family had walked to the edge of the pavement every time a vehicle passed by. Each time they hoped to sell something, but no one stopped. The father finally gave up – they never sold much, but today it was nada – nothing. The little girl had gotten tired of lifting fruits up to each passing car, so she set them on the ground. Her father stooped to pick them up and noticed something. It looked like a folded-up piece of American money with a rubber band around it. He picked it up and unwrapped it.

What he found made his day. There was a twenty-dollar bill – more money than they'd made in a week! There was also a piece of paper with words on it and a tube of lip gloss. He looked inside and then tossed the tube on the ground. The note meant nothing to the man because he was illiterate. He didn't even know the words were in English. Thrilled at his incredible fortune, he put the money in his pocket and threw the note on the ground. The wind picked it up and whisked it away.

CHAPTER TWELVE

As the pickup drove away, the masked bandit ordered Julio to drive the bus. It became the guide's unpleasant task to unbuckle Manuel's body and drag it into the bushes. The head was next – the bandit kicked it off the bus like a soccer ball, and Julio vomited as he respectfully picked it up by the hair and laid it next to the man's corpse. He'd known this driver less than two days, but nobody deserved to die like this. He resolved to think of a way out of the hostage situation. He'd wait for the right time. It would come. Their captors would make a mistake eventually.

Mark was astonished at the situation they were in. He'd always felt comfortable in this area of Mexico; it was very familiar to him. The archaeologist had been to this area dozens of times in the past five years, guiding tours or leading university digs. He'd never seen even one act of violence by the Zapatistas. Now and then they would set an old car on fire or block a highway with barbed wire and concrete blocks, but that was child's play compared to today. This morning he'd witnessed an execution.

He thought this looked more like the action of Guatemalan guerrillas thirty years ago than the Zapatistas of today. This could have happened during the brutal terrorist attacks of the 1980s, but incursions into Mexican territory by Guatemalan terrorists just didn't happen anymore. He had no idea who these men represented or what they wanted. What was the motive of this cold-blooded killer who stood three feet in front of him with an automatic rifle, watching the passengers closely through the eye slits of his mask? Was ransom what he wanted? Was he seeking publicity for his cause? Or was there something else behind the murder of one person and the kidnapping of thirteen others?

As the hours passed, the passengers stayed remarkably calm, each lost in thoughts of the day's horrific events and what might lie ahead for him or her personally.

The bandits took turns, one standing and watching the passengers while the other sat on the step. After they'd been driving for two hours, Julio asked the leader for a bathroom break. A few minutes later he was ordered to park the bus. The passengers were allowed off three at a time. Both rebels stood outside and watched as everyone, male and female, was forced to urinate together on the ground beside the bus. Julio thought briefly about trying to flag down a passing motorist but decided it was too risky to bring more people into the equation. They could be murdered too, and anyway he'd seen only three cars in the past two hours on this desolate stretch of road.

Once they were back on the highway, Mark asked the leader in Spanish, "What should we call you?"

"Call me Rolando," he replied with a smirk.

"As in Rolando Moran?" Mark had studied the politics of terrorism in Central America and knew well the history of the border skirmishes between Mexico and Guatemala over the past fifty years. He knew about Rolando Moran, a pseudonym adopted by the head of a

Marxist Guatemalan terror group called the Guerrilla Army of the Poor, or EGP. Moran had died in 1997.

"Ah, an educated man, I see. You know about our region. Yes, call me Rolando. What is your name? Are you the leader of this group?"

Mark said he was a university professor and an archaeologist. He pointed across the aisle and said, "This is Ted. He's the tour director, but he doesn't speak Spanish. It would be best for you to communicate through me."

"Thank you for telling me what is best," the man replied sarcastically.

"So your mission is to hold us for ransom?"

Rolando's eyes turned fiery. "My mission is not your business, Dr. Linebarger. You will learn my goals only when I am ready to tell you. Now it is *best* for you to shut up. I've had enough questions."

About an hour later Rolando told the driver he would be turning left soon. Once they left the main highway, several people on the bus understood where they were going. They were on a side road that went only one place – the Usumacinta River, the border between Mexico and Guatemala. It appeared they were going to the tiny river town called Frontera Corozal.

The twenty-mile trip took nearly an hour on the poorly maintained road. Dense jungle encroached on both sides. Massive trees reaching to the sky blocked the late afternoon sun. Julio turned on his headlights, slowed to a crawl and maneuvered around potholes.

A green hand-lettered sign welcomed them to the town and its one wide street paved with concrete. Dirt side roads led to crude houses with smoke curling from pipes in their roofs. Makeshift shacks along the main road offered fruits or vegetables or cerveza for sale. Men sat outdoors smoking and drinking, and lazy dogs lay on the warm pavement. The local people waved as the bus passed, unaware that this wasn't a typical group of tourists. These people were hostages.

Frontera Corozal was a fairly new town created with one purpose – to facilitate boat traffic. Many people crossed the Usumacinta River every day, heading from Mexico to Guatemala a quarter mile away to work, shop or for some other reason. A similar town was on the Guatemala side, equally poor and equally uninteresting, and boats from there made the same crossings. Even when the river flooded, the crossing took less than ten minutes. All day long boats big and small ferried goods and people back and forth. There were no border guards, no customs inspectors, no records of who came and went from one country to another.

The river also supported one other industry – tourism. Boats carried tourists on a forty-minute ride to see the ancient Mayan site of Yaxchilan. The imposing ruins, situated right along the river on the Mexico side, were beautiful but rarely visited due to the remoteness of both the docking facility and the site itself. Thirty longboats that resembled wide canoes with engines were tied up to a dock that looked as if children had thrown it together. To get to the boats, tourists maneuvered down a cliff high above the water, using a conglomeration of concrete stairs that were started but never finished and sandbags tossed here and there, presumably to help facilitate foot traffic. At last passengers crossed a swinging bridge to get to a rickety dock.

Each boat carried fourteen tourists, who boarded and sped downstream forty minutes to the ruins, seeing imposing jungles and the occasional monkey or crocodile along the way. It was a pleasant ride and provided a good income for the boat jockeys, who sometimes managed fifteen round trips a day.

It was nearly nine p.m. when the bus pulled into a parking lot high above the river. Three hundred yards away was the only sign of activity in the area, the lights and sounds of people at a rustic lodge called Escudo Jaguar. It served as the only rest stop for tourists headed to Yaxchilan. Once you got to Frontera Corozal, you had to spend the night either before or after your visit to the ruins. The town was simply too remote to fit in a day trip and have time to go anywhere else for the night. Escudo Jaguar was the only place for a hundred miles to get a mostly clean room, a functioning private shower, a decent meal and a cerveza or two.

Rolando and his partner ordered Julio off the bus and told him to start unloading bags. As soon as their captors were outside, Mark asked Ted, "You know where we are, right?"

"Sure. Frontera Corozal." They were here together last year, taking a group like this one to Yaxchilan. That time they'd spent the night next door at Escudo Jaguar.

The archaeologist pointed to a truck sitting in the parking lot nearby. "There's the old pickup two of them drove off in this afternoon, but there's nobody in it. What do you think these guys are up to?"

"I've been trying to figure out what's going on. Coming here makes it even crazier. Why would they bring us here?"

Others in the bus heard them talking. "Where are we?" one asked anxiously. "Where are they taking us?"

"We're in a settlement called Frontera Corozal. Just in front of us down a cliff is the Usumacinta River."

Bart Free shouted in desperation, "The Usumacinta? The border with Guatemala? What are we doing *here*?" Free was an anthropologist from UNLV – four years ago while on a backpacking trip his group had crossed the river here.

"Holy crap! Are they taking us to *Guatemala?*" Alison Barton moaned, her stomach churning with fear. She hadn't wanted to come to Mexico in the first place. She was a computer guru working at the Apple Store in Waco, Texas. Her boyfriend, Win Phillips, invited her to join him on an adventure in the jungle, all expenses paid. He was a psychology professor at Baylor and he knew the power of persuasion. Even though she'd met him just a few months earlier, she impetuously agreed on the spot to come with him. But as the weeks passed and the departure date grew nearer, she began dreading everything about this trip even before it started.

You? In the jungle? Are you insane? she'd said to herself after agreeing to come, but she decided to stick with her commitment. He'd already paid the fees for both of them, so he'd be out three thousand dollars if she didn't go. That didn't make her any less apprehensive. She was a city girl, born and raised in San Francisco, and she'd settled in Waco after graduation. She didn't belong in the jungle – she'd known it from the beginning, and now that she was a captive, she realized what an awful mistake she'd made in coming here. She was terrified and began to cry softly. Win tried to put his arm around her, but she pushed him away. She just wanted to be home. By herself. Without Win and without the sickening feeling that she could be the next one to die.

I only met this guy six months ago and I agreed to let him bring me here to this godforsaken place to be murdered? What was I thinking? Dear Lord, just get me out of here and I promise I'll never do anything this stupid again.

She quietly spoke words she hadn't thought of in a long, long time.

"The Lord is my shepherd, I shall not want."

CHAPTER THIRTEEN

Rolando barked instructions to Mark, who translated for the others. As Julio unloaded suitcases from the underbelly of the tour bus, the others picked up their bags. In the darkness and confusion, no one noticed a man retrieve his suitcase and backpack, toss them under the bus, and duck behind it.

Paul wriggled his way underneath the bus from the opposite side, pulled his luggage out, and disappeared into a thicket of trees at the edge of the dimly lit parking lot. There was no doubt Rolando was taking the hostages to the river. There was really no place else to go, and that was exactly what he did. Pulling and dragging their suitcases, the twelve hostages stumbled down the concrete stairway to the dock far below.

The bus engine started up suddenly and Paul ducked down, watching Rolando's lieutenant, Diego, pull out of the parking lot. In less than ten minutes he was back. He'd parked the bus somewhere nearby, probably out of sight of curious passersby.

Diego went down to the dock with the others, and the parking lot was deserted. Paul left his luggage in the brush and skirted around to the cliff, avoiding a couple of overhead lights and hugging the darkness. He memorized the numbers on two longboats that were backing away from their slips, loaded with people. Within minutes they had rounded a bend and were gone. He hadn't been missed. He'd observed Rolando all day long and never saw the rebel count hostages. Whatever Rolando was, he wasn't a professional. He didn't even know how many prisoners he'd taken.

The professional in this situation was Juan Carlos himself. He'd assumed many identities in the past. Paul Silver was the latest and the one he'd hoped to use from now on. This one was easy; on a tour bus people tended to take others at their words. His fabricated tale about a guy from the Northeast working for the oil company Pemex in Villahermosa was accepted without question. And if anyone did a cursory check, they'd see Paul Silver actually was what he claimed. He knew how to create new personas. He'd done it a lot in the past, and this time he'd done it perfectly. Paul was an accomplished linguist, fluent in several languages. His flawless American English made his new identity believable. He not only sounded like a New Yorker, euphemisms and all, he appeared to be one in every respect.

Paul Silver was his name, at least for now. He'd been born Slava Sergenko, a Ukrainian child prostitute turned multimillionaire. That was long ago and that was a name he'd never use again. There was nothing about Slava's life he cared about. Except the money, of course.

He'd used a dozen names in the past. His time as Juan Carlos Sebastian in Prague had been the best of his life. Even now it was that persona who stepped forward when things got difficult. He was Paul Silver, but in situations like this, the assassin in him was plotting and executing the next move.

Since he didn't know where the boats had gone, there was no way to know exactly when or if they'd return. The usual destination from Frontera Corozal was Yaxchilan, forty minutes downstream. But that Mayan site would be alive with employees and tourists by nine a.m. tomorrow. There would be no place for them to hide.

He'd seen extra gasoline cans in each longboat; it appeared they were going much further than Yaxchilan. The kidnappers could have built a camp somewhere along the river, but he doubted it. That would have required a lot of men and backbreaking work. The jungle here was truly a living thing, full of tremendous trees, vines as thick as a telephone pole and a plethora of dangerous creatures. Snakes, insects and animals would make life miserable for anyone trying to hack living quarters out of the dense vegetation.

But one destination made sense – the long-abandoned site of Piedras Negras four hours away by boat. Other than those ruins, there was nothing but miles and miles of uncharted territory and dense, impenetrable jungle on both sides of the river.

They were going to Piedras Negras. Paul was certain of it. He glanced at his watch. Ten p.m. If he was right, if the boats dropped off the prisoners and came directly back, they'd be here by daybreak. He'd be waiting for them.

Paul walked to the bushes where he'd put his luggage, opened his suitcase, and took out the Sig Sauer pistol he always carried. Since he'd joined the archaeological tour in Villahermosa, he'd had no air travel and consequently no problem with a weapon in his bag. All day long he'd waited for an opportunity to get into his suitcase stowed in the hold of the bus. Finally the chance had come. Julio was offloading bags. No one paid him any attention; they were all shaken, scared and trying to find their own luggage. In the darkness, it had been simple to throw his bags under the bus.

The other helpful thing he had was a second phone. Like the others, he'd handed over his phone, but he had another one fully charged and ready to go. The primary purpose of his joining the tour was to go to Piedras Negras, so he'd packed an Iridium satellite phone. Cell service in the vast jungle was spotty, only near the occasional tower put up by Claro, the Guatemalan phone company. His sat phone would work anywhere.

He considered leaving a message at the archaeological tour office in Durango to let them know what had happened, but he decided against it. For now he had nothing to report except his own position. He knew nothing about the motive behind the kidnapping, where the people had been taken, how many rebels there were – nothing.

Getting the US government involved might help save the captives, but it could also backfire. Boats of armed militia searching the riverbanks might spook Rolando. Who knew what he already planned for the hostages, much less what might happen if he felt trapped? Paul had to wait until he knew more. He wanted to talk to the boat drivers. Then he'd handle things himself.

He settled back against a tree and dozed, knowing he couldn't miss the sound of the boats when they returned.

CHAPTER FOURTEEN

One Year Ago
London

Roberto Maas held his breath for as long as he could, fighting the urge to take a huge, enveloping wonderful breath of air. Hot, dense, acrid smoke filled the tunnel almost completely. Every time he involuntarily sucked in a tiny bit of air, literally dying for just one more breath, he instead got the bitter taste of soot. His eyes burned from ash particles. He gripped the ancient iron bars that imprisoned him mere inches from fresh air and freedom. Growing clumps of ash and cinders floating down the passageway fired the hot metal of the bars. The bars scorched his hands.

The man behind him was dead. His hand had gripped Roberto's leg, but now there was nothing. Roberto would be dead too in a minute or so. He'd gotten out of many perilous situations before, but this was the end. How crazy was it that he couldn't break through a set of iron bars the Romans erected over a thousand years ago to block this end of the tunnel? But he couldn't. His strength was ebbing fast. This was almost over.

His lungs were bursting. There was time for just one last thrust, one last attempt, one last try at saving his own life. He was losing consciousness; his brain began to swirl in a dizzy kaleidoscope of color as he ran out of air. Consciousness faded into a soft lightness. *This is what dying feels like,* he thought as he pushed on the bars as hard as he could. Finally he could wait no longer. It was finished. In a second or two he'd have to breathe. In a final effort he stood, backed up, and ran headlong toward the ancient iron bars as he succumbed to the overwhelming requirement for oxygen. When his body hit the bars, he involuntarily sucked in a huge gasp of hot smoky air. He felt a giddy sensation of floating, sailing, falling and falling.

After that there was nothing.

―――――

A bird chirped gaily nearby. Was he in heaven? Doubtful, Roberto thought idly as he struggled to clear his fuzzy brain. He carefully opened first one eye, then the other. It was a painful exercise – they were bloodshot and full of ashes. He lifted his hand to rub them and saw his filthy, grimy, dirt-encrusted skin. It was so black with soot that he resisted putting more nasty stuff into his already throbbing eyeballs.

Roberto was caught in the jumbled branches of a tree. He could hear the Thames River lapping at the shore somewhere close by. He looked down; he was stuck maybe ten feet above the ground. He tested his perch and found it surprisingly secure, so he took a few minutes to think.

The last thing he remembered was the wall of iron bars at the end of the ancient Roman passageway beneath St Mary Axe Street. There had been a fire, he recalled; he and Edward Russell were trapped in the crypt. He remembered running to the end of the tunnel, which from the outside was simply a hole in the embankment a hundred feet above the Thames. The Roman workmen who built it had secured that exit. They wanted the crypt to be safe from intruders. A thick growth of trees covered it over the ensuing centuries; today no one had any idea it was there.

He'd gotten out somehow. He hazily remembered desperately struggling to hold his breath and running with all his strength at the bars, but what had happened next?

He was here in a tree where he must have fallen from the tunnel above. It had been night when they were trapped by the fire – wasn't that right? He thought so, but he couldn't remember. Now it was daytime – he looked at his watch. Six o'clock. Morning or evening? Surely he hadn't lain here twenty-four hours. It had to be six a.m.

As his mind cleared, he listened to the sounds of traffic somewhere above him. Buses were driving in the City of London, hauling passengers to work, everyone totally unaware that one man, Roberto Maas, had almost died but now was alive, hanging in a tree by the river.

For the first time in his life, Roberto Maas was completely free, truly unleashed. He'd reinvented himself time and again in the years since Russia. Despite his efforts, his pursuers had always caught up with him. This time was different. He was dead. He was alive.

CHAPTER FIFTEEN

The hardest part about shedding an identity was dealing with things you wish you didn't have to leave behind.

Roberto Maas had been the latest identity of a man accustomed to recreating himself. He was young, incredibly wealthy and had no family and no close friends. His collection of ancient artifacts was the one joy and love in his life. He was passionate about history, and he had accumulated some truly amazing objects. There was the female pharaoh Hatshepsut's long dagger made in 1478 BC. The unique weapon was sheathed in a golden scabbard and buried with her 3500 years ago. It had been removed by robbers several hundred years after that. A cartouche on the blade linked the dagger to the queen – any museum would have paid millions for it. It was one of thirty relics displayed in a flat in Lucerne that was owned by a shell corporation. That company, one of many Roberto used to hide his own identity, had been left behind along with the artifacts and Roberto's previous personas on that fateful day in London when he got his life back.

The day Roberto Maas died in the fire.

As much as he ran, as carefully as he hid, as much money as he used to create new identities, a few people had always managed to find him. They wanted him tortured in a gruesome, painful manner. Then they wanted him dead, once and for all. He was an assassin – at least that was what Juan Carlos Sebastian was. He was trained to kill without being detected, but he couldn't shake the people whom he'd blackmailed as a teenager. Men pursued him even when the trail ran cold. They were driven by hatred and fear. They'd caught up with Roberto and were probably responsible for the fire that trapped him.

When Roberto had apparently perished in the massive blaze that burned two blocks of St Mary Axe Street in London, he became Paul Silver, an American citizen living in New York City. He performed a corporate and personal makeover as he'd done more than once before. He had safety deposit boxes in a dozen banks around the world. Each contained a wad of cash and everything he needed to become someone else: credit cards, passport and an identity card – everything required for a new life in a new place. Those things were the mechanical parts of becoming someone else, and Roberto had prepared well for this eventuality.

He also had access to hundreds of millions of dollars in cash and had investments worldwide. There were over a thousand separate accounts at banks, brokerage firms, real estate companies and financial services operations, each in a different shell name, each protected by a series of passwords. The access information was securely encrypted and loaded on two flash drives. One was made into an Egyptian falcon amulet that Paul wore around his neck. The other was in a safety deposit box in New Orleans.

He could have lost much of his fortune a year ago in Lucerne. He did, in fact, lose four hundred thousand dollars in a massive theft orchestrated by his second-in-command Philippe Lepescu. The greedy Romanian who was Roberto Maas's financial officer siphoned funds to his own accounts. After his bold betrayal of both Roberto's friendship and his trust, Philippe disappeared, leaving Roberto to change a thousand passwords and put safeguards in place. Almost another hundred thousand dollars disappeared during the time it took to switch everything, but that was nothing to Roberto. What concerned him were the people looking for him – did his cheating partner give them what was required to locate him?

Roberto was betrayed by a man he considered his friend – and he didn't have friends to lose. That wouldn't happen again. He'd let Philippe get too close. Friends were liabilities, not assets.

Philippe believed Roberto Maas died in the fire in St Mary Axe Street. His next step would be to seize his boss's assets – he had the passwords he needed and he'd already started moving money – so Paul had to move fast.

Working round the clock, he changed account names and access codes, created new shell corporations and moved his assets out of Philippe's reach. It was an incredible amount of work, but Paul had to ensure his fortune was secure. Finally it was done. Wherever he was, Philippe would never find the new Paul Silver or the millions that had belonged to Roberto Maas. All Philippe would see if he tried to steal more money now was that someone – presumably Roberto's lawyer – had changed the passwords.

Roberto left no heirs and no will. Informed of his death, his lawyers in Geneva had no idea what provision he'd made for his assets, but in truth there was nothing required. Roberto, Juan Carlos, Slava – every person he had been – owned nothing at all. Not a single piece of furniture in one of a half-dozen furnished apartments around the world. Not a bottle of expensive vodka. Not a cherished artifact proudly displayed in a living room cabinet in Lucerne. Corporations owned everything, and Roberto walked away from all those personal items. He'd been handed a new life. He couldn't risk any link to the past.

When the apartment leases began to expire and after exhaustive attempts to locate a will, his Geneva law firm sold all the personal property. For years they'd held a retainer and instructions to settle things in case Roberto disappeared. Since the corporate shell owners of everything were never located, most of the proceeds went into unclaimed property funds in various locales and eventually would enhance the treasuries of one country or another. It was unfortunate to lose several million dollars, Paul mused at the time, but the money he'd given up on those was part of his new anonymity. It was also a drop in the bucket; there were hundreds of millions in his vast investment portfolio, now shielded inside webs of new shell corporations worldwide.

CHAPTER SIXTEEN

When the bus full of hostages pulled into the parking lot next door, a few guests still lingered in the dining room at Escudo Jaguar, finishing a last beer before hitting the sack. At daybreak they were all going in longboats to Yaxchilan. No one gave the bus a thought; they could barely see the dark parking lot anyway from the bright dining room.

Once the bags were unloaded, Rolando and his *compadre* ushered the remaining people off the bus and divided them into two groups to make it easier to keep an eye on them. The hostages could hear the sounds of talking and laughter coming from the veranda of Escudo Jaguar. With people so close, some thought about screaming for help.

Rolando uttered a sharp command and Mark translated. "Don't make a sound or he'll kill one of us." He added, "It's unlikely the people at the lodge have weapons, and it's certain they won't react fast enough to save us. We have to do what he says."

Each person took his suitcases. The bandits herded their captives down the steep stairway, the light of a nearly full moon illuminating the path. They had to cross a maze of sandbags and work their way to the dock. *Most of these people are young*, Rolando thought idly. *They can haul suitcases down a hill, and maybe they'll think next time about packing so much. Damn Americans.* That made him smile. He saw the two older people were having a hard time.

He yelled at them, "*Mas rapido*." Faster. He saw the man named Ted, the leader, stop to help the lady with her bags.

Two men stood on the dock in the darkness. Rolando greeted them with hugs, and they pointed to two boats, each with a driver and several cans of gasoline in the back. "These are ours," his man said. "We've rented them for twenty-four hours."

Rolando did a quick head count as the people clumsily tossed their suitcases into the long canoes ahead of them, then boarded. Twelve hostages sat down, six on each boat. Soon Diego, Rolando's second-in-command, came running down the dock. He'd parked the bus in a grove of trees a quarter mile from town where it wouldn't be seen for a while.

He and one of his men jumped into the first one, and the driver started the engine. Diego and another rebel boarded the second boat, and they putted away down the Usumacinta River.

The leader checked his watch. It was 9:30 p.m. They'd be at their destination in four hours if things went smoothly. It was dangerous doing this run at night, but the boatmen had navigated the rapids a thousand times. They'd get there with no problem. Everything had worked perfectly up to now. Nothing would go wrong tonight.

Ignoring his prisoners, he removed the ski mask and wiped his face with a dirty bandana. He took a swig of water, poured more on his head, and sat back, his pistol still in his hand. Something nagged at his brain. What wasn't exactly right? Something, but he couldn't put his finger on it. What was it? He'd made sure all the luggage was off the bus, and he'd counted all twelve people ... Wait. Was that it? How many people had there been earlier? The driver was gone and there were twelve now. But weren't there fourteen when they started?

Rolando had done a cursory count on the bus. He thought he counted fourteen, but he could be wrong. It had been a long day and he'd been occupied watching the hostages. There must have been only thirteen to start with. Now there were twelve.

Let it go. All is well. Focus for just a few more hours. Once we get to Piedras, we sleep. Now you must concentrate.

Ted was on the second boat. He knew exactly how many people had been on the bus – they were his responsibility. Before Manuel was murdered, there had been fourteen. Including Ted, there were six hostages on this boat. It was so dark he couldn't see the captives boarding the second one, but there had to be seven.

That was incorrect. There were only six.

———

Forty minutes after they'd left the dock, the captives saw dim lights flickering on the left bank ahead. "Yaxchilan," Ted said. "Those are the lights of the buildings at the entrance to the site. I wondered if they were taking us there ..."

"No talk!" the masked rebel in the back of the boat yelled over the buzz of the outboard motor.

Yaxchilan wasn't their destination. The boats sped past a long dock without slowing. Mark wasn't surprised.

Yaxchilan didn't make sense for this operation. There were too many people around. It would be very difficult to hide a group of hostages. There were acres of cleared and maintained ground, many temples in various stages of reconstruction, a visitor center, and dense jungle everywhere else. It simply couldn't work.

He figured they were going to be held for ransom. If that were true, the rebels would need a remote location far from the river and sufficient manpower to guard hostages twenty-four hours a day. He hoped that was the plan. He didn't want to consider what else their captors might be planning. Although they could have built a rebel camp virtually anywhere on either side, by now the archaeologist had a pretty good idea where they were going. If he was right, they'd be there in around three hours.

Despite the perilous situation, the monotonous hum of the engine lulled some of the captives to sleep. In the front of Rolando's boat, David Tremont, a thirty-seven-year-old insurance agent from Kansas City, thought through his plan one last time. This was crazy, but he had to try it.

David devoured books about archaeological discoveries. This was his first trip to Mexico and he'd been excited to see the ruins he'd heard about for years. He didn't think of himself as particularly brave, but as they sped downriver, he decided what to do.

He had no idea who these guys were or what they wanted, but he was convinced none of the hostages would survive. David chose to try something now rather than being killed in the jungle, having missed an opportunity. He talked himself into doing something proactive instead of waiting for eventual execution like they'd done to the bus driver. He would escape, make his way back to Yaxchilan, and hide until morning when the tourists arrived. He hoped he could save the others by contacting the authorities.

For once in my life I have the chance to help other people. Not like a Boy Scout helps people. I can hopefully help save lives.

Rolando saw quick movement at the front of his boat. He saw a man dive over the side into the dark river. Several people screamed, but the rebel laughed at the man who was paddling briskly toward shore. Both drivers cut their engines and aimed spotlights at the place where David was swimming.

He aimed his pistol as the hostages screamed, "Don't shoot him!"

Smiling, he replied in Spanish, and the archaeologist translated grimly. "He's not going to shoot. You may want to turn your heads. If what's going to happen next is what he thinks, you won't want to watch."

The leader took the spotlight and played it sideways along the riverbank. What appeared to be a huge black log lay on the sand a few feet from the water. Suddenly it became tragically obvious what was going to happen. David's splashing made a lot of noise; a scaly head with a long snout slowly turned to watch him paddle furiously toward shore. Then the crocodile smoothly slid into the water.

In shock the horrified tourists watched the ripples as the creature moved quietly along.

"David! David!" someone yelled. "There's a croc!"

Both boats sat dead in the water. With the engines silenced, the noises of the jungle were amazingly loud. Howler monkeys screeched, the roars of nocturnal felines and the buzz of giant insects merged in a surreal cacophony that was performed nightly in the forest. The denizens of the forest simply ignored the scene playing out in the river. It was the same as always – survival of the fittest.

"Let's make an example of our foolish guest," Rolando said to his driver. He yelled to the other boat; both drivers aimed lights at the swimmer. The hostages sobbed helplessly, shocked as they numbly watched the giant reptile close in on David.

"Swim! Swim, for God's sake!" Dick yelled.

Then most turned away, unable to watch.

In the beams of the spotlights David finally noticed the crocodile. His terrified scream echoed eerily; the hostages would never forget the sound. He started to paddle crazily toward the bank just ten yards in front of him. Finally his feet struck bottom. He stood and began to walk, splashing awkwardly through the water.

"Big mistake," Rolando idly commented.

Like a submarine the huge creature slid effortlessly beneath the surface, and within three seconds David disappeared too, pulled under and taken to the bottom to drown. He'd almost made it – he had only ten feet to go – but now he was gone.

CHAPTER SEVENTEEN

The boats stank with vomit as people reacted in horror to David Tremont's death. No one really knew him – they had all met just forty-eight hours earlier – but suddenly one of *them*, one of a group who'd signed up for a simple trip to Mexico, was dead. The execution of the bus driver had been a shock, but this death was more personal to the rest of the hostages. He was an American tourist, just like they were. And he was dead. *Just like each of us will be*, many of them now thought.

Three and a half hours into their trip, they reached the rapids. Ted and Mark knew of them; when the river was low, they could be treacherous. Sometimes the drivers hauled the boats by hand through the swirling waters while the passengers walked on shore. This time of year the rains came almost every day and the river was high. There would still be tricky rapids, but the boatmen were used to it.

When they hit the whirling, agitated foam, the people held on, many screaming as the boat rocked wildly. One wrong move and they'd be upside down. Though it looked as though they'd capsize, the boatmen steered expertly through the foamy water and around jutting, jagged rocks. Finally they popped out into calm water on the other side.

The time dragged by, slowed by the endless repetition of shoreline, water and engine noise. By now many of the captives were dozing, heads lolling up and down, but everyone became alert when they heard the engines throttle down. It was nearly two in the morning and they'd been on the river over four hours. Rolando stood in the rear of the lead boat, staring intently ahead. He saw a signal – somewhere onshore a light blinked on and off three times.

"*Ahi esta!*" he said to the boat driver, pointing. *There it is.*

The light blinked its signal twice more as the boats drew near and turned toward the shore, moving at a snail's pace through very shallow water. In the moonlight the tourists saw a tall rock structure – three stones stacked like a snowman, the top one clearly resembling the skull of a huge bird with a long, protruding beak made of rock. It was impossible to miss.

Bird Monster, Mark thought to himself. The ancient Olmecs believed it was the statue of a god.

There were a dozen men waiting for them. Rolando jumped out and waded onshore. He was greeted with hearty rounds of congratulations and backslapping from the band of grubby, sloppy ruffians. Mark understood their raucous banter.

"You did it! You actually kidnapped them! We're rich! We're rich!"

When Hailey had been ordered into the first boat, she'd hoped Paul would be there too, but he wasn't. She was disappointed, but even more, she was afraid; even after such a short time she somehow felt safer with him around. She couldn't put words to her feelings; he was a different kind of man than she'd ever met before. He exuded confidence and had a take-charge attitude that made others comfortable. *He seems like the kind of guy who could plan our escape,* she thought to herself, although she couldn't figure out why she felt that way. *I really don't know him at all.*

Now that everyone was standing on the beach in the moonlight, she looked around. *Where is he? He isn't here! What the hell? What if he tried something on the other boat like that guy did on ours? What if he tried to resist and they killed him?* Bile rose in her throat as she thought what could have happened. Should she say something to the others?

Wait, something inside her cautioned.

Rolando barked orders to his lieutenant. "Diego, you know what to do now. Get started. Quickly – we only have a few hours before daybreak."

His men knew their assignments. Some started unloading luggage from the boats, stacking bags on crude wooden wheelbarrows. Others picked up rifles leaning against nearby trees and herded the group toward a path leading into the jungle. Rolando, one of his men and the two drivers stayed on the rugged beach. As they walked away, the leader counted again. There were eleven. All accounted for.

Diego walked at the front, guards were interspersed among the hostages, and two men pushing the carts brought up the rear as they marched single file into the bush.

Gavin was in front of Hailey. He knew Paul – he'd sat next to him when they did introductions the other evening. She whispered, "Gavin, was Paul on the boat with you?"

"No. Wasn't he with you?"

"No! What do you think they've done with him?"

"Dear God, with these murderers I can only imagine. I hope to God he's all right. He seemed like a great guy. Look at me, talking in the past tense about him already. He *seems* like a great guy. Let's not jump to conclusions. He's around somewhere. Our hosts seem pretty good at keeping up with everyone."

"Good Lord, Gavin. Do you think they've killed him —"

"*Silencio!*" one of the guards yelled. She began to panic and struggled to think positively.

After an hour they came to an area that was cleared on both sides of the trail. Moonbeams played across huge ruined temples that soared a hundred feet into the sky.

Hailey murmured, "Where are we? What are these ruins?"

"Piedras Negras," Gavin whispered. "Guatemala side of the river. The lost city of the Maya, built maybe a thousand years ago. Last excavated in 2005 or so and abandoned since then. Except for the bandidos, I hear."

"How do you know all that?"

"I wrote a novel about this place once. After we passed Yaxchilan, I figured we were coming here. There's nothing else for miles, far as I know. This site is four hours by boat from Frontera Corozal, so that matches. Piedras Negras is also the only excavated ruin on this side of the river. I'd hoped to see it someday …"

"Bet you never hoped to see it like this."

One of the guards approached and jabbed her side sharply with the butt of his rifle. "*Silencio, puta!* No talk."

"Fuck you," she muttered, grimacing from the blow.

As they left the ruins, the trail narrowed again; the bushes on both sides were close enough to touch. It was inky – no moonlight penetrated the thick trees. Only the guards' flashlights indicated where the path was.

Gavin pressed a button on his watch and saw they'd been walking about two miles. The author was a fitness buff – his watch measured heart rate and blood pressure, but it also had a pedometer. He'd set that when this forced march began in hopes the knowledge might come in handy later.

The guards dropped their efforts to keep people quiet. Some were complaining about the long hike, most vocally Alison Barton, whose boyfriend Win's calm reassurance kept her moving ahead. No one knew what the guards had been told to do with stragglers, and no one wanted to be the first to find out.

At last they arrived at a large, roughly circular campsite. Gavin clicked his pedometer off at 2.1 miles.

Three rebels sat in rickety chairs around a blazing campfire. When they saw the group marching in one by one, they stood and drew their pistols.

The suitcases were dumped and Diego shouted, "Take bags!"

The captives gathered their luggage. Only David Tremont's suitcases were left, a sobering reminder that one of them was gone. Win and Alison carried his bags along with their own. Whatever he'd packed might help the others survive.

"Go there!" He pointed to the edge of the clearing, where they saw a yawning black hole – the entrance to a cave. Lanterns hung inside, their glow casting flickering shadows on the stone walls.

The cavern was thirty feet wide and fifty long. The ceiling was twenty feet or more above them. The weary captives were ushered inside, where twenty filthy cots were set up in two rows. There were no pillows or sheets, but at least they wouldn't be sleeping on the dirt floor of the cave.

"Sleep now!" Diego yelled at them. "Take place!"

Hailey walked to the back of the cave, glancing here and there to confirm what she already knew. Paul was gone. She hoped for the best; maybe he was alive. Maybe he'd escaped and was working on a plan right now.

She picked a cot at the end of the room, and Alison immediately claimed the one next to it.

"Aren't you bunking by your boyfriend?" she asked.

"I hate him for bringing me into all this," the girl sputtered, tears forming in her eyes. "I hate caves. I can't stay in here! I need to use the bathroom. Where is it?"

Oh boy, Hailey thought, rolling her eyes. *I'm no backpacker, but this little baby is going to have a hard time.* "If I had to bet, I'd say that's the bathroom." She pointed to a bucket on the floor in a corner. There was no privacy whatsoever.

"Oh God, you're right." Alison sobbed pitifully. "I can't ... I can't use that. There's not even ..."

"What? Any toilet paper?" Hailey snapped. She'd had enough. "Listen to me, sweetie. We have to try to stay alive here. I don't care if they make me poop in a can and eat it for breakfast. I just want to get out of here and do it fast. So quit your whining and get with the program. You're either part of the problem or part of the solution. Buck up, for God's sake. We have a long, long way to go." She turned and began to unpack her bag.

Doc Spence helped his wife use the bathroom while the rest – the men, Hailey and Alison – went outside. The girls squatted nearby while the men walked a few feet away to give them some semblance of privacy.

"That's better than using the pot inside," Hailey said to the girl when they were done, trying to assuage her earlier comments. "We can always come out here if we need to go to the bathroom."

"Aren't there wild animals? Do you think –"

Hailey interrupted gently. "Around here the human wild animals are the ones I'd be afraid of. That guy Rolando's a psycho, and you can bet his band of merry men is too. We haven't even figured out why we're here yet. Getting eaten by a jaguar's the least of our problems."

Within moments the sound of snores filled the cavern. The people had used whatever they'd brought to fashion makeshift pillows. It was so hot that the men stripped down to shorts and T-shirts. Modesty not being one of her hang-ups, Hailey knew the less she had on, the cooler she'd be. By the time she crawled onto the dirty cot, she was in a T-shirt and panties with two cotton shirts spread underneath her for a bottom sheet and a jacket forming a makeshift pillow. As she closed her eyes, Alison whispered. She said she admired Hailey – you've got a lot of courage, she said – but Hailey didn't respond. If Alison only knew. Hailey always put up a great front – she was good at keeping her emotions to herself. Right now she was scared to death. But she was too bullheaded to let anyone know.

As she rolled over, Hailey noticed a guard sitting at the entrance to the cave. She felt strangely relieved that animals actually wouldn't be able to just stroll in. Sleep came at last among grunts, farts and snores mixed with jungle noises just feet away from the exhausted travelers. A roomful of strangers had taken the first step in a long journey. They'd get to know each other a lot better before it was over.

Rolando and one other rebel had stayed behind while the hostages were marched to the camp. They carefully swept the beach to remove footprints and smoothed out the two notches in the sand where the boat prows had dug into it. When they finished, there was nothing to indicate a group of bandits had taken eleven hostages ashore. They headed off to join the others.

CHAPTER EIGHTEEN

The buzz of motors jolted Paul awake. He was sitting stiffly upright, leaning against a tree at the top of the cliff. Two boats rounded the bend with drivers but no passengers. He checked their numbers. These were the same boats that took the hostages away.

It was 6:30 a.m. and the sun was popping over the horizon, bathing the river and the verdant jungle in light. Paul stood and stretched; his back ached. He stuck the pistol and phone in his pocket and waited. The men tied up their longboats and started up the hill. It was good timing. Although breakfast was being prepared and the smells of bacon and coffee were wafting from the lodge's kitchen, there were no guests up yet. No one saw him walk over to the concrete stairway. He greeted the boatmen in Spanish as they reached the top of the stairs.

"Good morning. Long night, eh?"

He surprised them. Weary from an eight-hour round trip in the dark, they simply wanted to go to bed. Their part in this affair was over; what these bandits wanted with a bunch of Americans was none of their business. That man who was the leader had made it clear they'd better keep things that way if they wanted to stay safe.

The boatmen were paid handsomely for hauling everyone to Piedras Negras – two hundred American dollars each, more than a month's wages in this dreary town. When they got there last night, they'd been surprised to see a band of rebels on the shore. There must be a camp near the ruins, they figured. But they'd been paid to drive a boat, not to think about what they'd seen. It was safer for them and their families to forget everything that had happened.

Now here was some guy, probably an American, inquiring about their long night. What was this about?

"*Hola*," one of the men replied casually as he kept walking.

Paul stepped in front of them. "I want to know where you went."

"*Vete a la chingada, gringo. I'm tired." Go screw yourself.* He turned to walk away.

Suddenly Paul jerked the man's arm, knocking him to the ground. In a sweeping move he brought the pistol up and aimed it at the other man.

"There's no need for disrespect. I asked you a simple question. Where did you take the people?"

"Piedras –"

"Shut up, you ass!" the other man screamed. "He'll kill us!"

"Who, Rolando, or whatever his name is?" Paul responded. "I wouldn't worry about him. It's *me* you have to worry about. *I'll* kill you. Right now. You have ten seconds to tell me where my friends are."

The first man started to get up. Paul pushed him down with his foot. "Stay where you are. Where did Rolando go?"

They looked at him quizzically. They didn't recognize the name.

"What's the boss's name?" Paul asked.

"We don't know. One of his guys hired us. We just drove the boats."

"Did they get off at Piedras Negras?"

He didn't answer. The other man was sitting on the asphalt, shaking his head. Their jubilation over making a small fortune last night was forgotten. They were far more afraid of retaliation by the rebel leader than anything this gringo might do.

The first man started to stand. "You won't shoot us. There are people over there at the lodge. You can't risk firing your pistol."

"You're right," Paul replied. With a quick swipe, he hit the man squarely in the forehead with the butt of his gun. The boatman fell backwards, unconscious. He turned to the other driver. "You're next. Talk to me or you'll wish you had."

The man was exhausted from a long night and suddenly afraid of what this man might do next. He talked.

"We drove them to the landing place that leads to Piedras Negras. A lot of men were waiting there and they took the gringos off into the jungle. Others carried the people's suitcases on barrows. The leader ... the man you call Rolando ... he stayed on the shore and didn't go with the others. He paid us our money and told us to come back here. So we did. That's all I know, *señor*. I swear it."

"How much did he pay you?"

"Two hundred dollars." He pulled the money from his pocket. "See, here it is. You can have it."

Paul believed the man. He knew roughly where the boats had dropped their human cargo. From there Piedras

81

Negras was a mile's trek through the jungle. He handed the boat driver a hundred-dollar bill.

"Keep your money. You earned it. Here's an extra hundred for the information you gave me. Tell no one about me. That will keep you and your family safe."

He kicked the unconscious man on the ground. "Tell your friend to do the same thing. If you want to make five hundred dollars more, come back alone tonight at sundown and take me to Piedras Negras. If you're afraid and don't want to come, I will understand. I promise I won't betray you – I won't tell anyone what you did last night. You must promise me the same thing. I want to save my friends and you can help me. I hope I see you tonight. I will be waiting."

As the boatman knelt to revive his unconscious friend, Paul walked away without looking back. When he reached the trees where he'd hidden earlier, he glanced at the parking lot. The men were gone.

An hour later Paul had rented a room, unpacked his bags, eaten breakfast, stripped naked, dived under the covers and gone fast asleep. Now that Rolando had sent both boats back, he likely had no means of returning himself. For the moment it appeared to be safe to emerge from hiding. Wherever he saw Rolando next, Paul would be ready. Whoever he was, Paul was far better at this sort of thing than the rebel could ever be.

When he awoke, it was afternoon. Paul began crafting a strategy. He'd wanted to visit Piedras Negras on this trip. Now that would definitely happen, whether it was with last night's boat driver or another one. He simply had a little extra work to do since twelve people had been kidnapped.

CHAPTER NINETEEN

Dressed in black, Paul waited in the same thicket of trees near the parking lot. He had packs and a collapsible duffel. They were packed solid with food, water, batteries, flashlights and blankets he'd bought in town this afternoon. He had no idea what lay ahead, but he'd better be prepared for anything.

It was nine p.m. Paul's hiding place was shrouded in darkness. Less than a hundred yards away there were lights and conversation. Several people sat on the outdoor patio, having a beer and sharing memories of their trip to Yaxchilan today. The lighthearted tourists had no idea eleven people were being held captive in the jungle.

Now and then people wandered through the parking lot. A couple walked to their bus, retrieved something they'd forgotten, and returned to Escudo Jaguar. Others strolled to the cliff to see the river glistening in the moonlight. One passed within five feet of Paul without ever realizing he was there.

Soon a man on a bicycle rode up. It was the boat driver; he chained his bike to a tree and walked to the steps leading to the dock. As he did, Paul stepped out and gave a low whistle. The man turned, nodded imperceptibly and started down the stairway.

BILL THOMPSON

Paul gave him a five-minute head start. He watched from the cliff until he was satisfied nothing was out of the ordinary. The few people around were engrossed in their own situations, and no one gave him a glance. He walked down to the dock, saw the man prepping the motor of a longboat, got on board, and they moved out into the dark river without saying a word.

The trip was long and monotonous. The jungle was beautiful, but at night there was nothing but blackness. Creatures howled, cawed, roared and otherwise confirmed their dominance in a realm intended for them, not for humans.

When they hit the rapids, the boat jerked back and forth as the driver maneuvered skillfully through raging water and dark rocks jutting above the river's surface. Once that part was over, things settled down.

"Maybe thirty minutes now." Those were the driver's first words.

"Stop here for a minute," Paul ordered. The man killed the engine and they drifted silently. "Tell me what was at the place where you landed the boat last night."

The man said a signal had guided them in, but it really hadn't been necessary. The place they'd landed was where any visitor going to the abandoned ruins would disembark.

"We landed at Bird Monster's statue. There were many men on the shore, all armed with rifles or pistols. They took the hostages on the trail to Piedras Negras. I watched them go. They disappeared into the jungle while the leader and another stayed on the beach."

Paul didn't know what to expect when he arrived. Why had Rolando, obviously the leader, not gone with the hostages? Were his men guarding the shore? Paul had to arrive undetected. He gave instructions to the driver, who started up the motor and continued.

When there was about ten minutes left, the driver pulled close to shore and idled the engine. The boat putted almost silently down the river, so closely hugging the shore they could touch overhanging branches.

"*Tenga cuidado con las serpientes,*" the driver cautioned. *Be careful of the snakes.* Huge constrictors liked to rest on tree limbs; one wrong move and a ten-foot snake could end up in the boat.

A jaguar howled furiously nearby as the boat moved quietly, just three feet from the bank. They were hidden here; moonlight bathed the river, but the branches provided perfect cover.

They rounded a small bend, and the driver cut the engine, pulled out a weathered oar, and began to paddle. Paul saw a sandy beach about fifty feet ahead; they had reached their destination. He took out his pistol and flipped off the safety.

As soon as the prow dug into the sand, the driver slipped into the water, pulling the boat onshore with a rope. Paul looked around cautiously, pistol ready. There was nothing but the harsh noise of the living, breathing jungle.

He jumped out and offloaded his packs. He looked at the sandy beach, puzzled. He asked, "Are you sure this is the right place? There's nothing to indicate people have been on this beach."

The boatman pointed to three stacked rocks, the top one shaped like a beak. "Bird Monster's statue. They got off here."

Then he walked to where the beach stopped and the dark jungle began. He pointed out a pathway leading into the bush. "They have brushed it clean. They walked into the woods here, on this trail. I must go now." He glanced anxiously about, fearful that one of the bandits might be around.

Paul pulled five hundred-dollar bills from his pocket. "Thank you for your bravery in coming back here. I may be able to save lives because of you."

The man stuck the money in his shirt pocket. "How will you get back?" he asked as he prepared to push off.

"I'll work that out later."

The man handed Paul a piece of paper. "Just in case, that's the number at the store by my house. Leave a message for me. I am Pablo. I will come."

Paul stuck out his hand and the man shook it. "Thanks, Pablo. I'm Pablo too – Paul in English. Safe travels."

"You too, *amigo*."

The driver pushed off without looking back. Paul hid in a grove of trees as the man's oars clipped the water silently. Finally, far away, he heard the motor crank up. Pablo guided the boat through the night back to Frontera Corozal. His mission was complete; Paul's was just beginning.

CHAPTER TWENTY

The front desk manager of the Palacio Hotel in Palenque was frustrated at having lost the revenue from eleven rooms that were no-shows last night. He had a deposit of five hundred pesos from Crestmark, the tour company in Colorado that had made the booking, but that was a fraction of the total cost. If Crestmark refused to pay, his employers would be out a lot of money.

He called the company's headquarters and spoke to Carla, Ted Pettigrew's executive assistant. She was as surprised as he was that the group didn't show up. She assured the hotel manager they'd pay for the unused rooms.

Tense and apprehensive, Carla texted Ted. According to their itinerary they should be on the road to Bonampak now, but after their no-show, she had no idea what might have happened. It could have been anything – a mechanical breakdown, a blocked highway or something else. There was no reason to get worried yet, she told herself. Ted had led over fifty of these tours and he knew how to handle things in rural Mexico. But she couldn't help being a little worried. What if they'd broken down far from a cell tower and were stuck? What if they'd had an accident? What if … She stopped herself. This wasn't productive.

Ted's iPhone vibrated as Carla's text appeared. No one saw it; his phone and all the others were in the underbrush a hundred miles away.

After a half hour and no text response, Carla began backtracking. She called the hotel in Villahermosa and confirmed that the group had spent two nights. They'd had a welcoming party and dinner on the second evening, and the bus had pulled out of the parking lot around 8:30 yesterday morning, loaded with box lunches for their noon meal. The desk clerk heard Ted say they'd stop to eat somewhere along the road to Palenque.

Next Carla called the visitor center at the Palenque site. Between her broken Spanish and the man's similarly poor English, it took a while, but she learned that although the group had a reservation to tour the ruins, they had never arrived.

Carla walked into the assistant director's office and said, "Ted and the group have been AWOL since sometime yesterday. I'm really worried about them."

Abe Birnbaum, the president and owner of Crestmark Tours, also owned a dozen other companies, one of which was a successful travel agency in Colorado Springs. Abe's father had made millions in Colorado real estate and his son had made much more. He'd served as mayor of Colorado Springs, and he was very active in Democratic politics, hosting fund-raisers at his lavish mountain retreat in the Rockies near Vail. In turn, his travel agency enjoyed a lot of business from many politicians and their staffs. Abe cultivated powerful friends over the years, and until today he'd asked for nothing in return for all his time and money that had helped some folks become very important indeed. Now Abe needed something from Washington, and his friends were happy to help.

By lunchtime things were starting to happen. Harry Longmire was the senior senator from Colorado, the Senate Majority Leader, and one of Abe Birnbaum's close friends. He responded immediately to Abe's urgent call about the missing tour group. Within an hour the director of the FBI, a senior official at the State Department and the Mexican ambassador to the USA had been briefed and were developing a plan. The Secretary of State made a courtesy call to the White House so the president, an acquaintance of Birnbaum's and occasional recipient of his fund-raising talents, would be aware of the situation. The US Embassy attaché for legal affairs in Mexico City was instructed by State to spare no resources in searching for the missing Americans. This evening a Lear jet owned by the US government would fly a senior embassy official and a cadre of FBI agents to Villahermosa. Tomorrow they'd join Federal Police to begin the search for a busload of archaeology buffs who'd seemingly vanished.

At five p.m. Abe stopped thinking about the missing group for the first time since he'd gotten the news. He went home, poured a stiff Scotch and water, and sat on his patio. He glanced at CNN's broadcast of the missing Americans – it was the top story of the evening – but he muted the volume. He couldn't deal with any more right now. His bones ached from the stress and he had a hard knot in his stomach. He'd done all he could. He'd enlisted help at the highest levels of the federal government. He'd spent an hour on the phone with the FBI and had blocked most of tomorrow morning for a face-to-face with agents. He knew it would be an exhausting meeting, repeating facts and details endlessly, but he would do anything to help find his group. At least he had this evening to wind down and relax. Tomorrow the nightmare would begin all over again.

Before he fell asleep, he prayed for his partner Ted Pettigrew, his friend Mark Linebarger, whom he'd known for twenty years, and all the people on that bus somewhere in Mexico.

Earlier this afternoon the FBI had contacted the company that owned the tour bus. Its president didn't know the bus was missing; he quickly responded to the agency's request for a picture and description of the bus and its license number. Within an hour the FBI created a flyer containing both bus and passenger information and offering a ten-thousand-dollar reward for information. That was Abe's idea, and the FBI thought it would be a big motivator in the impoverished areas of rural Mexico where the bus was last known to have been. The flyer was emailed to Federal Police headquarters in Mexico City.

They emailed the flyer to every single police station in Mexico. From sprawling metropolitan cities to the smallest communities in remote areas, the police were asked to watch for the bus and its foreign passengers.

The US ambassador to Mexico himself had called the director of the Federal Police in Mexico City, requesting cooperation, and apparently it worked. Things were moving much more quickly and efficiently than usual in the land of "*mañana*." Everyone down the line was aware that this case had been initiated from the very top. Everyone – Americans and Mexicans alike – sprang into action.

By the time Abe Birnbaum drifted into fitful sleep, a massive nighttime search was underway in streets, parking lots, garages and public areas everywhere throughout Mexico. It was as though the small police departments wanted to prove themselves as diligent as their big-city counterparts. Everyone was searching, and every police car had a copy of the flyer on its dashboard. Like CNN had done all day, the government news channel Aguascalientes TV made the missing bus its top story.

About the only one who wasn't searching for the unaccounted-for tourists was the one person who should have been: the lone policeman in Frontera Corozal, where the bus sat abandoned in a grove of trees just outside of town. He glanced at the story on TV but paid it no attention, thinking it had nothing to do with him. He also never received the Federal Police's email or the descriptive flyer. If he had, the ten-thousand-dollar reward would have motivated him to look around. If he had, chances are he would have found the bus.

This wasn't the only email he missed. He actually hadn't gotten any mail at all in three weeks – his computer wasn't working, and his brother-in-law, the only person in town who had any idea how to fix a computer, was off visiting relatives in the Yucatan. The fact that his computer was broken wasn't a big deal, the policeman reasoned. He never got anything interesting on it anyway. Mostly it was routine flyers about criminals in Tuxtla Gutierrez, the capital of Chiapas. The stuff he got never had anything to do with him or his village. So the broken computer would wait until his relative came back from his trip.

CHAPTER TWENTY-ONE

Ruben Ochoa had been driving his longboat up and down the Usumacinta for twenty years. An illiterate man of thirty-four, he had a common-law wife and four kids at home and, given his lack of education, he made a good living. His family had indoor plumbing, running water and electricity. They also had a seventeen-inch black-and-white television with a set of rabbit ears made from coat hangers and aluminum foil. They could receive just two channels. One happened to be Aguascalientes TV.

Ruben saw the news story. He heard the reporter say that thirteen North Americans and their tour bus were missing and there was a huge reward for finding them. He was smart enough to realize how high profile this case must be if it was on national television. So he knew that very important people wanted these people found quickly.

The boat driver also knew exactly where along the river he and his cousin Pablo had dropped off the hostages and their captors. What he knew terrified him.

He told his wife he'd be back later and rode his bike to Pablo's house. Soon the policeman in their little town would come calling. He was their friend, but that didn't matter. This was a huge deal. They needed an alibi. Fast.

CHAPTER TWENTY-TWO

At seven a.m. Rolando walked into the cave that was his captives' bunkhouse and ordered Mark outside. The rebel no longer wore a ski mask, apparently seeing no need to hide his identity any longer. That was disconcerting; it meant he no longer cared that someone could identify him.

Mark and Rolando sat in two lawn chairs near a campfire over which a coffee pot sat bubbling. Men were working at various tasks around the site; a pair of donkeys was tethered nearby, casually chomping on the wet grass. Despite his circumstances, the archaeologist couldn't help savoring the aroma of the coffee.

Mark took in his surroundings. He noticed the entrance to a second cave fifty feet away at the edge of the clearing. It had been invisible last night, but now he saw its opening was even larger than the one where they'd slept. Rolando's crew was going in and out of it, carrying boxes and cloth bags.

Rolando handed the archaeologist a cup of coffee and said, "Your people are free to walk around today, but if someone tries to escape or challenges my men, he will be killed. My men have orders to shoot if they are concerned in the least. I want you to explain that to the other gringos."

He pointed to a building where two guards sat in chairs at its door. "No one can go there."

Mark figured that was the rebels' command center. He could hear faint static, probably from a shortwave radio. A large tree trunk that had been stripped of its branches stood next to the shack. A wire snaked out of a window, ran up the tree and connected to a metal rod on top. It was almost certainly a makeshift antenna.

Mark pointed to the cave. "What's in there?"

"Storage for food and supplies. Your people are not allowed in there either. Tell them to stay out."

"I'm not the leader of this group. Ted Pettigrew is. You should be talking to him about all this instead of me."

"You speak Spanish and you're an intelligent man whom I believe thinks logically instead of impetuously. I will talk to you. Then you can tell the others."

"All right. What's going on? Exactly what are we doing here?"

"What are you *doing* here? Is that a joke? You have been kidnapped. Is that not obvious?"

"Is this about money? The American government won't negotiate, you know."

Rolando smiled. "Please don't worry yourself about the American government, Dr. Linebarger. I know what I'm doing."

"I saw the ruins of Piedras Negras last night as we marched through the jungle. As long as you're holding us captive here, may I take some of our group to see the site?" Mark had lain awake, trying to think of any way to separate the captives from the rebels. *If a small contingency of guards accompanied several of us, maybe we could overpower them.* But it was a long shot. *What would we do if we were successful? We're still stuck in the jungle miles and miles from any other human beings, with no food, no water, and no way to communicate with the outside world.*

It was immaterial; the rebel flatly refused. "You are no longer on an archaeological trip. You are prisoners. No sightseeing. You will be our guests for a week, maybe more, depending on what happens. No one knows where you are or how you got here. Don't think of escaping. It's foolish. Going into the jungle without weapons and transportation would be insane. You must explain that to the others. No heroics. You will all obey orders or you will be killed. It's that simple."

"Perhaps some of us can help with the ransom. These people have families ..."

"You're too kind," Rolando replied sarcastically. "Please leave the details to me. I'm capable of extracting ransom for hostages. I've done it before."

Back in the cave-cum-bunkhouse, Mark gathered the people. He told them what Rolando had said. Even though the rebel chose to communicate through him, Mark emphasized that Ted remained their leader.

"Ted will make the final decision on everything we do. Although he and I can't control your actions, I strongly urge you not to do anything rash. We know this man will kill without compunction. That's not to say we can't use our brains and come up with ideas. I'm just asking that we discuss things before anyone gets himself – or the rest of us – killed. We have to be a team – none of us expected to be in this place, and together we can survive."

His voice dropped to a whisper. "Gather around closely."

Everyone knew what was coming next. Someone was missing and two people already knew who it was. Gavin and Hailey had gotten to know Paul Silver best. He'd been on the bus when it arrived in Frontera Corozal last night, but he hadn't been seen since.

"We don't know what happened to Paul," Ted explained softly. "You'll recall he's the Pemex consultant, a guy from New York living in Villahermosa. We know that he wasn't on either boat last night. I don't think Rolando left any of his men back at the town, although I'm not sure. I'm wondering if they could have separated Paul for some reason."

"I hope they didn't kill him," Mary Spence blurted out.

Her husband, Doc, the surgeon from Dallas, patted her hand. "Let's stay positive, dear. We have enough to be concerned about without worrying about things that might not have even happened."

Doc asked if the luggage was all accounted for. "When we left the parking lot, we all had to carry our bags down to the boat ramp. Are there any extra suitcases around here somewhere? Did anybody bring Paul's?"

No extra luggage had been brought on the longboats. Wherever Paul was, his bags were missing too. Was that a good sign or not? No one knew what to make of it. Gavin wondered if he might have escaped, but everyone thought that was impossible with the rebels watching their every move. And how could he have both escaped *and* taken his suitcases?

But then again, if he didn't escape, where were his bags? They discussed if Rolando could have separated Paul and his suitcases from the rest of them? That scenario didn't fly. Why, where and when could that have happened? Focused on their own dire situations, none of them had paid that much attention, but everyone agreed they'd have noticed if Paul had been forcibly taken away. Especially if he'd also been carrying his luggage.

The consensus was that somehow he'd managed to get away. Gavin said, "No one really knows anything about him. Think about it. All you really know about *me* is what I told you the other night during introductions. I could have made everything up. So could he. Who knows what this guy Paul Silver really is? Maybe he works for the CIA. That would be helpful."

"Yeah, helpful if you're using his story as part of your next book," Alison shot back in a scornful tone. "We're all going to die here. If you haven't figured that out by now, you're all a bunch of idiots." She began to cry.

Bart whispered calmly, "Let's take it easy, folks. Who knows how long we're going to be together. This isn't the time or place for accusations or ridicule. Like Ted said, we have to be a team in order to beat these guys. On our own, we can't make it. But if we stay strong and united, we can make it through this. We're *not* all going to die here, Alison. I'm not going to accept that. I'm choosing to think that whatever Paul Silver is, he managed to do one thing none of the rest of us did. Somehow he's gotten away, and it appears these guys don't even know he's gone. That could work really well for us."

Several people nodded in agreement.

Ted urged the others to keep quiet about Paul, even among themselves. "We have no idea if these guys speak English; they may understand everything we say. We also don't know if Paul can help us or not. If he really works for the state oil company, it's possible he can get help from the Mexican government. But how would he know where we are right now? We just need to be calm and wait. If it's your thing, a little praying wouldn't hurt either."

CHAPTER TWENTY-THREE

The first day in camp passed slowly for the hostages. They wandered around and explored the place, a cleared circle about three hundred feet in diameter. In the center of the clearing there was a fire pit. Four shacks sat around the perimeter. One was the off-limits building they dubbed the "office." It was guarded twenty-four seven. A stovepipe stuck out of the roof of another, the cook shack. Food was prepared and served there, but they ate outside. The other buildings housed Rolando and his men. The leader had a small hut to himself, and his men slept in the other one. A generator sputtered behind the office, and extension cords ran to the kitchen.

Everyone steered clear of Rolando. First there had been the callous murder of the bus driver, then the death of David Tremont in the river. That scene had been horribly played out in the beam of a spotlight aimed at the doomed man by Rolando himself. They were shocked and physically sickened at what this maniac was capable of. They were also afraid. He was ruthless, capable of anything, and no one wanted to attract attention.

They were grateful to have the things from their luggage. A few played cards; others read books. Each of them used one diversion or another to escape from the reality of imprisonment, even if for only an hour here or there. At midday they were guided to a line and served a lunch of some kind of meat, a tuber vegetable and some rice. Despite having no idea what it was, but ravenous after twenty-four hours without food, they ate everything on their plates.

That afternoon Gavin Michaels pulled out a briar pipe and stuck it in his mouth. Soon the smell of tobacco wafted through the camp; most of the captives were pleased with the aroma. To some it brought back memories of childhood, grandfathers and the good old days. Alison predictably complained, saying she wasn't going to be subjected to second-hand smoke. She stormed off into the cave, where she sat alone. She didn't like that either, but she pouted, refusing to come back outside. That would be admitting she'd made a mistake.

Win walked in to check on her. They hadn't spoken since her tantrum earlier, the one where she'd let everyone know he was the sole reason she was going to die in this godforsaken place and she should never have come with him.

"Alison, we need to talk."

"So talk, then," she shouted. "What do you have to say? You're sorry? Yeah, I'll bet you are. You're an asshole for making me come here! When Paul rescues us –"

"God, Alison! Shut up! We can't talk about that!"

She was sullen. Here she was in a dank cave, angry that a man she now detested had called her down for shouting Paul's name. And he was right. That made it even worse.

"Get out. I don't want to talk to you. If I ever get home, I never want to lay eyes on you again."

"Alison, I hate that all this happened. But there was no way I could have known –"

She fired back sarcastically, "Do you think, just maybe, if I'd been in Waco working at the store right now, I would have been kidnapped by a sadistic murderer and taken to the jungle? Do you *think,* Win? Of course not. People are safe in America. Why am I here, not there? One reason. You. That's why. Get out."

He walked out, disappointed by her petulant attitude. Now he knew how she was when it came down to things that mattered.

Hailey listened to Alison's outburst – with the shouting, no one could miss her side of it – and she felt sorry for this poor guy. He'd merely invited his girlfriend on a trip to the jungle, as simple as that. It had gone horribly wrong. It had turned into a terrifying, unbelievable situation none of them would have wished on another person. But it was what it was. Acting like a child wasn't going to help anything. She'd talk to Alison later, to try to help her understand she needed to calm down and go with the flow.

Around four it rained buckets for thirty minutes. Everyone scurried inside when it started, then emerged again when the sun came out. The storm had done nothing but make the humidity soar and the insects attack with a vengeance.

After the rainstorm, things got really steamy. Everyone sat in the shade, thankful for every bit of breeze. The suntan lotion and insect repellent came out, and everyone slathered it on. They shed as many clothes as possible – the men wore only shorts and shoes. The females stripped to their bras and panties, even the sixty-something Mary Spence. It was too hot to care – they were all in the same boat anyway. Seeing someone naked didn't matter much when you were concerned about dying.

Rolando observed the two young women from the window in the office shack. They were dramatically different – the whiny blond one was beautiful like a movie star, lean and with a great figure. She cried a lot – he would give her something to moan about, for sure!

He lingered over the other one, the brunette named Hailey. She was gorgeous too, with longer legs and smaller breasts than Alison. Hailey was assertive – she had a fire in her belly. She would be a handful to deal with, but he was ready for the challenge. It had been a while and he was looking forward to it. He felt himself stirring as he thought about what he would have her do to him.

He wished there had been more women in this group. He would have liked the diversity. There actually was one more female – the older one – but Rolando would enjoy these two young beauties. That would be plenty. He didn't need to take the older one with her husband here too. That would just be wrong, he thought sarcastically.

He watched them a bit longer and then made his choice for tonight.

The hostages went through the evening buffet line, if it could be called that, where two grubby cooks slopped the same food on their plates they'd had for lunch. Hailey wondered idly if the plates had been washed, then smiled. That was the least of their worries. If they died here, it wouldn't be from food poisoning.

Mark asked Rolando what the meat was.

"Javelina. You like it?"

"It's okay. Some of the people were asking, that's all."

He told the others that they were eating a piglike mammal called a javelina. The meat understandably resembled pork. Even if everyone might not like it, they all ate it because they were hungry. They were also determined to stay strong and ready, just in case of an opportunity.

The kidnappers had rigged a makeshift shower by hanging a hose from a tree branch. The hose ran into a large barrel filled with rainwater. It wasn't great and the flow was weak, but it beat nothing. Since there were no walls, most people waited until dusk to clean up. As darkness fell, they walked one by one to the shower. Some turned their backs to the others, some didn't. Most of the captives averted their eyes, showing respect for the others, especially the two beautiful young women. The guards merely stared lasciviously and grinned.

By eight p.m. the sun had slipped behind the tall trees that encircled the camp. The captives sat together around the campfire as their guards stood nearby. One counted the hostages. These head counts occurred randomly throughout the day; Rolando obviously didn't want to have anyone go missing. Most of them were afraid to leave anyway; unarmed, they'd rather face the known perils here than the things lurking in the jungle.

One of the guards approached and pointed at Alison. "You. Come with me," he said in broken English. Six other guards took up positions around the hostages.

She didn't move. "Why? Where do you want me to go?"

"Come," he harshly insisted.

"No. You can't –"

Suddenly he grabbed her hair, lifting her bodily off the ground. She screamed. Win jumped up to help her and a guard stuck a pistol in his face.

"Sit!"

He had no choice. He sat down.

The man let go of Alison's hair and said angrily, "Come. Now."

She began to cry softly. "Please don't. I don't want to go. Please."

Hailey looked at the man. "Take me. I'll go."

"She'll go!" Alison pointed at Hailey. "Tell him in Spanish," Alison sobbed. "Tell him you'll go so he won't take me."

Amazed that this girl would so easily throw her into peril, Hailey looked at Mark. "Tell him I'll go."

The guard started pulling Alison up by her arm, and Mark said in Spanish, "Take the other one."

He shook his head and pointed at Alison. "*Este. Ahora, este va.*" *Now, this one goes.*

Ten people watched helplessly as the guard dragged a sobbing Alison to Rolando's hut. He took her inside, came back out, pulled up a chair and guarded the door.

"I can't let him do anything to her. It's my fault she's here." Win wanted to step in – to rescue the girl he'd brought to Mexico – but there was no way it could happen with six armed guards nearby.

Ted shook his head. "As bad as it is, you can't forfeit your own life. It's not your fault this happened. We can only hope this isn't as bad ..." He stopped. No one had to be reminded about Rolando's savage murder of the bus driver.

At first they could hear deep sobs coming from inside Rolando's shack. Then there was conversation so quiet no one could make it out. For the last ten minutes there had been silence.

After what seemed like an hour to the hostages, Alison came out of the hut. She walked unsteadily back to the campfire and sat down next to Hailey.

Win said, "I'm so sorry ..."

She began to cry uncontrollably. Win started to move toward her, and she held up her hand. "Don't come near me. Don't ever come near me again."

Hailey put her arm around the girl. She wasn't very good at this emotional stuff, but it seemed like the thing to do, even though the selfish girl had been completely willing to sacrifice Hailey. Alison laid her head on Hailey's shoulder as she heaved sobs of anguish. Finally she whispered, "I need another shower. Will you come with me? I don't want ... I can't bear the thought of one of those awful men watching me. I don't know ... if I can ever be with a man again."

They walked to the shower and Alison stripped naked. She turned on the hose and asked Hailey to block the view of her fellow hostages, even though it was so dark no one could see anything anyway. As the girl showered, Hailey kept an eye out both for rebel guards and the creatures of the night. She was glad to see neither.

"You need to tell the others something," Alison said in a whisper as they walked back to their sleeping quarters.

"Rolando ... Rolando speaks English. Perfect English."

CHAPTER TWENTY-FOUR

The next morning Mark and Ted were up and out of the bunkhouse by sunrise. They were drinking coffee when Rolando came out.

"I hear we don't need to speak Spanish any longer," Ted said tersely as the rebel leader sat down. "I hope you're proud of yourself for what you did to that girl last night ..."

"What I do is not your affair, *Señor* Pettigrew," Rolando answered in English. "I need no advice from you. I will use you and the others as I wish in order to achieve what I have to do."

Mark said, "And what is that?"

"Ah, the same questions every morning, Dr. Linebarger! You will have to wait a bit longer for the answer, I'm afraid. I'm not ready to reveal my hand just yet."

"Where did you learn English?" Ted asked.

"Aren't you both the inquisitive ones." He laughed without humor. "Keep your people under control, gentlemen, and you may all make it out of this situation alive. Whether you live or die is only partially my decision. Your actions, and the actions of other people who do not yet know of your peril, will also determine if one or more of you dies. It matters little to me; I have a goal and you are merely part of the pathway to achieving it."

He walked to the office shack. Soon the men could hear crackling, then bits and pieces of words in Spanish. Rolando was using the shortwave radio.

CHAPTER TWENTY-FIVE

Paul walked noiselessly along the trail. It was so dense that it was impossible to see where he was going much of the time. Here and there moonlight filtered through the trees, but more often there was darkness. His eyes adjusted to the gloom as he flicked on a small LED flashlight he held in one hand, his pistol in the other. Firing the weapon would make his presence known to anyone within miles, but Paul couldn't ignore the dangers around him. You had to watch for humans, but the animals were something else entirely. He'd risk the noise – he'd shoot a cat before he'd be mauled to death.

An hour later he came to the same imposing ruins of Piedras Negras the others had seen twenty-four hours before. It was a beautiful sight, one he would have enjoyed under different circumstances. He wanted to come back here once this was all over. This place was an important part of the plans he'd had for this trip. First he had to find out the situation with the others. Were they still alive? Why were they brought here? Where were they?

Paul had heard the tales about bandits who lived among the ruins at Piedras Negras, occupying the crude buildings built by Brigham Young archaeologists in the late nineties and robbing foolish tourists who ventured this far up the river. The occasional daring adventurer who paid a fortune for a boat ride to Piedras Negras was almost guaranteed to encounter trouble. The boat drivers knew the program – they got their fare before they dropped a passenger on the beach. They waited without concern – the robbers wouldn't bother the locals. They wanted the tourists, the brave Americans or Canadians or Europeans. Those people usually came back to their boat with nothing left but the clothes on their backs. They no longer had money, jewelry, cell phones or personal possessions. And God forbid if the visitor was a pretty young female. That one would likely leave without her virginity as well. Fortunately there were very, very few women who braved this part of the Usumacinta River.

Many of the victims insisted on filing a police report back in Frontera Corozal. Other than arresting a drunk local now and then, one of the policeman's duties was to solemnly listen to tourists who should have known better than to go there in the first place. Everybody knew what went on at Piedras Negras. People got killed there on a regular basis. It wasn't his jurisdiction and the policeman damned sure wasn't going to get involved. But he listened as though it made a difference and wrote down the descriptions of robbers, the location where it happened and whatever else a tourist wanted to say. Once they left Frontera Corozal on their big fancy buses, he filed the report in the place he filed all the others – the trash can by his desk.

Paul heard nothing but the night noises of the forest as he snaked through the ruins of Piedras Negras. He passed ancient temples and the abandoned archaeological shacks from ten years ago. There were no bandits. Except Rolando himself, of course. Maybe he'd started his criminal career right here with the other thieves who frequently occupied Piedras. Paul knew nothing about the rebel except that somewhere further along this trail he'd find the man and the hostages. That was what Paul hoped would happen. If it didn't – if the boatman had lied to him – he'd have a long trip back to civilization and no clue where the hostages were. This was his only shot, and it depended on the veracity of a native boat driver. He'd taken a stranger's word that this was the trail Rolando took. The driver could have sent him into a trap, leaving him stranded out here alone to die. But this was all he had. He kept walking.

After the ruins, the trail narrowed even more. It had been recently cleared, probably with machetes. The jungle would reclaim it if it were left untended for even a month. He tripped on the stubs of small trees growing in the walkway. He carefully shielded the flashlight with his palm and kept it aimed at the ground.

A half hour later he noticed a faint glow around a bend ahead. He switched off the flashlight, made the turn and stopped suddenly. There was a clearing directly in front of him. Three men who were probably sentries sat around a campfire, smoking cigarettes and talking quietly. Each had a rifle next to his chair and a pistol holstered on his belt. Paul glanced at his watch; it was 1:30 a.m.

In the combination of moonlight and a flickering fire, he saw small wooden buildings here and there but no hostages. He felt sure this was where Rolando had taken them; it was perfect. Miles from civilization, two miles from the river along a single trail cut through otherwise impassable jungle, this place would be hard for rescuers to find and incredibly dangerous to anyone who tried to escape without a weapon.

Suddenly he saw movement fifty feet away. Someone stepped out of a dark hole and walked around another guard who sat in a chair. Paul recognized the guide Julio, who'd come into the clearing to relieve himself. Julio stood for a moment, his back to the guards by the fire, finished and went back into what must be a cave. That had to be where the people were.

His packs by his side, Paul spent two tedious hours standing noiselessly in the jungle, studying the guards' routine. Finally he'd seen enough. There was nothing more he could do until morning. Now that he knew the situation, he would come back after daybreak and formulate a plan.

Paul counted his steps back to the ruins. Counting for thirty minutes was tough, but he had to know exactly how far it was. Tomorrow he'd come back to the rebel camp; he had to be on alert when he reached the turn in the trail just before the campsite. In the daylight if he were standing as close as he'd been tonight, anyone in the clearing would spot him instantly. Tomorrow morning he'd have to be hidden.

At Piedras Negras there were wooden buildings that had been the BYU archaeologists' sleeping and working quarters. They had screen netting that allowed a little breeze inside. The screens should have rotted long ago, but they were mostly intact, probably because bandits had been here recently. He stopped and listened, heard no sounds that would indicate humans were present, then opened the rickety door to the first cabin.

There was an old picnic table and chairs, beer bottles and trash tossed here and there, and a hammock in one corner. That was a surprise; Paul had expected to catch a few hours of sleep sitting up, but instead he tested the hammock. It was in decent shape and bore his weight.

Although this shack was too close to the trail for a long-term hiding place, he was glad to have it tonight. Tomorrow he'd find something else. He crawled into the hammock and dozed until dawn.

Paul could hear activity ahead of him as he neared the rebel camp. It was nine a.m.; he'd purposely waited until the sun was well up. The day would be long regardless, and he reasoned there'd be nothing to observe until people were up and about. As he'd walked the trail, he kept his eye out for hiding places. This pathway was the only connection between the rebel camp and the river; Rolando's men would have to use it to move supplies. It also ran right through Piedras Negras, where he'd spent the night. He was lucky not to have seen anyone on the trail, but luck wasn't what Paul depended upon. He relied on the skills, training and instinct of the assassin he was, but most of all he needed a plan. Today. He needed a better hideout at the ruins, and he had to rescue the hostages.

He knew from the steps he'd counted that the clearing was just around the next bend. He stepped into the forest, crept noiselessly through bushes and vines, and ended up in a tight thicket of leaves fifty feet from the campfire. It was a good place – he was close to the activity but totally hidden by the foliage. He put down his pack and prepared for what would likely be a long day.

He reconnoitered the area and saw ten rebels doing routine tasks. Some gathered wood; others carried boxes from another cave entrance he hadn't seen last night. A few men were acting as guards, but everyone appeared basically unconcerned about security. This place was as remote as it got – there was no place to escape to. He counted ten rebels. Plus Rolando and maybe one or two he couldn't see. That was a lot, but Paul had dealt with more.

115

He was pleased to see some of the captives. Mark and Ted sat by the campfire, drinking coffee and talking. Doc and Mary Spence were hanging out clothes on a line, and Gavin, the author Paul had become friends with, was just coming out of the cavern, which apparently was where they slept.

If he hadn't known they were prisoners, he'd have thought they were friends roughing it on a campout. No one looked harried or concerned, the rebels had no interaction with the hostages at all, and Rolando was nowhere in sight.

Suddenly he stepped out of a shack, wearing a T-shirt and shorts. He walked to the campfire and sat next to Ted and Mark. Paul saw that Rolando no longer wore a mask. He had rough-hewn, ruggedly handsome features and a nose that looked as though a prizefighter had had his way with it in the past. He was muscular and lean – obviously life in the jungle kept him fit and trim.

When Rolando spoke, Paul was close enough to hear everything. He was surprised that the rebel spoke English. Shortly Paul knew exactly what was going on here.

"I have just sent a radio transmission to the United States Embassy in Mexico City. I have informed them that I require a ransom of one hundred thousand US dollars for each of the ten of you. Your guide, Julio, is not a part of this. I will release him unharmed once this is all over."

Ted pleaded with the kidnapper. "I don't know anything about the financial situation of the other people, but I do know there's nobody who can pay a hundred thousand bucks to ransom me. Mark" – he looked at the archaeologist – "what about you?"

"No way that's going to happen," Mark replied honestly. "I'm a teacher, an academic. We don't make shit. I maybe have twenty grand in my retirement account. It's all yours. If you want more than that, you might as well shoot me now."

Rolando stared at Mark for a few seconds. *These idiots don't take me seriously.* So he told them more. As he explained what was going to happen, their faces reflected the horror of their impending situation.

"I've given your families an incentive. Some people might not act as quickly as they should to raise the money. Others, like Dr. Spence, might be wealthy. I might get his money quickly. I am a patient man, but I also must be firm. You don't want to spend weeks here in the jungle, and I don't want to keep you longer than I must. So there is a deadline."

He stood with a cruel smile. "Three days from now someone, one of your friends or family, must have paid the first one hundred thousand. It doesn't matter who, but I must have at least the first payment. After that, I require the rest by the tenth day. On that day, I will see where we stand. The ones who have been ransomed will be fine. I will release them as a group when this is over. The unfortunate ones whose families do not pay will be eliminated. Executed, every one of them on the morning of the eleventh day. Should a family pay sometime later, I will gladly accept it even though they won't get their loved one back. Because they missed the deadline, you see. Their fault, not mine."

"Are you crazy?" Ted was shocked and astounded. He spoke more loudly than he intended; some of the others heard him. They turned to watch and Mark shooed them away.

Tears rolled down Mark's cheeks as he thought of what was going to happen to the others. "Three days to raise a hundred grand is unreasonable. I don't think you'll get anything by then …"

"You could be right." Rolando laughed. "But maybe that will work in my favor. A picture of the first execution, as you Americans say it, will be worth a thousand words. Don't you think people will take me more seriously then? Gentlemen, I am going to kill one of you four days from now if I haven't received one hundred thousand dollars."

Ted and Mark were speechless. They couldn't believe the casual manner in which their kidnapper had outlined a program to execute perhaps every one of them. If he was serious – and they had to believe he was – they had very little time to work on an escape. Their minds were reeling, already searching for a way out of this horrific nightmare.

Paul was way ahead of them. His mind was clear and steady. His plan was already coming together. And he knew he was their only hope.

Rolando turned to leave. "Gather the people, gentlemen. Tell them what I've told you. If anyone has something to say to someone who can pay the money, write it on a piece of paper and give it to me today. I will transmit your messages to the embassy."

Ted and Mark cried as the others ran to see what had happened. Soon everyone was in tears. Paul watched the people react to the stunning news. More of them would be murdered soon. Some were undoubtedly going to die. Wails of tortured heartbreak echoed through the camp.

As he saw the people grieve, Paul watched Rolando standing in the doorway of his hut. He was smiling at them. *Not for long,* Paul vowed. *You won't smile for long, you bastard. I promise you.*

CHAPTER TWENTY-SIX

Paul watched all day long. Most of the time the captives had sat in grim silence. As the sun began to set, Paul could smell food cooking. When they were told it was ready, none of the hostages went to the cook shack. Only Rolando and his men ate. The others appeared to have lost their appetites after hearing that their lives might end in a few days. As darkness descended on the camp, they sat around the fire, seeking solace in each other's company.

Alison and Hailey huddled close together. Although nothing had happened for two days, Alison was more afraid she'd be taken to Rolando's shack again than she was scared to die. The girl hadn't uttered a single word about what had happened that night, even to Hailey. She'd buried the entire episode deep in her mind, as if bringing it back to the surface might make it happen all over again. She felt so violated she was certain she'd never get over it. She hadn't ever given rape victims much thought. Now that Alison was one herself, she hoped somehow to get past it, but she didn't know if she ever could. While others pondered their own mortality, Alison worried about the fate she considered even worse – more sexual abuse by their evil captor. Little did she imagine what she would agree to do tomorrow in order to purchase her own life.

Bart and Dick talked quietly while Gavin sat alone with the comfort of his pipe. Julio lit a cigarette, took a long drag and settled back against a tree. Paul didn't see the others – Ted, Mark and the Spences. They must already be in the sleeping cave.

One of the rebels came out of Rolando's shack and walked across the clearing directly to where Hailey and Alison sat. Alison shrank down, cowering against Hailey, as if that would make her disappear.

"No! God, no! Get away. Please don't take me!"

The man grinned and pointed at Hailey. "You. You go."

Hailey had mentally prepared herself for this, even while she processed the earlier jolt about the ransom demand. She knew she'd be next, and she decided to learn as much as she could while enduring whatever was going to happen. Maybe she'd see or hear something that could help them overpower the rebels.

"My turn? Before he kills us, he wants to screw us, is that it? What kind of sick bastard is your boss?" Her words meant nothing to the guard, who spoke no English. She gently withdrew from Alison. The girl's hands clutched at Hailey's T-shirt like vises as she pried them away.

"It's okay. I'll be all right. There's never been a man I couldn't handle." As she stood, some of the others said they were sorry.

"Don't worry about me," she responded in a tone too upbeat for the reality of what was going to happen. She was putting up a good front, and she had to keep doing it until Rolando was finished with her. She'd damn sure give it a try. Even if things worked out badly, she'd never let him know he'd beaten her. Whatever he made her do, she'd keep her wits about her. Anything – even something small –

might help them figure out how to beat this psychopath before he killed them all.

She stepped inside his shack and the guard took a position outside the door, the same way he'd done when Alison was taken here two nights ago. Hailey looked around the nasty, cluttered twelve-by-twelve room illuminated by a single lantern hanging from a rafter. Rolando sat at a small desk across the room, wearing the same T-shirt and ragged shorts he'd had on since they arrived at the camp. He looked up and smiled as she came in.

Hailey returned the smile as best she could. She had experience faking a good time with partners – she'd done it more than once – so she'd have to think of this one like that. It meant nothing and she'd get through it. She might be able to learn something helpful if she convinced this guy she liked him. That would make everything worth it. Maybe.

"Hey, hotshot. Nice shithole you have here."

"Hotshot?" he replied with a puzzled look. "What is the meaning of that word?" He ignored the comment about his shack.

"It doesn't matter. I guess you didn't invite me for tea, and I guess it's not time to kill me yet, so let's get this over with. What do you have in mind?"

"You Americans are so businesslike! How do you say it, slam bam? I can do it that way too. Take off your clothes and show me how you look with nothing on. If I like you, maybe I won't kill you at all. Or at least until the end. We can have some fun until then, right?"

She didn't answer. As much as she hated it, she had to do whatever she could to stay alive. Every day she didn't die was one more opportunity to escape. She wouldn't show how much she detested whatever he was going to do to her.

Hailey slowly unbuttoned her shirt; she'd quit wearing her bra two days ago. She kept her shirt provocatively open without taking it off, and undid the top button of her shorts. She lowered the zipper halfway, then stopped. She was wearing nothing underneath, and he could see the beginning wisps of pubic hair.

This was one of the most difficult things she'd ever done, but her life was at stake. She forced a seductive smile, ready to go on with whatever he wanted just to get this part over. It would be pure sex. Not fun, not exciting, not … sexy. But she damn sure would make it good enough to keep him coming back.

She swallowed hard and sighed. "Do I get to see anything too, or do I have to show and tell all by myself?"

"Of course." He stood, pulled his T-shirt over his head, stepped out of a pair of old sandals and unzipped his shorts in one quick move. They fell to the floor, revealing his swollen erection. "All yours," he said with a scornful laugh.

Just keep your mind on something else and it'll be done before you know it.

Hailey slowly pulled off her shirt and he ogled her breasts, their pert nipples involuntarily hard despite her circumstances. She lowered the zipper of her shorts, kicked off her shoes and took a deep breath. Her pants hit the floor. She stepped out of them and stood naked in front of her kidnapper.

He walked to her and cupped a breast in each of his dirty hands. He began to massage them slowly. She reached down to take him in her hand. The sooner this all happened, the faster she'd be finished with this episode. She stroked him, and then he said the words she'd hoped not to hear.

"Get on your knees in front of me. You know what to do."

Fifteen minutes ago Paul was watching as the guard delivered Hailey to Rolando's shack. He had no doubt what was about to happen. He regretted that he couldn't help her, but the fate of the entire group rested in his ability to remain hidden. He had to continue observing the routine of the rebels to see where there were opportunities. His mind raced with ideas for a plan, but it hadn't come together yet. There were too many guards to deal with at one time. He could extricate a hostage here, a hostage there, but he wasn't sure what that would accomplish. They'd be missed at the next head count and the others would be punished … or worse. This far from civilization, everyone's best chance for survival was here in the camp, where the food and shelter were. He needed time for a plan, but time was running out for the captives. If Rolando followed through with his threat, the executions could begin in three days. He had to act quickly.

Hailey walked out of Rolando's cabin, buttoning her shirt as she passed everyone without a word. She went to the water bag, grabbed a cup, took a huge drink, rinsed and spit it on the ground. She sat down next to Alison and they embraced. Alison sobbed – so did some of the others. But Hailey didn't. Paul saw furious determination in her clenched jaw, her angry face. The man may have gotten what he wanted, but this female was someone to reckon with. She had stamina whereas many of the others didn't. She could be a huge help when the time came for action.

Paul moved stealthily through the woods along the fringe of the campsite, watching the hostages go into the cave for the night. Mark and Ted went last, making sure everyone was accounted for. They'd done the same thing yesterday, and now Paul waited, hoping something else he'd observed last night would happen again. And it did. Bringing up the rear, the archaeologist walked away from the sentry at the cave entrance. He stopped at the water bag and filled his cup.

In a split second Paul made his move. He emerged from the jungle right in front of Mark, his finger on his lips. Less than twenty feet away, eight rebels talked and smoked around the dying campfire. A ninth was even closer, talking to the one guarding the cave entrance. Paul handed Mark a piece of paper; then he disappeared back into the forest. Mark stuck it in his pocket and walked nonchalantly back to the cave.

CHAPTER TWENTY-SEVEN

Ten exhausted people lay stunned on their cots, each lost in thought. Most were convinced they were going to die. They all had reached that sobering conclusion independently after hearing what Rolando had planned for those whose ransoms weren't paid. Several people doubted their families could raise the money in time, if at all. Others could only hope that the money would arrive and Rolando would honor his commitment to release them. That was a long shot few believed would happen. A few others pondered how to escape into a jungle full of equally frightening dangers as what they faced from the rebel leader.

Mark sat on his cot and read Paul's note. Then he rested, glancing at his watch every few minutes. In less than an hour the others were in some form of restless slumber. Some were having tortured dreams – they groaned or called out. Others tossed and turned on the crude, uncomfortable cots. At exactly eleven o'clock, Mark put on his shoes and walked quietly to the entrance, careful not to wake the others. From here he could see the guard sitting in his chair, smoking a cigarette. Per Paul's instructions, he waited just inside the front of the dark cave.

Paul's job was to distract the guard. From observation last night he knew the sentry left his post frequently to relieve himself, talk to a perimeter guard or just walk around. After all, no one in the cave was going anywhere, so he didn't see the need to be particularly diligent about guarding them when they were asleep. Five minutes passed as the guard puffed his smoke then did something he did ten times a night, every time he had a cigarette. He tossed the butt into the bushes a foot from where Paul was standing. That was what Paul had waited for. He pulled out a lighter, bent down and cupped the flame with his hand. He lit the leaves around the cigarette butt. As soon as they caught, he crept silently toward the cave entrance.

Soon the guard noticed a plume of smoke coming from where he'd tossed the butt. Cursing, he got up, walked to the spot and stamped out the burning leaves. When he did, Mark slipped out of the cave, saw Paul standing nearby, and followed him.

The men sneaked through the bushes until they reached the trail that led back to Piedras Negras. Giving him a signal for silence, Paul motioned for Mark to follow. They walked for ten minutes then stopped and sat, sufficiently far from the camp to talk in whispers.

Mark asked, "How did you get away, and how did you find us?"

"There's no time to go into it now. I've been watching you all day and I'll be back tomorrow. I'll get you out of here. Here's what we're going to do."

In a few minutes Paul outlined the plan he'd created during his hours in the jungle today. Mark listened, saying nothing until he was finished. He asked a few questions and nodded. There was really no alternative since Paul was the only one of them who was free.

Paul said, "I need your help. It's not a good idea to tell anyone else I'm here – there's too big a chance someone might be coerced or tortured into telling Rolando about me. Also please don't let anyone attempt anything crazy in the next three days. Just tell them you're working on a plan. Very soon Rolando's going to know I'm here anyway – I just want to lie low for now to get the upper hand. My idea may not work, but give it a chance. Right now it's all we have. As long as Rolando doesn't know I exist, I can help. As bad as it is, we can get out of this. There are things in my past that will serve all of us well."

"Your past? What exactly ..."

Paul shook his head. "I can't tell you that – you know the old joke 'I'd have to kill you'? That's what I'm talking about."

"So you're CIA or something ..."

"Or something. And I *was*, but not anymore." Little white lies were the least of Paul's concerns right now.

The last thing they worked out was a way to communicate. Mark was to go to the water bag every evening before bedtime to see if Paul wanted to pass information along.

Thirty minutes later the guard got up, stretched and strolled around the campsite. Mark sneaked back into the cave and Paul slipped away into the night.

CHAPTER TWENTY-EIGHT

The United States Embassy in Mexico City was already on full alert when Rolando's shortwave radio transmission arrived. Three days earlier the ambassador had briefed his senior staff about the missing Americans. Even the White House was involved in this one, he advised, stressing the urgency and importance of the situation. Five additional FBI agents fluent in Spanish came in yesterday – they and two senior embassy people had immediately been sent to Villahermosa to assist the others in the so far fruitless search. Today they'd all driven to Palenque, following the route of the missing bus.

Like most outposts in third world countries, this embassy had a shortwave radio. It was so rarely used that when Rolando began talking that morning, the transmission startled the person in the office where it sat. The radio's messages were recorded like every other communication coming into the embassy. Within minutes the US Department of State and the FBI knew the missing Americans had been kidnapped and their captor wanted a ransom. Messages from each captive to his or her own family were sent too – from that the FBI knew this was the real thing, not an unconnected con artist trying to make money off a busload of missing persons.

The search was ramped up and the hostage messages were passed along to their loved ones. The victims' families were asked to keep the ransom demands confidential for a few days. The FBI wanted to find the hostages quickly and without the high-profile pressure that would come from this news.

The kidnapper instructed that ransoms be wired to a small bank in Venezuela, a country generally unfriendly to US interests and unwilling to cooperate with criminal investigations. Although US authorities didn't know it, Rolando had set up two more transfers, in Nicaragua and Costa Rica. That was enough to keep the US government from learning who was getting the money or where it was ultimately headed.

Now that they knew a crime had been committed, the embassy's switchboard operators were put on full alert. Any call about the situation was given top priority. Attachés were on duty twenty-four hours a day.

The day after the kidnapper sent the shortwave transmission, the telephone operator on duty took a call. A man's voice said, "Transfer me to whoever is handling the missing Americans. Now!"

She sent the call immediately to a monitored, recorded line. As soon as the attaché answered, an FBI agent at the next desk put on headphones. A computer began a GPS search for the caller's location.

The voice said, "Listen closely because I don't have much time. I'm on your side – I'm going to help rescue the hostages and I need the kidnapper's instructions about where to send the money."

The FBI agent believed the caller was a man speaking Americanized English like TV newscasters – with no hint of a regional accent. This could mean more than one thing. Maybe a person had learned English as a second language, but it could also point to someone born or raised in the Midwestern USA.

"First let me get your name," the attaché said calmly, reading the first line of a script in front of him.

"Did you hear me? There's very little time. Give me the information."

"How do you know that the hostages are being ransomed? That information's not −"

The caller interrupted curtly. "If one of these people dies because of your stupidity, then you can live with that the rest of your life. Tell me how to pay the ransom. NOW!"

The FBI agent nodded his head and the attaché picked up a second sheet. With a lump in his throat, he began to read the instructions. It was a sobering thought to know that the words you were saying might save an American life. Or lose one.

As soon as Paul had the wire transfer information, he disconnected. People sprang into action, analyzing the call word by word and attempting to learn the phone's location. They got very little from the analysis and nothing at all from GPS. Paul's satellite phone was equipped with a feature that bounced his location from place to place across the globe every three seconds. All the FBI got was a frustrating list with dozens of random city names.

Next Paul sent an email to his bank in Rome. The message contained twenty-two words and a series of numbers. It was short, but hopefully it would work.

CHAPTER TWENTY-NINE

Days after it was abandoned, the nearly new tour bus still sat in the woods near Frontera Corozal. By now it was getting grimy and dusty.

A couple of middle-aged village ladies who sold trinkets to the tourists lived on the outskirts of town. They walked from home to the river and back every day, passing less than twenty feet from the hidden coach each time. On the sixth morning after it had been abandoned, they got started a little later than usual. The sun was already climbing into the sky and they saw a bright reflection in the trees.

They ran to the tree line to see what it might be. There sat a huge motor coach. One of them screamed with delight, "There's been a story on TV about a missing bus and a big reward!" Their day selling trinkets now forgotten, they rushed back to their houses and told their teenage sons, who rushed to check it out. They tested the bus door and found it unlocked. That was a pleasant surprise; they had been prepared to break in. The boys rummaged around in the seats, finding sacks, water bottles and even a pair of binoculars. These tourists must have left in a hurry. The boys took everything that was loose, stuffing it into a bag they'd brought. Then one of them noticed something else.

"Look at this! There's a note in this seat."

Mark Linebarger had scribbled a letter on a piece of paper. It described his group of Americans and explained everything that had happened, beginning with the hijacking by the man called Rolando. He told about the execution of the driver and surmised they were going to go on the river. He had carefully folded the letter; then he wrote large words on the outside in Spanish. "GIVE THIS TO THE POLICE IMMEDIATELY. THERE HAS BEEN A MURDER!"

The archaeologist had no way to know if Rolando and the other rebels might do a last walk-through before abandoning the bus. If they did, they'd surely find his note and destroy it. If they didn't, he could only hope someone else might come across it and do as he asked.

Fortunately it worked. The anxious looters first took their spoils home, and then they headed straight to the house of the one police officer in their town. They banged on the tin door of his house that doubled as the police station. He read the note and ordered the boys to take him to the bus. He did a quick walk-through and then he called the superintendent of Federal Police in Tuxtla Gutierrez, the capital.

The policeman was instructed to guard the bus until the *federales* arrived. This morning he sat on the first step of the coach with his gun drawn and a stern look on his face as he brushed inquisitive townspeople away. Everyone had heard that the bus, the subject of a national search, had been found right here in their very town. It was the most exciting day in history.

"This is a crime scene!" he yelled to anyone who approached. "I will arrest you if you come closer!" He was enjoying his important role.

134

No one liked him. He was always full of himself because he got to carry a gun and he had a car furnished by the state of Chiapas. No matter that it was ten years old and belched smoke. You'd have thought he was the mayor of Tuxtla the way he treated other people with disdain.

Despite his threats, people nosed around the bus, asked him questions, and pushed his buttons, knowing he wasn't going to shoot anyone or arrest them. Despite that, the cop did a good job keeping the crowds away, which wasn't hard because there weren't many people in Frontera Corozal.

By nightfall the local cop's role was over and the little river town had almost doubled in population. It was so remote – so far from a major highway – that getting there had been a major task involving hours of driving. There were officials from the American Embassy in Mexico City, federal agents from Tuxtla Gutierrez, and enough police and militia to battle a small army. Most had come by plane to Palenque airport, where some hired floatplanes to bring them on to Frontera Corozal.

The visitors booked every room at the lodge, many bunking two or three to a room, but there were far more people than accommodations. The locals opened up extra bedrooms in their homes. By midnight all the newcomers had beds and knew the plan for tomorrow.

People congregated in the dining room the next morning at six. The lodge's manager called in extra staff to fix breakfast and coffee for the dozens of guests. Around ten a satellite news truck from Aguascalientes TV arrived from Palenque, only a hundred miles away but requiring over nine hours of driving on poorly maintained roads. They'd been driving all night and were thrilled to smell hot coffee and bacon as they piled out of their truck. By noon the network's crew was beaming coverage from a field close to the bus that was still being scoured by *federales* and the FBI.

The note had said the hostages might be taken away by boat, so the investigation started there. Many of the men who drove the longboats also owned them, although hired drivers operated a few. The officers quickly realized that there was no official list of boats or drivers, no licensing process, and no way to know exactly how many drivers or boats there were. Today there were twelve longboats tied up at the dock. Several other slips were empty; the police were told those boats were already downriver, ferrying early-bird tourists to Yaxchilan. Ten drivers were on the dock; two more hadn't shown up yet. Those two were Ruben and Pablo Ochoa. The local policeman was dispatched to bring them in for questioning.

The authorities commandeered two of the lodge's rooms, where police and Spanish-speaking FBI agents interrogated each boat driver. Meanwhile, floatplanes scoured the river all afternoon, searching for signs of habitation but finding nothing.

Ruben and Pablo considered themselves fortunate. On the night they'd been hired to go to Piedras Negras, it had been late. All the other drivers were already at home, so no one saw them. The one thing Ruben didn't know was that Pablo had made the same trip again the very next night, ferrying another American downriver and returning alone before dawn. Pablo kept that trip – and the five hundred dollars Paul had paid for the ride – to himself.

Days ago when Ruben first saw the newscast, he had gone straight to Pablo's house. Ruben was upset that they couldn't claim the ten-thousand-dollar reward. They didn't know exactly where the bus was, but they had a good idea where the hostages had been taken. They'd even seen the kidnappers. Ruben figured with a little searching they could have found the bus somewhere nearby.

As enticing as the reward money was, they couldn't risk it. They couldn't say anything without implicating themselves. They'd end up in prison as accessories to a crime instead of becoming the wealthiest citizens of Frontera Corozal.

Now, instead of planning how to spend ten thousand dollars themselves, they knew two teenaged thieves would get it instead. The Ochoas, the ones who deserved the reward, sat in Pablo's yard, creating an alibi. They knew eventually someone would find the abandoned bus. They fretted, sweated and practiced their story for nearly a week, but nothing happened.

Yesterday the whole thing had blown up. Sitting at the dock waiting for a fare, Ruben and his cousin heard about it around noon – news traveled fast around the small community. The two kids found a note on the bus, told the cop, and he searched it. Now Frontera Corozal had more activity and more police than anyone had ever seen before. It wouldn't be long before they would talk to the boat drivers.

The cousins left the dock immediately, but they couldn't hide forever. Undoubtedly they were missed already; they hung out there every day. When the knock on Pablo's door finally came, they trembled. The local cop stood on the doorstep.

CHAPTER THIRTY

With a good deal of pomposity, the local policeman brought in the two "suspects" who also were his childhood friends – men he'd grown up with. He, Ruben and Pablo all played together as ragged children before Frontera Corozal even existed. Fifteen years ago their fathers made a living hauling potatoes, corn, beans and livestock across the river to Guatemala. When they became teenagers, the Ochoa cousins followed in the family business, inheriting the longboats from their fathers.

The policeman took a different path; in a highly unusual move for this rural area, his parents kept him in school until he was sixteen. He was suddenly the most educated person for miles around, and he landed a comfortable job as the sole lawman for the tiny river town.

Today friendships were forgotten. News cameras were rolling and it was the policeman's fifteen minutes of fame. He wished he'd had shackles – it would have made a great photo – but he hadn't even gotten handcuffs from the state, so he had to be content to push the Ochoas along roughly. He thought about drawing his gun but decided against it. He didn't even know how to use it; he'd skipped the mandatory firearms training so many times the officials in Tuxtla had stopped asking.

The *federales* took Ruben into one of the cabanas and Pablo to the other. There were two officials in each room – a Federal Policeman and an FBI agent.

The interrogators were tired. The cabanas were hot and stuffy; a fan lazily moved air, but nothing could ease the humidity. For hours they'd interviewed honest and sincere boatmen who knew absolutely nothing. The lawmen were ready for cervezas as soon as they finished these last two interviews. Two to go before Corona time.

Thirty minutes later the interviews were over. Pablo walked home, confident that it went well and their alibi was solid. He said he and Ruben had been fishing and drinking beer that evening. They didn't see or hear anything because they were more than a mile upriver in Ruben's longboat. They hadn't returned to the dock until around 11:30 p.m. Ruben's story was identical.

"Did you notice the tour bus sitting in the parking lot for days?" Pablo had been asked.

"Not really. There are buses here all the time. They all look the same to me."

"Do you have any thoughts how more than a dozen people with luggage could have been taken somewhere on the river, or where they might have gone?"

"They might have gone to Yaxchilan," he offered, hoping to sound helpful. "Lots of people do."

"Is there anything else you want to add?"

"Nothing else, *Señor*."

For today the interrogations were finished.

CHAPTER THIRTY-ONE

A week ago today the people had been taken hostage, and it was four days since Rolando made the ransom demand. Nine of the ten captives had sent personal messages to relatives in the States via shortwave radio. The tenth, the archaeologist Mark Linebarger, prepared a note to his girlfriend in Toronto, telling her he was okay. He didn't mention the ransom. It might as well be a million – he wasn't kidding when he told Rolando it was fruitless. He didn't have money – he didn't even *know* people who had money. Mark's life was divided among teaching, being with friends, and leading groups into the jungle. It was a satisfying existence, but he'd never be wealthy doing it.

When Rolando read Mark's message, he thrust it back and said, "Ask her for money."

"No. All that'll do is make a bunch of my friends scramble around to do something they can't make happen. I'm not asking for money. You ever hear the phrase 'blood from a turnip'?"

Rolando ignored the question. This man puzzled him. He stayed calm – he wasn't afraid. He was stronger than many of the others.

"Have it your way. I'll pass your message along. After all, it's your funeral."

"Actually, I suppose that part's up to you."

The ransom would be no problem for a few of the hostages. Doc and Mary Spence, Dick Mansfield, the real estate man from New York, and the author Gavin Michaels had sent detailed instructions on how to access funds. Their problem was the short time frame. Three days wasn't much, especially with the US Embassy acting as middleman. Since Rolando's demand for ransom had been made through the embassy and he'd also sent the hostage messages there, the ambassador and the FBI would facilitate the money transfers to pay the kidnappers.

Today was the fourth day – the deadline for a ransom payment. Every day the hostages knew someone could die, but Mark and Ted tried to keep spirits positive. Today was different. From the moment they awoke, every one of them knew that someone would die today if at least one ransom payment didn't arrive.

Ted and Mark tried to calm concerns as the hours ticked by far more slowly than usual. Most of the questions had no answers. How would the kidnappers find out the money was paid? They were here in the jungle, not in a city with banks and communications. What if something delayed a payment accidentally? Would Rolando give them any leeway?

Not a chance. They all knew that.

Mark and Ted set a deadline of their own. At three p.m. they confronted Rolando.

"So what's the plan? How do you find out if you got your damned ransom money or not?"

Rolando smirked. "Ted! Are you getting a little worried?"

Mark snapped back, "You're a sick bastard! I'm sure you know kidnapping ten North Americans and murdering our driver is going to land you in prison or, even better, get you killed. You'll never get away with it."

Rolando paused and decided to tell them what this was all about.

"Everything will be worth it when Chiapas is ours again."

"Whose? Guatemala's? Do you really think that's going to happen? Do you think this senseless act of violence against innocent tourists will attract people to your cause? Get real, man. What you're doing here sets you back. It simply proves to the world what sadistic savages you are. You're not interested in politics or unity for Chiapas. You're a brutal murderer. What's your real agenda, 'Rolando'?" Mark spat the alias out like vomit.

"I'm going to be a wealthy man in a few days, Dr. Linebarger. And the freedom fighters will be wealthy too. I plan to share with them, you see. I'll take my commission for arranging the deal; then they'll have money to buy guns, ammunition, everything they need to kill the police and the militia. Then, contrary to what you think, we *will* cause Chiapas state to secede."

"So did you get the ransom money you demanded today? Are you going to spare us a little longer?" Ted was surprised at the hatred in Mark's words. "Do you get to have some fun today killing another innocent person? That sounds exciting, don't you think, Ted?"

Ted said nothing. Rolando's jaw was clenched – it was clear he wasn't going to take much more of this.

"You have a very negative attitude," the rebel said calmly. "I don't like you at all. You've already told me you can't raise the money. I think it will be you who goes first. That would make life easier for me. And yes, as you said, it would be fun."

Mark stood his ground. He'd never faced death before. He'd never even had a crime committed against him. Now he found an inner strength he didn't realize he had.

"If that's your decision, I'm ready. I just want to know when we'll get the news."

"Trust me. You'll hear as soon as I do. I sent a man to La Tecnica this morning …" He stopped, deciding he'd said enough, and walked away.

The others ran to Mark. They'd watched and listened to the whole thing.

"What's La Tecnica?" Alison asked.

"It's a village on the Guatemala side just across from Frontera Corozal."

"Why did he send someone there?"

Mark's answer was pure speculation, but he'd given some thought to the logistics of the ransom demands. Rolando had to receive confirmation of bank deposits somehow. The radio wouldn't help and there was no cell service here. The last tower Mark had seen was Claro's, a mile from Frontera Corozal on the side of the river.

Rolando sent his man to the Guatemala town, Mark suggested, because it was even less populated than Frontera Corozal was. No one would pay any attention to just another Guatemalan checking email.

The hostages anxiously waited. No one had eaten; on a day when someone was going to die, nobody had an appetite. It was almost dusk when one of the rebels walked into the camp. The hostages perked up and watched as he went directly to Rolando's shack.

In seconds the rebel leader came out. Everyone saw the pistol on his hip. It hadn't been there earlier today. As Rolando walked toward them, Alison began to cry uncontrollably. A few of them stood up, but Rolando waved them back to the ground.

"Listen to me, all of you. I have good news and bad news." He smiled broadly. "Since everyone likes jokes, I will make the American joke, 'do you want the good news or the bad news first?'"

"Are you fucking kidding me?" Dick Mansfield muttered.

"No, I am not. All right then, I will choose for you. I will give you the good news first. My men and I thank you for your generosity. The first money has been paid." He stopped, crossed his arms over his chest and waited.

Ted spoke up. "And?"

"And what? What more do you want to know?" He was enjoying himself immensely, as the others were literally scared witless.

"Who gets to live? Whose money did you get?"

"Ah, you remember my plan! *Excellente!* Actually I received three ransoms today. I think one of these may surprise someone. It certainly surprised me." He paused for effect then pulled a scrap of paper from his pocket.

"Dr. and Mrs. Spence, you're safe. Nice to know you have funds to help our cause, don't you agree? And we appreciate your generosity very much." He laughed mirthlessly.

"Now for the surprise. Dr. Linebarger, you tricked me."

Mark looked up sharply. "What are you talking about?"

"I'm disappointed because I was looking forward to killing you. But I have your ransom too."

CHAPTER THIRTY-TWO

That's impossible, Mark thought to himself. "So what's the bad news?" he asked caustically.

"As usual, I can always depend on you to be the pushy one. But, in fact, your ransom has mysteriously been paid. Now I have to spare you. At least that's what I said I would do. And speaking of things I promised, I'm afraid I must change my plans. I've thought carefully about the ransom schedule. Let's review what I told you earlier."

He enumerated the points from four days before. "I promised if someone paid by the fourth day, which is today, none of you would die today. If someone paid – anyone – then all of you would live until ten days total have passed. On the eleventh day those who haven't been ransomed will be executed en masse. I believe that was the plan. Am I correct, Dr. Linebarger?" He smirked at the archaeologist.

"So what's the bad news, Rolando? I'm sure there's something you've decided to renege on. Are you going to kill us all now and wait for the money to come in?"

Several people gasped and Bart shouted, "For God's sake, shut up! Do you *want* him to kill us?"

Mark responded bluntly. "Do you think anything any of us does is going to make him act differently? He's a maniac." That made Rolando smile.

Dick yelled, "That's easy for you to say. You're safe."

"Not if his bad news is that he's going to kill one of us anyway. It may be me, you know. I appear to be numero uno on your list," he said to the rebel.

Rolando held up his hand. "If I may have the floor, gentlemen, I'll try to ease your minds. Most of your minds, that is." He paused as Alison continued sobbing. Hailey took her hand.

"Although I greatly appreciate the help of the Spence family in following my orders to quickly pay the money, I think many of you don't have the resources they do. I'm leaving Dr. Linebarger out of this. I have no idea how his ransom got paid and I doubt he knows either." Mark said nothing.

"So I must make an example. Except for two more of you who have instructed payment be sent – that would be Mr. Michaels and Mr. Mansfield – the rest have friends or family who are desperately trying to raise a large sum of money. I want them to be perfectly clear about my instructions. I want them to know that I actually do intend to kill every single one of you whose ransoms are not here six days from now. How can I deliver that message? Originally I had thought four days wasn't sufficient time for the ransoms to arrive. And I said one of you would die today if it didn't come. But here we are, much to my surprise. Three ransoms have been paid, but I still need to prove to the outside world I'm serious. I need to send them a picture."

He continued with a heartless smile. "I apologize for changing the plans. If none of you creates a problem, this will probably be the last change. After this I will wait until the tenth day passes. On that eleventh morning those who have paid will go free and those who have not will leave us in a different way."

He took out the ski mask he'd worn on the bus. As he pulled it over his head, he whistled to one of the guards. The rebel moved closer and raised a camera he was holding.

Rolando took out his pistol and everyone shrank back in fear. Alison and Hailey screamed. A couple of others fainted. Mark and Doc Spence sat impassively.

"Please, dear God, please don't." Ted's plea went unheeded.

Rolando spoke to his associate. "Ready for a picture?"

The man with the camera nodded.

Rolando pointed the gun at Win Phillips and calmly shot him in the head. He fell backwards into the dirt.

"That was my example. That should show everyone we are serious, don't you think?"

The leader ordered his men to remove the body and walked to his shack as nonchalantly as if he'd just brushed off a fly.

———

"We're all going to die. You all know that by now. We know what Rolando looks like. He doesn't wear the mask anymore. We're trapped out here in the jungle and he's going to kill us all."

The hostages huddled together in the cavern as Alison choked her words through heaving sobs of anguish.

149

She'd just witnessed the murder of the man who brought her here – the man who'd once been her boyfriend. The others nodded as she ranted. A few sat with heads bowed, consumed by thoughts of their mortality. The trauma was tormenting each of them in a different way, and some were losing their grips quickly.

Mark understood their anguish. These people couldn't take much more, and everyone knew Rolando's promise they'd be alive for six more days was worthless. He'd reneged already and a third person had died. Everything Alison said was right. Rolando wasn't a bit concerned that they could identify him. No one was going to leave here alive. Mark wanted to calm the people's fears, to keep them from doing something stupid that might cost everyone's lives. They had to be united and wait for Paul. But these people didn't know Paul was even around. Should he tell them, even though Paul asked him not to?

"Alison, what you say makes sense. None of us knows what this guy's real plan is. I'm sorry Win's ... I'm sorry, Alison, that your friend is gone. What a sadistic, brutal madman."

He continued. "I'm thinking Paul Silver's out there somewhere working on a plan to help us. If he is, that could be –"

Dick interrupted. "What the hell are you saying? Are you living in a dream world? Sure, it'd be nice if Paul sweeps in here on a white horse and rescues everyone, but there's as much chance of that happening as Rolando inviting us all over for Christmas dinner. Paul's gone. Don't give these people false hope."

"It's not false hope. He *is* close by. He's working on a plan." *God, I hope this isn't a mistake.*

Gavin spoke up. "I don't know what you're talking about. I don't know Paul. I'd never laid eyes on him before this trip. Has anyone else ever met this guy before?" Nine people shook their heads. "What makes you think he's any better than you or I at saving us? What makes you think he's out here somewhere?"

"Because I met with him three nights ago. He told me there are things in his past that'll help him rescue us. CIA-type things. He wouldn't say more, but I trust him. Who else can I trust? I don't know where he is, but he's around. Listen, everyone. He asked me not to tell you. He's afraid that Rolando will retaliate against us if he knows Paul's around. Please, please keep this a secret. I only told you because God knows we all need some hope."

Dick said, "So you believe this guy's tale that he's some kind of spy? You're willing to trust him with your life? And you want me to trust him too? With *my* life? Because that's what you're asking us all to do."

"What can it hurt to give him a day or two?"

Alison began shaking violently. She hissed, "Because we don't *have* a day or two. He killed Win – he killed him after he said he wouldn't." From deep inside her came a banshee-like wail that tore at their hearts. "He's going to kill us all! Paul can't help us. You can't either. No one can. We're going to die. Don't you get it?"

Suddenly she jumped up and began to beat Mark's chest with her fists. "Leave us alone!"

Hailey pulled her away. "Alison, stop. This isn't helping anything. Paul's all we've got."

"Maybe it's all *you've* got," she said in a whisper Hailey didn't hear.

CHAPTER THIRTY-THREE

The next morning everyone rose as usual and Hailey immediately noticed Alison's empty bed.

"Hey, guys. Did anybody see Alison this morning?"

No one had, but by the time breakfast came around, the mystery was solved.

The hostages were sitting around the campfire as Rolando came out of his shack. This time he had company. Alison emerged behind him, her head bowed so she wouldn't have to face the others. She was nude.

"Good morning, everyone," Rolando said heartily. "I want to show you my new toy!" He snapped at Alison, "Turn around and show them everything you have. Men, this is quite a treat. Maybe when this is all over I'll share my new plaything with all of you!"

She turned slowly around, covering her eyes with her hands so she wouldn't have to face them.

"Go back inside, *mi gatita.*" *My kitten.* "Although you have made me very tired already, I can use more of what you have!" His words were laced with sarcasm; on his face was a cruel smile. She walked back to his hut while he casually poured a cup of coffee.

Ted said, "What're you doing to her?"

"I'm doing nothing except taking what she offered. She came voluntarily, you know. She is my sex toy now. She has given herself to me in exchange for freedom." He burst out in laughter. "What some people will do – eh? Pardon me now. I have to go back to bed for a while. She will do anything when she's desperate. Anything at all! Sorry I can't stay and visit. My imagination's already working!"

Halfway back to his hut, he stopped and turned. "I almost forgot. Two more ransoms arrived while we slept. Thanks to you, Gavin and Dick, I'm an even more wealthy man!" He roared with laughter.

Last night around midnight Alison had made a decision. Careful not to wake anyone for fear of being dissuaded, she walked to the sentry outside the entrance and pointed to Rolando's shack. He smiled and took her there.

El jefe va a ser feliz esta noche, the guard had thought to himself. *The boss will be happy tonight.*

Alison made a deal, trading her body to the rebel in exchange for a guarantee of freedom even if her ransom weren't paid. She had no hope left. In desperation she chose to trust a man who had no conscience, no morals, no sense of decency. A man who couldn't be trusted.

CHAPTER THIRTY-FOUR

Paul's only goal was freeing the hostages. The Spences, Gavin, Dick and Mark were safe in theory, because their ransoms had been paid. Everything depended on whether Rolando would keep a promise he'd already broken.

Maybe Alison was safe for now as well. Paul had no idea if she had a plan or if she had given herself to Rolando out of sheer desperation. As long as Rolando wanted her as his toy, it made sense he'd keep her around.

The Mexican guide, Julio, was also okay. Rolando didn't put him in the ransom pool at all, apparently because he was a native.

That left three whose futures were far less certain: Ted, Bart and Hailey. Paul picked Hailey to remove first. As a young female, she was most at risk.

Paul thought about how Rolando could have learned two more ransoms were paid "while you slept," as he had put it. He must have left someone back at the town with a shortwave radio, a man who could check a bank account and advise Rolando.

The guards left Hailey alone. Now that Alison was being paraded around naked, they lost interest in the other female because she still had her clothes on. Despite

Rolando's orders to watch everyone, when Hailey walked away to use the toilet, no one gave her a glance.

As Hailey peed near the cave entrance, she heard a rustling sound and stifled a scream. Paul stepped out of the bushes three feet from her and put a finger over his lips. She zipped her shorts and whispered, "Where have you been?"

He whispered and then he slipped back into the jungle.

The alarm on Hailey's watch vibrated at 12:55 a.m. Careful not to wake anyone, she tiptoed to the front of the cave. Soon she heard a dull clang and looked out. The guard was walking away across the campsite, just as Paul had promised. She sneaked around to where she'd seen Paul earlier. He was waiting and they slipped away to Piedras Negras.

At exactly one o'clock Paul had tipped over a barrel next to the cook tent. It made enough noise that both the perimeter guard and the sentry at the cave entrance went to investigate. They'd find nothing, of course, and chalk it up to some animal's nocturnal curiosity. They both returned to their posts, unaware that the first captive had been freed.

It was late morning when one of the guards decided to count the hostages. Then the proverbial caca hit the fan.

Paul was watching as the captives were pushed roughly into the center of camp. Rolando came out of his shack, a naked Alison stumbling along behind him. He dragged her by a rope tied around her neck. He spoke to his men – pistols were drawn and rifles raised. He pushed Alison to the ground, where she cowered like a beaten dog.

"You have made a very bad decision, *amigos*. Where is Hailey?"

Mark replied, "No one knows. She disappeared sometime last night. She didn't tell us anything –"

"Really?" Rolando interrupted harshly. "You expect me to believe an intelligent female like Hailey just decided to run away and take her chances out here in the jungle alone, unarmed and miles from civilization? I'll ask you one last time. Where. Is. She?"

Dick said evenly, "We really don't know. When we woke up, her bed was empty."

Rolando was livid. His eyes blazed and he screamed, "Perhaps this will help you remember where Hailey is." He pulled hard on the rope and jerked Alison to her feet. Then he hit her hard in the stomach with his fist. She screamed, doubled over in pain and fell to the ground, vomiting.

Several of the men started towards Rolando, but the armed guards stepped in front of their leader.

"For God's sake, stop!" Mary Spence yelled. "We can't tell you what we don't know. She's gone. We don't know any more about it than you do, but please don't hurt Alison any more. Haven't you done enough?"

"My dear Mrs. Spence –" he laughed cruelly "– I have hardly begun. I'm going to sacrifice her if you don't tell me where Hailey went. Do you understand this word *sacrifice?* I'm going to gut her while she's still alive, and all of you are going to watch her die. I'll give you some time to think about where Hailey is. Not long, though. You'd better start remembering. Shouldn't they, Alison?" He laughed at the pitiful girl.

Rolando told them he'd gotten two more ransom payments. Now there were seven. His hard words were uttered with a cold smile. "I was pleased to get money from Win Phillips's family. Isn't that hilarious? They paid money

157

to ransom a dead man!" He laughed exuberantly and then snapped instructions to his men. He told the guards to watch every hostage carefully. From now on, none could be alone. He dropped Alison's rope and left her curled in a fetal position, sobbing in pain.

"I don't want this bitch anymore. She's no fun. Tomorrow I'll kill her."

As Rolando walked off, Doc Spence gently turned Alison over, removed the noose from around her neck, and examined her stomach. He went to the cave to get a painkiller, a guard following behind him.

"Hey, asshole," Dick yelled.

Rolando turned sharply. "Are you talking to me?"

"I don't see any other assholes. Who else's ransom was paid?"

"Oh, my mistake. It was Alison's. Another hostage who dies tomorrow even though her family came through. Oh well, such is life! And *hey, asshole* ... I'm going to kill you tomorrow as well. Enjoy the hours you have left."

"Don't ... don't let ... him ... kill me," Alison wailed, heaving gasps of breath between her words. It was painful to inhale after the brutal punch to her midsection. The others tried to calm her fear, but no one had any idea what to do. Only Paul could save them now.

Mark leaned in close to Alison and whispered, "Did you tell Rolando about Paul?"

Alison shook her head. "But I am now. Paul rescued Hailey, didn't he? *DIDN'T HE?* I'm not going to let Rolando kill me. I'll tell him everything if he'll let me live."

"None of us knows where Hailey is, Alison. I have no idea if Paul rescued her. If he did, that's the first rescue – maybe we're all next. Regardless of what you tell that monster, it won't change his plans for us. Let's work on helping Paul instead of losing the only chance we have. Not a one of us is going to make it out of here alive if Rolando kills Paul. So please … I beg you … please don't betray Paul. All of our lives depend on that secret."

Paul listened to it all. He wasn't surprised about Rolando's outburst. He also knew the sadist would kill Alison – and Dick too – to make a point. He wasn't bluffing and he was a psychopath. The entire group was in mortal danger and there was very little time left.

Paul also heard what Mark said to Alison. He was disappointed the archaeologist had decided to tell them he was nearby. He wasn't mad – Mark was the most levelheaded one in the bunch. If he'd felt compelled to reveal the secret, then there must have been a good reason. It did make things much more difficult, though. Especially if Alison revealed the secret to Rolando.

He had to move quickly.

CHAPTER THIRTY-FIVE

As they walked to Piedras Negras last night, he'd told Hailey what had happened the past couple of days. He spent the first night in one of the archaeology shacks from ten years ago, but the next day he found a cave he'd read about. Shortly they were standing at the rim of the pit themselves.

"Be careful. We have to go down about twenty feet on a path. Just hang on to the branches that stick out of the side of the sinkhole and you'll be fine."

The rocky pathway was nearly four feet wide. It was simple during the day, but tonight it was a challenge. Paul pointed out each handhold as they carefully descended. The cavern wasn't visible from the surface; if Paul hadn't known from Isaiah Taylor's journal to look for it, he'd never have found it. It was the perfect hiding place; even if they built a fire, it couldn't be seen from above.

Paul pointed out the packs of supplies, glanced at his watch and said, "It's nearly two. I have to get some sleep so I can be back at the camp tomorrow. There's no telling what Rolando's going to do when he finds out you're gone, but I have to get the others out. Feel free to use whatever you want from the supplies I brought."

"Who are you? What part of your oil business training taught you how to rescue hostages?"

"Actually, the military did that. I was part of a search-and-rescue team for a while." More lies.

Hailey had escaped with nothing but the clothes she was wearing. Paul offered her a T-shirt and a pair of shorts. "They may be a little big, but if you want fresh clothes, go for it." She appreciated the gesture but hesitated to take some of the few clothes he must have with him.

"I'm okay. I've slept in my clothes for a week. I guess I can do it again!"

Paul took blankets from one of the packs and spread them on the floor. "It isn't home, but it'll do," he quipped. They lay three feet apart. Dead tired from the stress, both were asleep in seconds. It was the first full night's rest Hailey had gotten since the ordeal began.

Safe, she thought as she fell asleep. *Safe at last.*

She awoke refreshed around seven, heard him snoring, and went outside to use the bathroom. When she came back, she saw him rummaging through the supplies.

"Coffee," he muttered groggily. "Can you grab some wood out there?"

She collected some sticks and helped build a fire. Ten minutes later a metal army-issue canteen was functioning as a pan to heat water. Soon they had instant coffee. He tossed her a granola bar and said, "Eggs Benedict for milady."

She laughed and nibbled on it as he pulled a shirt and a pair of shorts from his pack.

"Time for a change," he said. "I think four days in the same clothes is enough, don't you?"

"Absolutely. I'll wash ours while you're gone."

162

"That would be great. Okay, here goes. Modesty's not one of my virtues, so if nudity bothers you, now would be a good time to turn away."

Hailey had liked Paul when she'd first met him, and she had great respect for him and what he was doing to help the others. He was a different guy than she'd ever known. Some people would consider her damaged merchandise after what Rolando had forced her to do. She didn't think Paul was like that, and she hoped she had a chance to get to know him better. Lots better, actually. She decided to just be herself.

"Naked's never been a problem for me. Go for it!" She sat cross-legged on the floor by the fire and watched as he unashamedly shrugged out of his T-shirt and dropped his shorts. She was surprised to see no underwear.

"Voila!" He chuckled, doing a spin.

Laughing too, she clapped at his little show. Then he put on clean clothes.

This feels good, she thought. *Even with the mayhem all around us, I feel really comfortable with him. And he's sure not bad looking either. He thinks he can save all of us. And I think he can too. There's something about him ... something different.*

Paul interrupted her reverie. "I have to go in a minute. I want to tell you something first. Do you know what a ushabti is?"

She snapped back with a grin, "Am I working on a PhD in Egyptology? Is that what you meant to ask? Of course I know what a ushabti is. Every first-year student knows that. It's a funerary figurine used in pharaonic burials. What does that have to do with us, here and now?"

"Because here and now, there's a ushabti in the tunnel back there. At least that's what I think we're going to find." He pointed to the back wall of the cave and she noticed the four-foot hole for the first time.

He told her what he'd read in the BYU archaeologist's notebook and cautioned her about going into the tunnel when he wasn't here. "I haven't had time to check it out. I have no idea where it leads or even if it's a passage at all. It could be collapsed a few feet in, or it could be full of poisonous snakes. There's no way to know what's back there until we can explore it, and we need to both be here when that happens, just in case.

"Right now my priority's getting people out before Rolando starts killing again. I'm going back to the camp – just stay here. You'll be safe until I get back. I wish I could leave you the gun, but I'd better keep it." He pulled out a Bowie knife. "I doubt you'll need this, but it might help your peace of mind."

Knowing even this early how impetuous she was, he added, "If you decide to start poking around by yourself and you happen to see the ushabti, please leave it in situ. If it's there, I'd like to see it where it lies." One last time he stressed the danger of crawling into the tunnel by herself, then smiled and handed her a headlamp.

"When you decide to ignore my warnings, you'll need this."

She promised to watch herself. Without thinking, she leaned up and kissed him on the cheek. "Be careful."

As soon as Paul left, Hailey went to the back of the cavern to have a look at the tunnel. She saw a small hole in the shadows, roughly circular and about four feet in diameter. She turned on her headlamp and slithered inside. Hailey wasn't prone to claustrophobia, but she did hope this very narrow crawl space didn't get any smaller or – even worse – stop entirely. She'd have to snake her way out backwards if that happened and she didn't look forward to it. Speaking of snaking, she also hoped that wasn't part of the agenda here in the cramped passage.

She crawled like an iguana on elbows and knees for six feet and then came to a sharp right turn. Resting against the wall was a small figurine. Clearly old. Almost certainly Egyptian.

The ushabti. I'll be damned. She looked at it but didn't touch. She left it against the wall exactly where she'd found it.

Around the corner the tunnel expanded, becoming wider and higher. If she crouched a little, she could walk now. There was another sharp turn and she popped into a room about twenty feet square with a fifteen-foot ceiling. Her headlamp battery was fading and she could barely see something on the far wall. Was it a carving? She walked across the room to see.

How's this possible?

She was dumbfounded. If she wasn't in a remote site in Guatemala ...

But she was. She was at Piedras Negras. And here was the confirmation of her theory, absolute proof of the connection between ancient Egypt and the peoples of Mesoamerica.

If she weren't in a remote site in Guatemala, she could easily be standing in a tomb in the Valley of the Kings.

I'll be damned.

She studied the single brightly painted wall more closely. It was covered with hundreds of beautiful, colorful hieroglyphs so akin to those she'd studied in one certain Egyptian tomb that they could be duplicates. There was even ... *Oh God*, she thought suddenly. *Is that what I think it is?* In the excitement, she'd failed to notice the faint outline of a door with light impressions all along its seams.

Déjà vu. I've seen all this before. Not just something similar – this exact thing. This is a duplicate.

She examined the seals closely. As she looked at one, then another, she knew what would come next and in what order. Anubis the jackal. The bound captives. Horus, the man-bird figure. Sobek, the crocodile-god. Seals carefully stamped into the mud while it was drying, all in the same order as the ones she'd seen before. These were necropolis seals – Egyptian seals marking a tomb. But who could possibly be buried here? Why were there Egyptian glyphs eight thousand miles west of Egypt? How old were they? Most importantly, why would this doorway be stamped with identical death seals to that of a tomb she knew well, a burial place in Egypt's Valley of the Kings?

Suddenly Hailey's heart began to pound. She felt blood rushing to her brain and started getting light-headed. She saw an additional seal – one she knew hadn't been on the tomb wall in Egypt.

A cartouche. Not just any but ... No. How can this be possible?

The mystery suddenly multiplied a thousandfold. Thoughts – crazy thoughts – flew into and out of her mind. Weak-kneed, she sat on the floor, close to fainting but unable to peel her eyes from the fantastic wall before her. Her headlamp was dying, so at last she looked away. Reluctantly she crawled back to the main cave to avoid being trapped in blackness when her light quit.

Hailey could hardly wait to show Paul what she'd found. He said he might be gone for hours, so she stayed busy while time passed slowly. Struggling to keep her mind off the exciting things she'd seen, she arranged everything he'd brought in the packs.

He must have spent a lot of time planning what he'd need. This certainly wasn't his first campout. There were plastic baggies filled with lighters and matches, a mirror, snakebite kit, insect repellent and biodegradable soap. He had army-style meals ready-to-eat and several packs of nonperishable staples like rice and beans. He'd included a few changes of clothes and a clothesline. There were two plastic bottles full of water – she figured he brought those empty and caught runoff from the daily rainstorms. She also found batteries for her headlamp, but forced herself not to grab them and go right back through the tunnel. This stuff was Paul's – they weren't her batteries to take.

The way he acts – the stuff he brought with him – it's like something a Green Beret would do. He'd mentioned the military, but there was more to him than that, she was sure. She'd never seen such confidence, such calm resolve, in a man before.

Who are you anyway, Paul Silver? You're not an oil consultant from New York City. I'll bet money on that.

Whoever he was, she had him to thank that she was free instead of the hostage of a homicidal rapist.

She gathered more wood, heated some water, stripped naked and did the laundry. She hadn't washed a man's clothes in a while, she reflected. It was a good feeling, doing something for someone else you were starting to care for. She'd had boyfriends, but they were never anything special. They came and went as she had doggedly pursued her education. She put up the clothesline and hung everything.

She splashed warm water on herself and used the soap Paul had packed. For the first time in days she felt relatively clean and presentable. While her clothes were drying, she put on the T-shirt Paul had offered last night. Now that she was clean she didn't mind using it. She was surprised how good it felt. And it smelled like him. Not a bad thing, she reflected with a grin.

She had a good idea what was behind the sealed door. It just had to be – everything fit together – and if it was what she believed, both she and Paul would be famous beyond imagination. They'd prove that a mythical, fabled civilization truly existed and actually did create an ancient Hall of Records in Guatemala ten thousand years ago. The obvious Egyptian connection was another story entirely. She had her theory and the glyph-filled wall verified it, but still it was crazy and unbelievable.

After days with little sleep and realizing she was finally safe, she succumbed to the exhaustion she'd fought. She lay on the pallet and dozed. When she awoke, she took paper and a pen from Paul's gear and began to write her thoughts. If they ran out of time before she could show him the wall, she wanted him to know her ideas about Egypt and the Olmecs. And Atlantis. It was time to reveal her theory about how they all fit together.

CHAPTER THIRTY-SIX

The Olmec city of La Venta
1322 BC

The Egyptians settled easily into life among the Olmec people. They learned each other's languages as the newcomers taught them building techniques. Soon La Venta had wooden buildings and the foundations of what would be a temple complex.

The Olmec chief and Maya spent considerable time together and became great friends. He learned why Maya had journeyed across the great sea. The high priest's king sent him on a one-way trip to hide a sacred urn. Maya asked if he had heard of a place marked by a statue topped by a bird's head. Maya didn't mention the map that called it the Place of the Skull.

The Olmec was surprised. "That is Bird Monster's home. There is his statue and also his cave. How do you know about it? It is a secret known to no outsiders."

Although no Olmec alive had been there, everyone knew of the sacred site where Bird Monster lived. It was the most magical and fearsome place in the Olmec world – a place spoken of in whispers.

"We have a legend about it as well. I think the bird statue has been there for a very long time, much longer than your people or mine have lived. The Ancients – a people who lived long ago – called it the Place of the Skull."

"That would be a good place to hide your vessel. Our legends say others have used it to protect their secrets. People from long, long ago, as you said. Ancient people. But it is a sacred place. I cannot give you permission to go there without approval of the gods. I will consult the shaman."

The shaman respected Maya – the Egyptian was his counterpart, the chief religious figure in an empire across the great sea. These strangers were already teaching the Olmec their sophisticated construction techniques, arts and crafts. The sorcerer believed the Egyptians had been sent to their land by the gods, so he agreed to let them go to Bird Monster's cave.

The chief would provide canoe bearers and guides. After several days' travel southeastward in the jungle, they would travel up a mighty river for many miles until they came to Bird Monster's statue. Then they had to go through the jungle to a sacred cavern. The Olmecs would stay at the river because the cave – Bird Monster's home – was forbidden. Once the Egyptians returned to the river, the Olmecs would guide them back to La Venta.

It would be a difficult and dangerous trip, the old sorcerer advised. Consulting a legend passed down for generations, he instructed Maya how to get from the river to the cave. Maya had the Atlantean map as well, but the Olmecs didn't know it.

Two days later the entourage marched into the forest. Maya brought two of his strongest men plus a cadre of artists. Four Olmecs carried two canoes above their heads, using padded yokes similar to the portage yokes of today. The guides and some bearers rounded out the expedition.

On the third day they came to a raging waterway nearly a hundred feet wide, cascading around dozens of rocks and creating a formidable barrier. The canoe bearers put the boats into the water and took up positions at the front and rear. The laborers loaded provisions, and everyone climbed aboard. The first five minutes was a thrilling ride in swirling eddies of powerful whirling water, but the rapids quickly eased to a steady current moving in the right direction. They settled down for the ride up what would a thousand years later be called the Usumacinta River.

The men were on the river for several days, camping each night. Finally they spotted their sign. Three large boulders on the eastern shoreline were arranged one on top of the other, rising over twenty feet in the air. It resembled a snowman topped by the skull of a bird with a long, sharp beak. They had found the statue of Bird Monster, the Atlantean Place of the Skull.

The men knelt on the sand. Maya thanked Amun for guidance and safe passage while the Olmec crew bowed before Bird Monster's statue. The Olmecs set up camp while the Egyptians set out into the jungle. According to the map, they would walk for an hour, then come to a sinkhole with a cave in its side. They also had the shaman's instructions. Both indicated the same direction. Maya was on the right track.

The jungle was so dense it took far more than an hour. The men tediously cut a path through twisted roots and vines, and it was late afternoon when they arrived at the huge cenote. It was three hundred feet in diameter and

171

very deep – they could see water more than a hundred feet below. This was the sinkhole!

Maya consulted his map and concentrated on the east side of the hole. He spied what might be the entrance to a cave. They stumbled down an old path and reached the cave entrance about twenty feet below ground level. They wearily walked inside and lit torches. Then they stopped, speechless and terrified.

In the gloom at the rear of the cave stood three brightly painted warriors, each holding a long spear.

Wishing he had a translator, Maya held up his hand in greeting. He spoke slowly in Egyptian. Even if the men didn't understand his words, perhaps his calm voice would help.

"We are here from a distant land. We come in peace and ask nothing of you. We have gifts from our people ..." He reached for trinkets in his pack.

The warriors stood in the shadows in silence. They hadn't moved a muscle.

"High Priest," one of the Egyptians whispered, "I think they are statues."

Maya took a tentative step forward, then another. When nothing happened, he walked confidently to the other end of the room and stood in front of them.

"Come," he said to his men. "They are indeed statues like the ones our craftsmen build for the tombs of the pharaohs." The impressive warriors were seven feet tall with plumed headdresses, bright loincloths and impressive metal-tipped spears.

Maya looked around the cave. Except for an old fire pit in the middle and the statues, the place was empty. He was disappointed; if this actually was the Crypt of the

Ancients, whatever the Atlanteans had left here had been stolen.

"Master!" one of his men shouted. "Come here! Look at this!"

The warrior statues had been positioned so as to hide something. Behind them was a hole in the cave wall, large enough for a man to crawl through.

On the other side of the tunnel, Maya found what he'd come for. Although it was almost invisible in the rough back wall of the next chamber, there was a faint outline. He studied the wall, determined there was a door cut into the rock, and called for silence. He began to chant softly, invoking a building process the Egyptians had learned centuries before. He was using telekinesis, a powerful tool given to his people by the Ancients. It was fitting that today that particular power would allow the heavy stone to move by itself. Behind it, he was certain, lay the Crypt of the Ancients, the knowledge repository of the same people who had taught Egyptians the wisdom of the ages.

The stone was out in less than ten minutes. Maya instructed the others to stay as he slipped alone through the opening into a room lined with shelves. In the center of the room were pedestals, each holding an unusual machine or instrument.

The Ancients are real. Maya was fascinated.

He ordered the artists to paint a wall of hieroglyphs around the rock door in the outside room. He handed the chief artisan a papyrus. "I want this wall," he instructed.

Creating a memorial to the boy-king here in this faraway land was sickening to the priest, but his pharaoh had commanded it. Despite Maya's hatred for the heretic king and his father, the pharaoh was still a god. A part of him would lie hidden in this steaming jungle. He must be honored.

The artists had no idea why they were duplicating identical glyphs they'd painted in the Valley of the Kings only a few months ago. They never questioned the high priest. They painted Tutankhamun's burial chamber wall all over again, eight thousand miles away from his tomb.

Maya stayed in the Crypt of the Ancients for hours. He pondered what the purposes of the complicated machines were, wondered what words were written on the sheets of metal, and thought about the people who built this room thousands of years ago. A doomed civilization had left its technology hidden for posterity.

He wished he could reveal this wonderful place to his people, to bring the inscribed plates to Egypt for study and translation – to show these amazing, enigmatic machines to the scientists for examination. He would be remembered as the high priest who found the secrets of the Ancients.

But Maya wasn't going home. So he walked around like a modern tourist in a museum. He absorbed everything about this wondrous hoard of information, to lock it in his mind for the rest of his life. Since childhood Maya had heard tales about the Halls of Records. None had heretofore been found, but right now he believed he was the first human in ten thousand years to see the repository of knowledge left by the Ancients – the inhabitants of Atlantis.

Finally he walked to the back of the room, carefully removed a long cylindrical object, and set it gently on the floor. He opened his pack, took out the jar bearing the likeness of Amun, and put it on the pedestal.

He knelt in front of it and finally recited the prayer he'd waited for years to say.

Amun, grant that the heart of Tutankhaten shall remain hidden in this ancient room forevermore. For, as the Gods have taught us, so long as the heart is missing, the soul may never enter Heaven.

If I have sinned by condemning this heretic to the underworld for eternity, may I be condemned also. I have done this act for one purpose only – to honor you, Amun, you who were shunned by Tutankhaten and his father Akhenaten.

He stood with a satisfied grunt, patted the urn, and left the room. Maya had completed his mission.

A day later the wall painting was complete, and the door was put back in place and covered with necropolis seals and more glyphs. The Egyptians returned to the river; a few days later they returned to La Venta.

"As the Ancient ones taught my people, so will I teach yours."

That became the high priest's mission for the remainder of his life.

The mind was limitless, the Atlanteans believed. Legends credited those ancient people with teaching technological skills so advanced many could not be recreated even today. They helped civilizations in Asia, Europe and Africa learn to govern, wage war against their enemies and create massive structures to honor their gods and kings. As they had taught the Egyptians, Maya passed knowledge along to these Mesoamerican peoples.

Maya lived at La Venta for fifteen years. He, his artisans and his builders taught construction techniques, art and the secret of telekinesis – the way to move heavy objects using nothing but the human mind. The high priest and his men also took their educational services on the road. They visited another tribe of indigenous Indians who would rename themselves *Maya* in memory of a stranger from a faraway land who taught them secrets beyond their limited imaginations.

Thanks to the education they got from Egyptian artisans and craftsmen, the formerly agrarian Mayans suddenly became temple builders, erecting vast city complexes with structures over a hundred feet tall at Chichen Itza, Tikal and a dozen other places throughout Mesoamerica – structures that would cause men to wonder how a primitive civilization could possibly accomplish such wondrous architecture.

CHAPTER THIRTY-SEVEN

The jungle near Piedras Negras
Present day

The first item in Paul's plan was completed when he paid Mark Linebarger's ransom. The archaeologist was critical – like Ted, he was a natural leader: dependable, intelligent and levelheaded. Unlike Ted, his fluency in Spanish was immensely valuable. Paul couldn't be around all the time to listen, but Mark could. He understood the rebels' language.

This morning he'd implement part two. Alison and Dick had to be rescued – they were going to die today if he didn't. He wasn't sure how it would happen, but he knew it had to work perfectly.

He also knew from experience that things never went perfectly. He was prepared for the unexpected, which was a good thing, since that was exactly what happened next.

Paul crept out of the brush and hid in the shadows by Rolando's shack. He knew the man was inside. The hostages huddled in small groups by the campfire, their captors carefully watching them.

When the time was right and the guards weren't looking his way, Paul would slip into Rolando's shack and overpower him. Even if one of the rebels saw Paul and gave a yell, he had the element of surprise – and a few seconds of lead time – on his side. In theory it should work.

Paul began to count the guards – there should be fourteen. Suddenly Gavin stood up. One of the guards brandished a rifle and said, "*Sientate!*" *Sit down.*

"Got to take a pee, my good man," Gavin replied casually. "Be right back."

Paul was astonished. *What the hell's he doing? The guard's going to shoot him!*

Suddenly Paul got it. Brilliant, if it worked. Gavin was counting on the guard's not having the authority to shoot without Rolando's order. It was risky – if Gavin was wrong, he was dead – but at least it separated him from the others.

All eyes were on Gavin as he walked toward the edge of the clearing where the men usually peed. Paul slipped back into the trees and crept toward Gavin. As Gavin walked across the clearing, the guard yelled at Rolando.

"This gringo's walking away!"

The leader stuck his head out, looked at Gavin and said, "Get back with the others."

"Taking a pee first." He kept on walking. When he reached the edge of the clearing, he stepped into the thick underbrush. He was gone.

"Pepe! Go after him!" Rolando screamed.

Dashing across the clearing, the guard yelled, "Do I shoot?"

"*Si!* Shoot! Kill him!"

THE CRYPT OF THE ANCIENTS

The hostages began yelling, "Gavin! Come back! Gavin!"

Pistol ready, the guard stepped into the forest where Gavin had disappeared. Seconds later a single shot rang out and a hundred birds flew wildly into the air. Then there was silence.

"Holy shit!" Dick crudely verbalized what each of them was thinking. *Another one of us is dead.* Rolando let David Tremont die in the river, he killed Win Phillips, and now Gavin was gone. Hailey was missing and Alison was supposed to die because nobody could say where Hailey went.

I'm going to die today too, Dick reflected, *since I called Rolando an asshole.*

Am I next? each one of them thought silently.

Rolando strode confidently to where the men had entered the jungle and called out, "*Pepe, esta bien?*" *Everything okay?*

No response.

"Pepe?"

He walked into the bushes for a split second then came out yelling orders. Two more guards ran into the jungle, pistols drawn and ready to fire.

Rolando waited.

Ted turned to Mark. "What the hell just happened? Where's Pepe?"

"Gavin got away. Pepe's dead, because Rolando just told his guys to find Gavin."

Suddenly the buzzing of insects stopped again as two more shots rang out, further away this time.

Rolando watched for his men to return. Five minutes passed. Then five more. Nothing.

179

He went back into the shack. *This isn't going well. I'm changing the plans. Now.*

The other guards were worried. One walked across to Rolando's shack and said, "*Juan! Donde estan los hombres?*" *Where are the men?*

Rolando didn't answer them.

No one knew where Pepe and the other two guards were, but the hostages knew Rolando's actual name was Juan. Mark cautioned the others not to use that name. No need to piss him off more than he already was.

CHAPTER THIRTY-EIGHT

When Pepe had run into the jungle, Paul was ready. He'd signaled Gavin to wait. Paul's single shot killed the guard instantly. He scooped up the man's pistol, and he and Gavin ran through the jungle toward the trail. Making noise wasn't an issue with all of the yelling and screaming coming from the campsite.

Rolando walked to where Pepe lay and saw the single shot to his head. Both Pepe's pistol and Gavin were gone. As hard as it was to believe, the author must have overpowered Pepe without a sound, taken his weapon and then killed him with it. Rolando immediately sent two more men to the jungle to bring Gavin back, dead or alive. The American wouldn't last long in the jungle anyway, but he wanted him as an example for the others.

When Paul and Gavin were a hundred yards away, they paused to see if other guards would come for Gavin. Suddenly two more came crashing through the thick vines. Paul took aim and shot these two rebels as easily as he had the first. He ran back, picked up their weapons and then took Gavin to the trail. After a short distance, he told Gavin to wait in the underbrush. Paul had to get back to the hostages. He gave Gavin all three of the rebels' guns, just in case. He kept his own Sig Sauer and an extra magazine of ammunition.

Rolando heard the two gunshots. Satisfied that the matter was now dealt with, he waited for his men to return. After ten minutes, he knew something crazy was happening. He'd lost three men in a flash. Inexplicably, Rolando now had only eleven left. With Gavin gone, there were eight hostages, still plenty of manpower to maintain order. And there would be fewer hostages very soon.

How could Gavin kill Pepe with his own gun? Rolando couldn't understand. Pepe was one of his best. He wouldn't have been an easy one to overpower, especially without a sound. And then Gavin, who was supposed to be an *author,* killed two more? This just didn't make sense.

He would fix this little problem. His hostages wouldn't be so bold next time, once they saw what he was capable of. He was ready for the next step. He went outside, looked at Alison and said, "Bitch. Come with me. You will pleasure me one more time before you die." He laughed heartily as she trembled.

"Why don't you pick on one of us instead?" Julio spat in Spanish. "Is she easy for you because she's weak? Does that make you feel more manly?"

"Watch yourself, *compadre.* I promised to let you live, but that can change. I'm taking her instead of you because she has what a man needs. Perhaps you find pleasure in other men, but for me, I'll stick with *mujeres.*" He looked at Dick, aimed his fingers and did a pistol shot. "You're next, *asshole.*"

He told a guard to bring Alison to the shack. As the man reached for her arm, Bart suddenly grabbed his leg and pulled his feet out from under him. The rebel fell to the ground with a grunt and dropped his rifle. Doc Spence snatched it and aimed it at Rolando, who stood defiantly and pointed at the doctor's elderly wife. Rolando's lieutenant, Diego, held a pistol two inches from Mary Spence's head.

"Drop your weapon or Diego will kill your wife."

"Shoot him!" Mary yelled. "Kill him! Don't worry about me!"

"A foolish request," Rolando commented fearlessly. "If you shoot me, my men will finish what I've started. Those are their orders. In the meantime, your wife will certainly die."

Defeated, the surgeon handed the rifle back to the guard Bart had taken down.

"Sorry, everyone ..."

Rolando laughed. "I'm sure they understand, Dr. Spence. You saved your wife but maybe lost everyone else. The price you have to pay, I suppose." He whispered something to one of his men, who walked away. Rolando jerked Alison by the hair and dragged her away like a caveman. With a swift kick he booted her inside his shack.

After leaving Gavin, Paul had returned just in time to see the scene play out. He admired Doc's courage, even though it hadn't worked. It was up to him now. He had to move fast; Rolando would make an example of Alison as soon as he'd gotten a last round of sex.

Paul knew there had been fifteen rebels at first, counting Rolando. He'd just killed three, so that left twelve. There were also eight hostages. The majority – Julio, Ted, Mark, Dick and Bart – were in their thirties or forties and agile. They could fight. The others – Doc, Mary and Alison – might help but likely couldn't. No way to know until it happened. The Spences were older, and Alison was volatile, fragile and unpredictable.

He again tried to count the guards, but he kept making mistakes. They were constantly milling around, talking and smoking while they encircled the seated hostages. It was hard to keep up with them long enough for a count. Now he put more effort into it.

He counted again and wondered if he'd made a mistake. There were ten, one less than there should have been. *Was one inside with Rolando?* He didn't think so. He started a third time. *One, two, three –*

"Your count was correct the first time, *Señor*." He heard quiet words from behind him and felt the barrel of a rifle in his back.

CHAPTER THIRTY-NINE

Paul quietly said, "I knew from my count there was one more of you bastards around somewhere."

Paul's response surprised the guard. He'd expected this gringo to be scared, but instead he seemed very much at ease. Whoever he was, this man was dangerous.

The guard said, "Juan sent me to find you. There had to be someone hiding in the jungle. Let's go show him what I've found." He jabbed the barrel hard into Paul's back.

Suddenly Paul whirled around, pushing the rifle aside and jamming his pointer and middle fingers into the rebel's throat at the top of his neck. He'd employed this technique before – a quick thrusting jab in exactly the right place would crush the larynx. The victim couldn't cry out for help – he couldn't say a word or take a breath. If a tracheotomy weren't performed immediately, he faced a brief but agonizing death.

Startled by Paul's quick movement, the rebel suddenly realized he was in deep trouble. He tried to suck in air as incredible hot waves of pain shot through his neck, but he couldn't breathe. He dropped his rifle and grabbed his throat, clawing desperately as if that would open his windpipe.

Paul could have saved him pain by crushing his skull with the butt of the rifle. Unfortunately for the rebel, Paul couldn't risk any noise, so he left the man to writhe on the ground in the throes of a horrible death by suffocation. Paul heard gurgling as he turned back to the people being held hostage. Within seconds, the man was still.

Rolando's sexual encounter with Alison had obviously been less than satisfying. That wasn't surprising, given her general condition and his promise to disembowel her in front of her fellow captives. Everyone could hear the screams coming from Rolando's hut. Not screams of ecstasy. Far from it. These were screams of pain, of horror, of revulsive terror. There was no sexual pleasure in the sounds that came from the shack. Paul waited, poised to strike when he saw an opening.

She came out first with Rolando trailing close behind. She was still naked, but the rope was gone. He pushed her roughly toward the campsite where her friends sat. She fell to the ground; everyone saw the cruel red marks on her face, breasts and back. Apparently when she wasn't able to do whatever it was he'd wanted, he'd beaten her mercilessly.

The strain on the hostages was almost too much to bear by now. Even the normally quiet Mary Spence had had enough. She yelled, "You're a savage. I hope you rot in hell for what you're doing."

Roberto ignored the insult. "Tie the whore to that tree," he ordered, pointing. Two guards grabbed Alison by the arms and jerked the naked girl to her feet. Her wailing protests cut to the hearts of the others, but none of them could help her. The rebels secured her to the tree with ropes.

In the heat of the moment, Rolando hadn't noticed that another of his men was missing. He sent one of his men to fetch his machete. Rolando walked to Alison and held it close to her chest. He ran its sharp tip carefully from her neck down to her breasts, barely ticking the skin. A tiny slit opened up and droplets of blood emerged.

"Please ..." she begged. "I tried to do what you wanted. I'll try again now. In front of everyone if it makes you happy. Please don't ..."

"Your time is up," Rolando said harshly. He brought the machete back, preparing to thrust it into her abdomen. "Are you ready?"

"Are YOU?" came a shout from the jungle.

Rolando pivoted around to see where the voice came from just as the top of his head blew backwards in a gush of bone, brains and blood. As he fell to the ground, Bart and Dick jumped up to untie Alison.

"*Deja o se muere!*" *Stop or you die!*

The command came from Diego, Rolando's lieutenant. The men didn't understand the words, but the intent was clear, as were the guns pointed at them. They paused, hoping Paul would fire again.

He couldn't. Diego was too close to the hostages to risk a shot. What had worked for Rolando wasn't feasible now. Bart and Dick sat down as Diego sent two guards into the jungle where the shout had come from. Still tied to the tree, Alison struggled to get loose.

Four gunshots rang out almost immediately, followed by a guttural scream.

"Diego!" A booming voice from the forest rang out in Spanish. "It's over. You can live or you can die."

The rebel was stunned. *Who the hell was talking?* He shot a glance at another of his men and nodded toward the clearing. The man slipped away, heading toward the jungle on the opposite side. He was going to circle around and ambush whoever was there.

Bart yelled, "Watch out! One's coming –"

A guard swung the butt of his rifle, connecting solidly with Bart's temple and knocking him unconscious. That brought more screams from the hostages. Ted and Mark started to get up, but the rebels pushed them back.

The guard reached the edge of the clearing, but never entered the jungle. Another gunshot – another dead man.

The voice spoke again. "Diego, think what you're doing. You're losing all your men. You only have seven left. Release the girl, put down your weapons, and you can all live."

"Who are you?" he yelled back. "*Where* are you?" He held his pistol in front of him with both hands, ready to shoot anything that moved. As his eyes scanned the perimeter, a shot rang out. This one came from a different direction, but it hit the mark perfectly.

Diego dropped his pistol. He looked down at the bloodstain rapidly spreading from a hole in the center of his shirt. Then he fell forward and hit the ground with a resounding thump.

"*Hombres!* Put down your weapons now or you're dead men!" Paul's voice again.

Mark jumped up and yelled, "Get their guns." Four of the six rebels, facing shooters in the jungle and outnumbered by hostages, dropped their weapons in defeat. They stood with hands held high in the air as their former captives scooped up weapons and gathered ropes to restrain the rebels. They tied them securely to a small tree and left Bart in charge of watching them.

The other two guards disappeared into the forest, running for their very lives. This time there were no gunshots.

"Good riddance," Ted muttered. "I hope the jaguars get the bastards."

Doc ran to Alison, grabbed the machete and cut her loose. Unconscious, she collapsed to the ground. The doctor knelt beside her, his fingers on her wrist.

"Mary! Bring me something to cover her with! Bring my med kit too!"

His wife ran to the cave and quickly returned. The doctor covered Alison with his wife's long skirt and began tending to the superficial cut Rolando had made down her breastbone. It was hardly more than a scratch, he noted with relief. The girl lay quietly as if asleep.

"Honey, is she ..." Mary Spence asked what the others also feared.

"She's in shock; she fainted from the stress. I'm going to let her rest until she wakes up."

Mark yelled, "Paul! Are you out there?"

Instead of one person emerging from the twisted jungle foliage, two appeared. Paul came from one side of the camp and Gavin from another. He had two pistols jammed in his belt and held another.

"You look like a gunslinger!" Julio said.

Paul met Gavin in the middle of the clearing. "I knew it was you. You killed Diego – right?"

"Yep."

"Good shot. Do you have a handgun at home?"

"No, but my dad gave me plenty of target practice growing up. He taught me to be comfortable around weapons. I haven't shot a gun in fifteen years, but I guess it's like riding a bicycle!"

The others rushed to hug them, thanking and praising them for their heroic efforts. Doc stayed on the ground, tending to Alison as she began to come around.

"How come you didn't shoot the two guards who escaped?" Mark asked.

"They surprised me, frankly," Paul replied. "They were so far away by the time I reacted that I couldn't see them through the undergrowth."

Ted said, "Where's Hailey? I hope she's safe."

"She is. She's hiding in a cave in the ruins at Piedras Negras. You might want to see this – I think there's a connection with the Olmecs somehow –"

Dick interrupted brusquely. "Hey, are you crazy? Alison and I were on this guy's death list ten minutes ago and you all sound like we're going to hop back on the bus as if none of this happened. I think some of us" – he swept his hand around the group – "might like to get the hell out of here and go home. Pronto. Does anybody know how to operate a shortwave radio?"

Paul replied, "We don't need it. I've got a satellite phone."

Suddenly Dick became aggressive. He poked his finger into Paul's chest roughly. "You had a sat phone all along? Why in hell didn't you call in the troops? What in God's name were you thinking, leaving us here? We could have been killed. We were out of time and you were hanging out in the woods." He was red-faced and furious.

Ted stepped between them. "Dick, what're you *doing?* If it weren't for Paul, we'd all be dead. Don't you understand that? He had to wait until the time was right."

"Calling in the authorities would have gotten everyone killed," Paul explained. "I was watching almost all the time, waiting for an opportunity. I'm glad I was able to slip away at the very first, and I apologize for how long it took to set you all free."

Bart was guarding the rebels. He shouted, "I'm glad you snuck off too. If that hadn't happened, we'd still be captives. I think we owe Paul a debt of gratitude. Who are you, anyway? Are you really with the CIA?"

Paul laughed dismissively. "Yeah, right. Actually, I got a merit badge in search and rescue when I was a Boy Scout. That and common sense, I guess."

He turned to Ted. "Shall I call for our limo to pick us up?"

The leader looked at him quizzically; he explained he had one of the boat drivers' contact information.

Ted gathered the group. "How does this sound? Paul will call for the boats. It'll take at least four hours to get here. Let's eat lunch; it'll be our last time to eat for a while. Then we can pack everything and head to the beach in an hour or so."

Paul cautioned them to be alert. "There are two rebels loose with pistols out there in the jungle somewhere. We have plenty of guns now, and everyone who's comfortable using one should take either a pistol or a rifle. We also have no idea how many more people Rolando has working for him. When you get to the river, stay hidden when you hear boats coming. Make sure you know it's the authorities and not more insurgents. I'll go get Hailey, and we'll be at the beach not long after you are."

By now Alison was sitting in the shade, Doc by her side. Mary and Gavin went to the cook shack to rustle up lunch, and everyone else returned to the cave where they'd slept the past ten nights. Paul walked the trail back to Piedras Negras carefully, watchful for the missing rebels.

He figured they were getting as far from this place as possible, but one could never be sure what they'd do.

CHAPTER FORTY

After two days in Frontera Corozal the authorities had almost nothing. The tour bus had been scoured top to bottom. There were bloodstains all around the driver's seat and the front platform, consistent with Mark Linebarger's note saying there had been a murder. There were so many fingerprints they were useless. Until the hostages were back, there was no way to tell whose prints they had. Still, the Federal Police meticulously gathered them one by one. Later they'd be run through the national databases in Mexico and the USA to check for matches.

Today all the floatplanes except one had been sent home. The remaining one spent all day scouring the river in both directions from the dock. Several officers searched the eighty-six ruined structures at Yaxchilan. It was a big job and over a hundred acres to cover. There was no sign that anyone except tourists and park officials had been there.

Although the FBI's special agent-in-charge at the scene still thought some of the boat drivers knew more than they were telling, the interviews had gotten them nowhere. The boatmen had nothing constructive to offer about that night. As for the Ochoa cousins Ruben and Pablo, their night-fishing alibi couldn't be confirmed and they'd been more nervous than the rest, but that alone was no reason to detain them. Still, something didn't add up. A dozen tourists disappeared. They had to have been taken away by boat. It was the only logical answer.

The SAC ordered his men to interview the twelve boat drivers again. They were interrogated in pairs this time in hopes the discussions might spark a memory, an idea, a thought – something that could help. Each pair of drivers met with agents for about an hour; Ruben and Pablo were last.

The cousins felt even more confident this time. They stuck to their alibi, said they knew nothing about anything just like all the other drivers, and were sorry they couldn't help. For the officers this round of questioning yielded nothing new.

Pablo and Ruben walked out of the cabana and headed to the dock. The agents walked right behind them across the parking lot, heading to the lodge. Suddenly a man ran up to Pablo. It was his friend, the man who owned the store next door to Pablo's house.

What is he doing here?

"Ah, Pablo, I'm glad I found you! This is important –"

Pablo gasped, suddenly understanding why he was here. "I'll talk with you later." Pablo brushed him off without stopping.

"No, wait! The man you took to Piedras Negras the other night called me. He wants –"

Pablo spoke more loudly than he intended. "Later!" *Shit! Shut up, hombre! Not now!*

The FBI agent heard everything. He asked Pablo, "What does he want?"

"Nothing." He tried to keep his hands from shaking. Ruben was unconcerned since he had no idea what Pablo's friend was talking about.

The agent observed Pablo trembling. He turned to the shopkeeper. "Who called for Pablo?"

"Paul. He said his name was Paul, the same as Pablo. Tell him that, the man said, so he will remember me. You know who he is, right, Pablo? He said to tell you he has thirteen people in all and to bring two boats. Come to the beach at Piedras Negras where you dropped him off."

Pablo was dumbfounded. He wanted to run and hide, but the agent was moving closer to him. "I don't know …"

Still trying to help, the man added, "Paul. Paul Silver, that's what he said. Now do you remember your passenger from the other night?"

For Pablo, everything suddenly became a blur, a dreamy haze. Someone grabbed one arm, someone else the other. He vaguely comprehended the same thing happening to his cousin Ruben. It felt surreal as someone jerked his hands behind his back and snapped on handcuffs. He began to feel ill and suddenly he vomited. Then he lost consciousness.

The FBI agents had their break. Paul Silver was on their list. He was one of the kidnapped Americans.

CHAPTER FORTY-ONE

Julio, Ted and the other seven sat on the sand by the river, where the longboats would pick them up in a couple of hours. They had put their luggage in the underbrush, and the four rebels had been gagged and tied to a tree where they couldn't be seen from the river.

The snowman-like statue of Bird Monster stood like a sentinel as the former hostages laughed and talked about going home. Everyone was anxious to return to civilization and normalcy.

They heard the distant drone of an engine. Ted sprang into action, yelling, "It's too soon for the boats! Quick! Get back in the jungle!"

Although most of them had the weapons they'd been given, they'd be no match against more of Rolando's gang in a fight. They hid in the undergrowth, watching the shoreline.

Ted wished Paul were here. He was comfortable leading people, but after all this, he'd have welcomed Paul's odd familiarity in dealing with armed killers. Everyone else in the group had had the jitters. Not Paul. He was cold, calculating, and he knew what he was doing. Ted wondered if he'd ever learn what that was all about.

The noise became much louder, and soon they saw a floatplane descending lazily. It landed on the river directly in front of them. Some of the group began to clap.

"Quiet!" Ted hissed. "We didn't call for a plane! Wait and see what's going on."

A side door opened and a man dressed in black jumped onto the strut and yelled, "FBI! Is anyone here?"

English! Good old American English!

Ted shouted back, "We're here! Come on, everyone! We're free!"

CHAPTER FORTY-TWO

Paul walked into the cave and saw Hailey sitting on the floor, eating cookies. She jumped up with a big grin when she saw him. It was impossible to miss that she was wearing his T-shirt. *Only* his T-shirt. With wet hair and almost no clothes, she looked totally seductive.

"Nice outfit. Been shopping while I was off at work?"

"This old thing? No, it's just something I threw on. I'm just having lunch! Boy, I'm glad you're back! I know you may be hungry, but first I have something really exciting –" She was positively buoyant.

"Wait. I have something to tell you first. It's over. It's all over."

For a second she thought the worst – the hostages were dead and Paul had escaped unseen and unharmed. She struggled for words as her joy turned instantly into terror.

"Oh God. Please, don't let it be. Are they dead?" She'd heard distant pops earlier that might have been gunfire, but they were so faint she'd dismissed them.

But he's happy. He's so upbeat. Surely things are all right.

Relief swept over her as Paul broke into a huge smile. "The ones who ought to be dead are dead. Rolando,

Diego and several of their men. They're dead. All of us are okay."

"Thank God! What about Alison?"

"Physically, she'll recover, Doc Spence says. She's been through hell, as you certainly know. She suffered more than any of the rest of us. She's an emotional wreck, especially after Rolando told her she was going to die today. But physically she's good. Everybody else is fine. They're packing up, getting ready to move out to the river. I called the number my boat guy gave me, and I also called the embassy. One way or another, we're going to be picked up this afternoon!"

She ran to Paul and hugged him tightly. She stood on tiptoes and gave him a kiss – then another. "Thank you. Thank you for being whoever you really are, Paul Silver. Thanks for bringing your own gun, knowing how to get away and then rescuing us. Whatever you've done in the past, I'm just glad you were here when we needed you!"

Paul suddenly felt things he'd kept suppressed for decades. Overpowering gushes of intensity flowed through him as he held her and kissed her deeply.

Holding her close, he said, "I ... uh, I don't know what you mean about being whoever I really am. Or what I've done in the past. This isn't a video game – I'm just me." The words came out groggily; he could hardly concentrate with this exciting woman in his arms.

Suddenly she brightened even more and hugged him tightly. "Hell! How could I forget what I have to show you? Are you ready for something incredible? Oh, gosh ... what's wrong with me? I'm only thinking about me ... and you." She pulled away from his embrace. "What about everyone else? What do we need to be doing to help the others?"

Paul responded in a husky voice, his passion rising fast. "Right now? At this exact second? They're fine. Here's what I think we need to be doing."

He pulled her back, kissed her deeply and enfolded her in his arms. She put hers around his neck and pushed her body as close as she could. She could feel him getting hard – what was about to happen made her excited too. His hands ran up and down her back, then moved to the front. Still locked in a kiss, she moaned as he pulled the flimsy T-shirt over her head, then lightly ran his fingertips over her nipples. Her body felt incredible, he thought dreamily. As his hands played up and down her body, she pulled his shirt off then moved to his shorts. The zipper and button were only a momentary impediment.

Fleeting thoughts about how dirty she'd felt with Rolando were replaced with ecstatic ideas of what was about to happen with Paul. She knelt on the floor in front of him, taking him in her mouth and slowly moving up and down. It was his turn to moan now. Soon they were on the floor, lying on the sheets, locked in a feverish embrace. The imprisonment, the fear and despair had turned into glorious freedom. They came together, simultaneously, in a rush of emotion and intense rapture.

She lay next to him, tears streaming down her face.

"Was it that bad?" He laughed.

"God, I'm so happy. I really thought we were all going to die. This is the first time I've felt safe in what – a week? Ten days? I can't even remember. I just am so happy we're free, thanks to you."

"Other people did their parts."

"But if it hadn't been for you ..."

They kissed again, started everything again, finished again. Finally she said, "I guess we'd better quit screwing around and get back to business." They laughed at that until they cried.

Once they were dressed, she said, "Back to my original question. What do we need to be doing now? Nonsexual things, I mean!"

"Tell me in twenty words or less what you have to show me; then I'll tell you what we need to do next. We have some time, so let's hear what's going on and decide if we can see it now or if we have to wait."

"Back there – back through that tunnel – there's something that's going to blow your mind. It's going to change everything archaeologists and anthropologists believe about the Old World-Mesoamerican connection. This won't take long to see. It'll take much longer – some other time – to study it."

Paul answered excitedly, "Let's see it. Now. We have to meet everyone at the river. It'll take an hour to walk there, but the boats won't come for at least two and a half hours after that. We've got plenty of time. Show me what you've got!"

"I already did that," she quipped. "I've shown you everything I have. Oh, pardon me! My mistake! You're talking about my discovery, aren't you?"

He laughed at her boundless enthusiasm. It was pointless to admonish her for having gone into the tunnel alone. He'd known it was going to happen. She was like that. She'd made some kind of discovery; that overshadowed his concern she might get trapped, which hadn't happened anyway. And he truly wanted to see what she'd found. Even more, he wanted *her*. He was enjoying these feelings, ones he'd once thought too dangerous to ever experience. It had been a long, long time since anyone meant anything to him. And no one had ever been this close

– ever in his life. He wanted Hailey Knox more than anything in the world. He wanted to feel something he'd never allowed himself to feel. Love.

He loaded her headlamp with fresh batteries and they duck-walked through the tunnel. At the turn she pointed out the ushabti.

"Here's your little man. Right where I found him!"

"Incredible! Isaiah Taylor's journal was right!"

Slithering through a tunnel four feet high wasn't easy for casual conversation – she grunted an affirmation and they kept moving. They ended up in the large room, and she shined her light toward the far wall. When he saw a thousand bright hieroglyphs, he was speechless. He stared in silence for several minutes, absorbing its magnificence.

"Holy shit. Look at this." He was incredulous, mystified at what he saw.

Hailey finally broke the reverie. "Can you read glyphs?"

"No. Can you?"

"I sure can! These actually are easier for me to read than most."

"Why's that? Aren't they all the same?"

"Yes, but there's something special about these. I know this sounds crazy, but it's true. I can read these because I've studied them at the university. I memorized these glyphs a few years ago."

Paul gave her a puzzled look. "I don't get it. Are you saying someone's been here before? Someone recorded these hieroglyphs and you've seen them in a textbook? How's that possible? How come I never knew there were Egyptian hieroglyphs here in Guatemala? I've researched the possible Olmec-African connection a lot. Why have I never heard about these?"

She shook her head with a smile. "Hold on and let me explain. You haven't heard about these glyphs because we probably *are* the first people to see them in over a thousand years. Maybe the Mayans who built Piedras Negras saw this wall, maybe not. It was undoubtedly here when they came. In fact, it'd been here for two thousand years when the Mayans built their temples here."

Paul was dumbfounded. *What the hell is she talking about?*

"These aren't the glyphs I memorized from a textbook. They're exact duplicates. With one exception, this wall is an identical replica – a carbon copy, if you will – of a wall in a thirty-five-hundred-year-old tomb in the Valley of the Kings."

"Bullshit. That's impossible."

"Don't be too hasty. This is exactly how archaeologists miss the important stuff. Don't categorically deny something could be true just because it doesn't fit traditional thinking. Think outside the box. See this?" She pointed to a group of symbols ringed by an oval. "Do you know what it is?"

"It's a cartouche. A royal name."

"Right. Do you know whose name it is?"

"Not a clue."

She paused. Her voice dropped to a whisper as she continued. "I can't explain this. I can't tell you how it's possible. But it's right there and it's absolutely fascinating. This is a very familiar name glyph to Egyptologists. This cartouche is the single thing that's different here. Other than this one cartouche, the whole wall is exactly the same as one in the Valley of the Kings. Any idea why a name would be inscribed here but not on the same wall drawing in Egypt?"

"I presume you're going to tell me." He grinned excitedly.

"There was no need to put the royal name on the wall in the Egyptian tomb because the king himself was buried there. Everything in the tomb was marked with his name. Here, thousands of miles away, it's a different story. Someone wanted to link this place with a pharaoh." She pointed again to the cartouche. "I know for a fact this guy isn't buried behind this wall. He's buried in Egypt. There's no disputing that. So what the hell *is* behind this wall? Something that belonged to him? You and I have to find out."

He pointed to the cartouche. "Okay, Agatha Christie. Thanks for the buildup and the suspense. Give me the news. Whose name is that?"

"Tutankhamun."

CHAPTER FORTY-THREE

The pilot, two FBI agents and a Mexican Federal Police officer who had come in by floatplane protected the group until the boats arrived. There were far more people than the plane could handle.

The officers loaded suitcases on the longboats as the passengers boarded one by one. Today's boats had new drivers – the Ochoa cousins were in custody of the *federales* in Tuxtla Gutierrez.

As his group boarded the first boat, Ted counted them off: Julio, Doc, Mary, Bart, Dick, and Alison. The four rebels, now in handcuffs, were ushered onto the second boat along with two lawmen and the luggage.

Mark, Gavin, Hailey and Paul stayed behind, waving goodbye as the two boats slowly turned upstream and began the journey back to town. The officers waded out to the plane as the pilot went through his preflight checklist. The four watched the floatplane taxi to the middle of the river and skim along the water faster and faster. Within seconds it lifted off and turned south.

The ones who were left were primed and ready to go back to the cave. Gavin and Mark grabbed the last two pieces of luggage – their backpacks. Once they knew they'd be staying, they'd repacked, keeping necessities and sending the rest back to Frontera in the longboat. Hailey's suitcases and Paul's gear were back at the cave; they'd bring them when the floatplane picked them up. Everyone had a pistol.

Mark was enthused and ready to move. "Let's get started! I want to see what Hailey found!"

As soon as he had seen the hieroglyphs, Paul knew he couldn't leave now. What she found was exactly what brought him to Mexico, and he wasn't going until he knew more about it. He also wanted to know a lot more about her. He was becoming more captivated with her by the minute.

Although Hailey had had enough adventure to last a lifetime, she wasn't ready to let this man go either. So they agreed they'd stay long enough to open what appeared to be a sealed door in the painted wall. They reluctantly agreed on one more thing. As much as they wanted to be alone, they had to offer the others a chance to see this discovery. Everyone on this trip had paid his dues a thousand times over. After what these archaeology buffs had endured, anyone who wanted deserved to see what Hailey had found.

When Paul and Hailey arrived at the beach empty-handed, Ted asked where their luggage was. "We're not going back yet," Hailey said excitedly. They explained they'd found a connection between the Mesoamerican people and ancient Egypt.

Paul said, "Anyone want to join us for a day or two longer? Just repack your bags and keep a light one with you. Send the others back to Frontera Corozal, and we'll pick them up later." He told Ted he'd call for a floatplane when they were ready to leave.

Mark had joined the tour to serve as a combination guide and Olmec-Maya expert. He'd ended up being the de facto leader of a group of hostages, enduring more than he would have imagined experiencing in a lifetime. But he was an adventurer and had no immediate family waiting at home.

"I'm in!" There wasn't a moment of hesitation in his answer.

His willingness to stay didn't surprise Paul, but Gavin's had.

The author said, "I'm in too. Hell, I couldn't dream up a plot as exciting as what we've just been through. Let's play this one out until the very end. This could put me on *The New York Times* bestseller list!"

One more person would have stayed if he could. Ted loved archaeology and was fascinated about the implications of what Hailey had found. As the group leader, he had an obligation to get them out of Mexico. They were all dead tired, their nerves frazzled and emotions raging. They simply wanted to go home, to be with family and away from the jungle. It had been too much, and even one more day was unthinkable. *Get us out of here!* That was the battle cry for the remaining people. Within twenty-four hours they'd be home – safely home.

Now four eager souls remained. Two were archaeologists. The third was a writer and the last – Paul Silver – was something, but no one knew exactly what.

Hailey gushed about what she'd found as they walked to Piedras Negras. "You're really not going to believe it!" she told Mark.

Paul agreed. "It's impossible to imagine what you're going to see! It's like being in the Valley of the Kings!"

"How all this fits together is beyond me," Paul told Mark as they hiked along the same path they'd been marched down as hostages only ten days before. "With your knowledge of these cultures, I can't wait to hear your ideas."

Paul talked about the journals he'd bought in Utah and the cave they'd explored. He told them about the ushabti, the Egyptian figurine that Isaiah Taylor had tossed into the tunnel.

"Hailey found it! Amazing!"

Mark laughed. "I don't know who's more excited – you or Hailey!"

As they walked, they discussed whether to open the door in the wall of glyphs. The scientist in Hailey said wait, but she knew it might be now or never. Even with far more years of archaeological experience, Mark agreed with her. He knew from experience how things worked in this part of the world. If they didn't open the door, someone else would.

Guatemalan law required that the authorities be contacted as soon as something of importance was discovered. The site would be sealed until archaeologists could be dispatched for a formal investigation. If Paul and his crew followed the rules, they'd be required to leave the site immediately. Given the number of unexcavated sites in the country and the government's minuscule budget for archaeology, no one would likely show up for months or even years. In the meantime, word would spread about the discovery. Looters would destroy the wall and take whatever was behind it. Its secrets would be lost to science forever.

They were in agreement. The door *would* be opened, period. If something significant were there, they would notify the government and protect the site until someone came.

Mark and Gavin dropped their gear in the cavern. Paul suggested they remove their pistols and holsters since there wasn't much room in the tunnel anyway. Everyone left the weapons except Paul. He stuck his gun in his waistband, in the small of his back. If anything happened, he was the one whose gun could save them. He'd killed before – time and time again. They hadn't.

"Ready?" Hailey asked excitedly.

"Ready! Lead the way!"

She grabbed Paul's hand and walked him to the tunnel. They put on headlamps, and Mark checked the LED flashlight in his pocket.

"Just before the first turn you'll notice the ushabti against the wall," Paul said as they crawled single-file into the hole. "I'll bring up the rear."

Hailey went first, then Mark, Gavin and Paul. She crawled out into the room and immediately focused her attention and her headlamp on the opposite wall.

"Mark, shine your flashlight over there," she said as he maneuvered himself out.

The archaeologist marveled at the sight before him. "It's even more exciting than I imagined," he said breathlessly. Gavin emerged next and stood speechless with the others as Paul came up behind them.

But it wasn't Paul.

"*Hola, señores*," they heard, then a sneering laugh.

The last two rebels had hidden in a dark corner. Now they stood behind them with pistols drawn. None of them had noticed – their attention was focused entirely on the beautiful wall twenty feet in front of them.

"What do you want?" Mark responded in Spanish. "You should have run away. Rolando will find you –"

211

"Shut up and raise your hands," one snapped. "Rolando is dead. We have seen the campsite. He and Diego are dead and everyone has gone away. Why did *you* stay? *You* should have run away!"

Mark turned slightly and the rebel yelled, "Stop! Do not move again or I will kill you. When my *amigo* and I came to this cave, we knew you would be back. We saw the supplies here. We also knew you would come to see this wall. You are archaeologists, after all. So we crawled in here and waited."

"How did you know this place was here?" Mark asked.

"Because this area is my home, *gringo*. I was born not two miles from here, in the jungle. I played in this cave as a child. Enough talk! We go back now!"

One of the rebels crawled into the tunnel first. The other prodded Mark and the others to follow. He went last, holding his gun as best he could while he crawled through.

Paul had been five seconds from emerging into the room when he heard words in Spanish. He pulled back into the darkness of the tunnel, took out his pistol and waited. He saw what was happening but couldn't shoot – everyone was so close together a bullet could kill one of his friends.

Paul turned and scrambled back to the main room when the others were ordered into the tunnel. When the first rebel emerged, Paul was ready. He jerked the man around, put his forearm around his throat and held a gun to his head.

"*Silencio, amigo*," he whispered.

Mark emerged first, then Gavin and Hailey. They saw him holding the rebel and said nothing. The second man crawled through with his pistol in his hand. He immediately saw what was happening and reacted quickly. He slipped behind Hailey and stuck his pistol to her temple.

"What do you Americans call this? A Mexican standoff?" He grinned. "Drop your gun, *señor*, or the lady is dead. Do you think I care if you kill my *compadre*? He means nothing to me. If he is dead, it means more ransom money for me."

Paul kept his gun on the rebel. Mark said, "Ransom? What are you talking about?"

"You're going to give me ransom money just like you did Rolando. We all saw how easy it was. You *Norteamericanos* all have money, much more money than we could dream of. I want ten thousand American dollars from each of you. You will be my hostages until I get it. Then I will take the girl for myself and let the rest of you go."

Paul immediately saw the futility of this man's poorly planned kidnapping. If not for the weapons, it would be sadly humorous. Rolando had been well equipped and well manned. But these two guys were drones, not leaders. They hadn't expected four Americans and now they had their hands full.

"It's not going to work," Paul explained. "How about this? You leave your weapons and walk away. Go wherever you want. Just leave us alone. I'll give you ten thousand dollars each. Wired to whatever bank you wish."

"Wired? *No entiendo*," the man responded, confused. *I don't understand.* "I just want the cash."

"How can we get cash when you're holding us hostage? It's not going to work."

The man hadn't thought that far ahead. He paused a moment. Suddenly the other rebel, Paul's arm still around his neck, spat angry words. "You were going to let him kill me. You want the money for yourself, *bastardo*."

Suddenly the first man turned his gun away from Hailey and aimed it in Paul's direction. It was the break Paul had been waiting for.

A shot rang out. Then another.

The rebel Paul was holding fell to the ground, shot in the shoulder. Paul instantly returned fire, hitting the shooter in the abdomen. The man clutched his stomach, started to fall, and swung his pistol crazily. As he dropped, he fired a random shot. Now he lay on the ground, writhing in pain.

Paul kicked the rebel's gun away then said, "Is everyone okay? Hailey! Are you all right?"

She had a quizzical look on her face. She was aware something had happened but couldn't process what it was. She looked down curiously. There was a hole in her shirt near her breast, and a rivulet of blood was flowing out. The right side of her shirt was quickly turning red.

"I'm … I'm hurt, I guess," she said groggily. She sank to the floor in a sitting position and then fell sideways to the ground.

Paul forgot everything but the horror of what was happening before his eyes. He ran to her side and knelt. She was losing blood – a lot of blood. Her head lolled back – she was fading in and out of consciousness.

"Hailey. Stay with me! Don't leave me! We'll get you back to town … I'll get help. Stay awake. Can you hear me?" Tears flowed down his cheeks as he touched her face. Her skin was cool, clammy, and her eyes were closed. "God, Hailey. I just found you! Don't go!"

The rebel who'd shot her was grunting in pain. He lay in a pool of blood. Paul couldn't have cared less. He had one thought – the man was going to die, period. If he didn't die by himself, Paul would do it for him. He caressed Hailey, stroking her hair gently.

He cradled her head in his lap and squeezed her hand. She responded with a barely perceptible squeeze back. Her glazed eyes opened and she looked up at him blankly.

"Paul, I'm so tired … so sleepy. I just want to go home."

She closed her eyes and released her grip on his hand.

She was gone.

"No! Noooooo …" His wailing scream died into anguished sobs.

CHAPTER FORTY-FOUR

Two months later

Paul sat alone in the gloomy cavern the Olmecs called Bird Monster's cave. He sipped a cognac and watched the small fire toss eerie glimmers on the walls. Tomorrow Mark would arrive and they'd open the sealed doorway in the wall of hieroglyphs that Hailey had found.

He hadn't been here since he freed the hostages two months ago. They had walked away without returning to the cavern at the end of the tunnel. Whatever secrets were behind the sealed door were left for another time.

Paul carried Hailey's body every step of the way back to the river, his emotions swinging between grieving pain and unbridled fury. Gavin and Mark took charge of the two rebels. The one Paul shot died along the trail.

"Leave the bastard for the jaguars," Paul said bitterly as he kept walking. They left his body where he'd fallen. The second rebel, merely grazed by a bullet to the shoulder, would end up in jail.

Paul arranged for sentries around the clock to guard the cave and whatever was behind the wall. Making that happen meant taking over Piedras Negras, no small feat since it was a governmentally protected archaeological site.

A newly formed Cayman Islands company called The Mesoamerican Research Group, or MRG, offered a significant contribution – two hundred thousand dollars – to aid the work of the severely underfunded Guatemalan Ministry of Archaeology. In a quiet, discreet side meeting with the ministry's director, a bit more cash changed hands, and soon MRG was the recipient of an exclusive one-year research concession to explore Piedras Negras. MRG's president – its face to the public – was the well-known archaeologist Mark Linebarger. Its actual owner and financial backer stayed out of the limelight. Paul Silver worked alongside Mark as one of MRG's patrons, but no one knew his true involvement.

The kidnapping and release of American hostages was the lead story on news channels worldwide, and Frontera Corozal became a household name. Ted was interviewed a dozen times. Without invading personal space, he gave a broad overview of the people who were captured, what happened to them, and how one man – an American named Paul Silver – played a key role in their release. Three others – Gavin, Doc and Julio – were also interviewed. The rest declined – they'd been through enough.

As much as they tried, the news channels were surprised to find almost no background information about Paul. There were snippets here and there, but an online search showed remarkably little for a supposed New York oil consultant currently living in Villahermosa. Fox was first to dub him the "mystery man" since no one knew how to contact him for an interview. Now all the others had picked up the moniker.

Paul saw the news from his condo in Villahermosa that was owned by a Panamanian corporation. Even though nothing was in his name, he still had to change his identity. Paul Silver hadn't lasted long, but he was suddenly far too popular, newsworthy and mysterious. Becoming someone else would be easier this time around; he'd learned how to smooth the process when he did it the last time.

Today he was back in Piedras Negras for the first time since Hailey's death. The floatplane that had brought Paul here today took his sentries back to Palenque for a week of vacation. He wanted the place to himself – and Mark. The archaeologist would be dropped here tomorrow, and they'd finally see what Hailey had been so excited about that afternoon two months ago when she showed Paul her discovery.

Paul went from Frontera Corozal back to his condo in Villahermosa. When he unpacked his suitcase, he found three pages of notes tucked inside. Hailey wrote them while she was alone that day in the cave. Just in case they ran out of time, she explained, she wanted him to understand her theory about the Egyptians, Mexico and one other connection she termed "wild."

While she was working on her thesis, she'd researched possible connections between Egyptians, Africans and the Olmec. As a side project she also turned up interesting ideas involving Edgar Cayce's prophecies about Atlantis. Except for the notes she left for Paul, she kept her theories about those ancient people confidential. They'd never be revealed to a doctoral committee – that would be a sure way towards rejection. Atlantis didn't warrant serious consideration by anyone in the mainstream, stodgy archaeological community.

She organized what she'd learned, linking both the Olmec and Atlantean names together:

The landing site on the river:
Olmec = Bird Monster's statue
Atlantis = Place of the Skull
Cave in cenote:
Olmec = Bird Monster's cave
Atlantis = Crypt of the Ancients?
Room with wall of glyphs
Never mentioned by either culture
Room behind the sealed door:
Olmec = the room is not mentioned*
Atlantis = Hall of Records (or Crypt of the Ancients?)

* Did they know it existed? Maybe, but nothing is recorded in legend

She believed "Hall of Records," the missing repository of books and documents from the doomed civilization, wasn't actually the Atlantean name for it. Edgar Cayce called the three libraries *Halls of Records*. Hailey believed the people of Atlantis called the Piedras Negras library the Crypt of the Ancients and that it would be found not far from a statue called the Place of the Skull. Bird Monster's statue to the Olmecs. The Atlanteans created a map – the one the Egyptian high priest had followed.

His tears fell on her notes as he read the things she'd been so eager for him to understand. *Everything fits with the cavern at Piedras Negras*, she concluded. Although she didn't understand the Egyptian connection, she predicted that the Atlantean Hall of Records was in a crypt behind the wall of brightly painted hieroglyphs.

Paul deliberately waited two months before coming back here. There was a lot that had to be done. First he'd covered his tracks, vanishing and leaving no way for the people who'd been on the bus to locate him. Everyone still wondered who and what Paul Silver was. Only one person knew anything, and he knew only a little. That person was Mark Linebarger.

Paul had revealed very little about himself. Mark didn't care; it was none of his business. Paul gave him an email address and a phone number so they could communicate. It was a necessary risk, one Paul was willing to take in order to find out what was in the Crypt of the Ancients. Paul was a rank amateur at archaeology, facing potential proof that an Olmec-Egyptian connection existed thousands of years ago.

The second part of all this was Atlantis. If it could also be proven that Atlantis existed, the discovery would be overwhelming, shaking the scientific community to its roots. Paul needed a front man, a person of reputation and standing in the archaeological community, a man who could present the discovery, take credit for it, and allow the public to learn what might have happened here at Piedras Negras. A man who could allow Paul Silver to be part of a discovery yet maintain his anonymity.

Paul sipped his cognac and reflected. A lot had happened in these eight weeks. Except for the four who didn't make it back, everyone who'd gotten on the bus that fateful morning in Villahermosa had returned to his or her home. Gavin had called Mark several times, trying to find out how to get in touch with Paul. As the archaeologist and Paul had agreed, Mark told him he didn't know anything, and Gavin was now off writing a book about his experiences on the Usumacinta River and in captivity.

Rolando's actual name was Juan Garcia. He was a Guatemalan national educated in Paris who'd worked with the Zapatista rebel movement for several years. The

221

kidnapping had been well planned and well executed, carried out ostensibly in the name of secession for the state of Chiapas, but Rolando's real intention had been to steal the ransom money and kill the hostages.

The money was another issue. The FBI tried to recover the seven ransom payments, but Rolando's plan had worked just as he expected. The money went to a bank in Venezuela, a country whose relations with the USA were less than cordial. For weeks the authorities got nowhere. The bank didn't have the money anyway, so ultimately it released records showing the funds were transferred to a bank in Nicaragua, per instructions on file from Juan Garcia, the man who'd opened the account.

The Nicaraguan bank refused to respond. What the FBI didn't know was that the funds weren't there either. They'd been moved again to a little bank in Costa Rica. Four months after Rolando's death, the bank received instructions along with the correct password and security code. They transferred seven hundred thousand dollars to another country. It would never be found.

Five members of the rebel band were in jail in Guatemala City, facing charges of kidnapping and terrorism. The wounded one who'd been in the cave joined the four who surrendered when Rolando died at the camp. The last rebel, the one Paul shot in the stomach, died before they could get him out of the jungle.

The Ochoa cousins Ruben and Pablo were the boat drivers that night. The authorities questioned them off and on for two weeks. The police wanted them charged as accessories, but the federal prosecutor declined to press charges, saying their involvement was at best incidental and their biggest error was failing to disclose what had happened. The two went free and still run boats on the Usumacinta today.

Then there were the funerals. Over four days Paul went to every one of them. Why, he didn't fully understand himself. It wasn't out of a sense of obligation. It was more to honor the people with whom he'd become bonded through fate – people who thought they knew him, but really didn't know anything at all.

The first funeral had been in a small town near Cuernavaca, Mexico. He had been the only non-Hispanic at the service for Manuel, the bus driver whom Paul had known for only two days. He'd stood outside the Catholic church, waiting to see if any of the others would come. When no one did, he went inside and paid his respects.

He flew from Mexico City to Kansas City the next day and drove to a Presbyterian church for a memorial service honoring David Tremont, the insurance agent and archaeology buff. David had been lost on the Usumacinta River that night when he tried to swim to shore. Paul stood across the street and watched. Just before the service started, Doc and Mary Spence arrived in a taxi. Paul walked away, hailed a cab and went back to the airport. He'd known he might run into some of the other people who'd been on the bus. These were the same people who still wondered what Paul Silver actually was all about. He'd begun the process of separation from everyone, and he couldn't allow that window to open again.

In Waco, Texas, there was a graveside service for Win Phillips, the Baylor psychology professor who'd brought his girlfriend, Alison Barton, along for a fun trip to Mexico. Rolando shot Win point-blank just to make an example. Doc and Mary showed up for that service too; they lived nearby, up I-35 in Dallas. Alison didn't come;

Mark later told him Alison's therapist thought it would be too difficult for her. Once he saw the Spences, Paul left once again.

Finally there was Hailey. That was the difficult one, the only one where he had a real connection. He had to attend her funeral. He had loved her spirit, her grit and determination, her enthusiasm for life. Maybe he loved her too. Who knew? That concept was so unfathomable he would never understand if it applied to her. What he did know was that he had lost something real, something tangible and he'd never have it again.

He went to a little congregational church in Napa, sat in a rental car across the street, and saw every other person still alive from the kidnapping arrive one by one. Mark gave a eulogy. He let Paul read it later. It was a tribute to a strong female who'd helped them all in different ways.

"You should have been there," Mark told Paul later, not knowing that he'd sat outside.

She was laid to rest in a beautiful cemetery surrounded by vineyards. The guests stood in a circle as the pastor gave his final remarks. No one noticed a person standing by a tree a hundred yards away. He watched them listen to the closing prayer – the last words for Hailey Knox. As her casket was lowered into the ground, he watched the one person he could have loved leave him forever.

From brutal experience Paul knew how dangerous it was to open himself to anyone – anyone at all. He'd let it happen with Hailey. He had never felt emotions like that in his entire life. Even his parents hadn't deserved nor received that kind of love: unconditional, caring and free. His father had sold him. That hurt lasted for decades, but he'd overcome it. Then Hailey showed up, and for the first time in his life he cared about someone. Now she had been ripped from his heart. Two months after it happened, he was handling things fairly well most of the time. Only rarely did he allow himself to open the little compartment in his brain that held the hurt, the memories, the thoughts of her – holding her, loving her, touching her face.

Sitting here tonight in this cave where he'd held her as she died, Paul allowed it to overwhelm him once again. This would be the last time. It had to be. He consciously let go, opening the memory box. Here came the tears. Here came the memories laced with stabs of pain – the vivid recollection of how he'd carried her out of the jungle in his arms, how he'd screamed at the others when they tried to help him. "She's mine! She's mine! You can't take her!" He'd yelled it over and over as they walked down the trail for an hour to the shoreline, Paul leading the way, carrying her lifeless body.

Tonight he let the emotions out for longer than ever before, because he was back here where it all happened and because this was the last time. He allowed himself to feel the torrential gushes of grief. He experienced his feelings like he'd savor a fine wine. He drank in the horror, the loss of the first person he'd ever cared for.

Then it was over. He forced out the pain, the anguish, the knife-slashing hurt that burned through him. He locked the compartment for the last time. He became cold and distant again, back to who he really was. He focused on tomorrow and the opening of the doorway. He returned to the reality of a future all by himself, with no feelings to complicate his life. Just him. Nobody else. Just like it had always been.

CHAPTER FORTY-FIVE

Paul sat on the beach at dawn, watching the floatplane land smoothly on the river. He saw Mark wave as the pilot pulled close to shore, opened the door and dropped an anchor. Mark jumped out, gave him a bear hug, and they waded back to help the pilot unload four large rolling suitcases.

After the plane left, Paul handed over a pistol and holster. "You know this place as well as I do. You've heard the stories about bandidos. We don't need any surprises."

Mark understood. He unbuckled his belt and put the weapon on his hip.

"Did you bring your rock collection?" Paul joked as they struggled to move the heavy bags.

"Gotta have the tools to open that door. You can thank me later that these bags are on wheels. These damn things weigh a ton. American Airlines is going to make a profit this quarter purely because of my overweight baggage fees!"

Even with wheels, the going was tough. First there was the sandy shore and then the trail itself. When Paul had arrived yesterday, he saw that his sentries hadn't kept it up in the past two months. He used a machete to clear the pathway better, but it was still rough going. Each of them tugged two large cases.

The trail that had earlier taken Paul an hour to walk took twice that long this time. When they finally got to the sinkhole, they decided it was too dangerous to maneuver the heavy cases down the steep, rocky pathway. They unloaded everything up on the surface. He'd brought along portable lights, saws, drills and an assortment of hand tools. He was ready for anything.

They hauled down his personal gear and the equipment they planned to use first. They pushed and pulled everything through the tunnel, and soon they were standing in front of the painted wall. Two strong LED lights lit the room like they were outside.

Mark and Paul took turns operating a tile saw with a diamond blade, cutting slowly along the seams of the doorway. They'd taken over a hundred pictures of the necropolis seals they were going to destroy in the process, an unfortunate but necessary step to open the door.

Two hours later they stopped for lunch and a beer, then they went back to work. By mid-afternoon they had sawed along each seam, and the room was filled with dust. They paused to let it settle, and then dragged a hand-operated ratchet lever winch – a come-along – into the room. They snaked wires with hooks on the ends through both sides of the stone they'd cut out and prepared the come-along. There was no way to know how long it would take to remove the door – if it were four feet thick, it might take days due to the weight, moving it an inch at a time.

They got a big surprise when they started turning the winch. The rock door slid forward easily. It wasn't that heavy! Only an hour or so using the winch and the rock would be out of the doorway. The exciting part – what at least they hoped was the exciting part – was about to begin.

Off and on all afternoon they'd tossed around ideas about what was behind the door. The hieroglyphs were indisputably Egyptian, and Hailey claimed they were the same as Tutankhamun's burial chamber glyphs. How in hell did they get here? Did Egyptians paint them? Why?

Earlier they'd discussed if there could have been Egyptian activity here. Paul found Mark refreshingly open-minded and willing to engage in lively debate. As Mark worked the winch, Paul asked, "What do you think about Atlantis?" Most academics would have shied away from that question like you'd asked if they believed in aliens.

"I think there could be something there. For millennia everyone thought Troy was fictional, created purely in the mind of Homer. Then Schliemann came along and discovered it was real. If the scientific community's going to accept that Atlantis existed, it was far advanced technologically and it sank into the ocean in a cataclysmic event, there needs to be proof. Somebody somewhere needs to find something that says, 'This is from Atlantis.' People have tried to put Atlantis everywhere – Thera or other places in the Mediterranean, outside the straits of Gibraltar or in the middle of the ocean. It's a fact that volcanic eruptions decimated cities like Pompeii and islands like Santorini. But who knows about Atlantis? You have to have proof. What that'll be and when it'll happen – if ever – who knows?"

"Maybe it'll happen in a matter of minutes, right behind this door," Paul said with a smile.

"Wouldn't that be exciting? After my fellow academics finish decades of ridiculing us and admit they were wrong, maybe we'd be famous!"

Suddenly the rock door slid out the rest of the way smoothly. It turned out to be far less thick than the walls surrounding it. With the door pulled out, there was a narrow opening a few inches around the sides and top, and darkness behind the door.

"Another few tugs with the winch and we can crawl through," Mark said.

Paul was excited. "Want to have a sneak peek? A little 'Howard Carter moment'? Let's get the floodlight and see if we can tell what's back there."

As eager as kids on the last day of school, they set up the light. Mark flipped a switch and the powerful beam was directed at the crack outlining the door. He gestured to Paul.

"Be my guest – you first. It's your find … Hailey's, actually," he corrected himself with a pat on Paul's shoulder. "I wish she were here …"

"Please don't …" Paul's voice quavered. He pushed away the thought, ducked under the light, pressed his face against the narrow crack, and looked inside.

"What do you see?"

"Wonderful things!" Paul laughed, using the answer Howard Carter gave Lord Carnarvon when they opened Tutankhamun's tomb in 1922. "Actually, the room's huge – much bigger than this one. The angle of the light's not great, and there's not much light getting through this little crack. I can't see the walls. There are some square stones out in the middle of the room, and there may be things sitting on top of them. They're like displays at a museum. Here, have a look."

The archaeologist was eager with anticipation. Whatever this was, he'd never expected to find it in Mesoamerica. He put his face against the rock and stared, waiting for his eyes to adjust to the half-light. Then he saw what Paul had described – pedestals maybe three feet square and four feet tall. He noticed that something was sitting on top of each one. There were maybe twenty of them in all.

"It does look like a display at a museum. How about we quit wondering about all this and get this damn rock pulled out enough so we can get in there?"

"Here's a few ideas. It's almost eight o'clock. We can stop where we are and have dinner, then come back and open it up, however long it takes. Or we can keep going and skip dinner until we're finished. Or we can stop now, eat, sleep and pick up tomorrow when we're fresh."

Mark smiled. "I'm going to assume you threw that last one in just for kicks. I'm a scientist, a professor. I don't get chances like this every day. If you think I'm going to vote to stop for the night, you're crazy!"

"Yeah, I figured that one wasn't really an option. I'm excited to see what's in there, but think about this. It could take another hour to finish winching the stone. After that, there's no way we're going to take a break until we've seen whatever there is to see. As much as I want to keep going now, I think the best idea is to stop and eat dinner. Let's take a break, come back, and keep going until we're finished." They crawled back into the other chamber.

There was much more camping gear now than before. When Paul hired twenty-four seven guards, he bought the basics to set up housekeeping. There was a camp stove, insulated packs, lister bags to capture rainwater, and basic provisions for months of occupancy.

"Everything your basic Boy Scout troop needs, we have," he said as he started water boiling on the stove. Soon they were eating military surplus freeze-dried MREs –

meals ready-to-eat. Mark thought they were surprisingly good. Coffee followed, then a bathroom break. Mark glanced at his watch. 8:45.

"Ready?"

"Getting antsy?" Paul smiled.

"Don't tell me you're changing your mind. Want to sleep now? If you do, I'll see you tomorrow. I'm going back!" He crawled into the tunnel with Paul close behind.

It took forty-five minutes to move the rock enough for them to slip behind it. Mark squeezed sideways into the room and Paul passed the light pedestal to him. He set it up and aimed it just as Paul came through.

The room was an enormous natural cavern. The ceiling was low, since they were only twenty feet below ground level, but the room itself was at least forty feet wide and twice that long. It was cool but not damp; the humidity was very low. That would be beneficial if there were papyrus or vellum documents in here.

They looked at the first of the pedestals. It was square with the kind of perfect corners that proved it was man-made. Sitting on top was a complex metal object about two feet tall. It had several round dials and sat on a base. It was covered in numerals and characters.

"What the hell is this?" Mark asked.

"Don't ask me how it could be here, but it looks like an astrolabe to me."

"I think you're right. You know the Greeks used them for astronomical calculations. Theirs were pretty complex, but I've never seen anything as complicated as this. It looks like an astrolabe on steroids. There are parts of this thing that make no sense to me. And it doesn't look that old – it's in remarkable condition. If I saw it in a museum, I'd say it's nineteenth century, given its physical appearance, its complexity and the intricacy of design. What do you think?"

Paul looked at the instrument from all sides. "I don't know anything about this. But I agree that it's as shiny as new, it's extremely complicated, and it looks like you could set it up and use it right now."

Mark added, "Since we're standing right here, we know this device has to be old. Ancient. It has to be at least as old as those hieroglyphs in the other room that sealed the doorway. Offhand, I can't see any other way to explain it. If those glyphs are duplicates of ones in Tut's tomb, they're thirty-three hundred years old. So this thing has to be at least that old. Right? That's crazy!"

Paul glanced around the room. He saw shelves lining every wall, each holding bright metal plates about a foot square. Etched markings in neat rows covered their surfaces. There were a hundred plates on this one shelf alone – the room held thousands. They examined the plates without touching them. Some had drawings – tiny pictures – that accompanied the strange etchings.

Paul pointed at one of the plates. "Does this look like writing to you?"

"Absolutely. If we can translate this, we're going to blow some theories off the planet! I'd say we've come a long way toward proving an ancient myth is true after all."

Mark joked, "Damn, I've enjoyed my academic reputation. Now I'm going to be laughed out of town."

"So you agree this place is what I think it is? That we've actually found it?"

"The Hall of Records? The Crypt of the Ancients?" Mark stuck out his hand. "Congratulations, partner. You can't imagine how hard these words are for me to say, because I've spent a lifetime insisting on concrete evidence, not fairy tales, myths and legends. Yeah, I think we've found it."

He swept his hand around the room. "If this isn't concrete evidence, I don't know what is. Obviously, a lot of work has to be done – someone has to translate a language we've never seen before. And we must figure out the other enigma. I have no idea why the Egyptians were here, but it's clear they were. These things on the shelves – these metal plates – I think they're some type of books. Definitely not Egyptian – but still books. That's my opinion.

"Here goes my career! My professional opinion is that these are the records of the Atlanteans."

CHAPTER FORTY-SIX

Time flew as they examined the things in the cavern. Every pedestal held a different object. Some were so similar to modern objects that they could guess what they were for. There were instruments with dials like a clock, a device that resembled a slide rule, and a boxlike contraption that might be an abacus. Other things were so unusual – so dramatically different than anything they'd seen – they couldn't fathom what they were. One of those was a metal box with an open hinged lid that was crammed full of interwoven dials and sprockets. It had wires connecting everything, and Paul noticed something that made him gasp.

"Take a look at this! Is this a power cable?"

Paul held a short ropelike extension made of some type of pliable material. It went outwards from the side of the box and had four metal prongs on its end.

"I'll be damned. I'd say that's a plug. An ancient plug. Until today, I'd have said that was impossible. Now I'm not so sure."

Paul agreed. "I'd say this place redefines the word impossible."

"No shit, my friend."

Paul was shooting pictures of the shelves when Mark gave a shout from the back of the chamber. "You need to see this."

The object that had once sat on the furthest stone pedestal to the rear of the room had been moved. It was a metal cylinder resembling a pocket telescope and it was sitting upright on the floor right next to the pedestal. In its place sat a jar eighteen inches high and six inches in diameter – a jar with the carved head of a man on its lid. Two vertical plumes extended out as a sort of hat above the man's head.

"Well, well," Paul said. "It seems we've finally found an Egyptian connection. Is it a canopic jar?"

"That's what it looks like, but it's clearly not. The Egyptians had only four canopic jars, each holding one of a dead king's organs, and each one with a different lid in the figure of a god. I think this one was created to look like a canopic jar, but why? Every pharaoh had only four jars; I've never heard of a fifth."

Mark held up the jar and pointed to the sculptured lid. "See this guy? Any idea who this is?"

Paul looked at it closely. "Not a clue. I've read a lot about ancient Egypt, but I'm certainly no expert."

"I'm not either, but I took enough courses to recognize this fellow. He's pretty well known, actually. He's not one of the gods that appears on the real canopic jars, so that's not what this is.

"Paul, meet Amun. Except for that brief period when Akhenaten and Tut practiced monotheism, Amun was numero uno of all the gods of Egypt."

Paul raised the vessel to eye level and tried the lid; it was sealed tightly.

"What on earth are you doing here?" he asked Amun.

CHAPTER FORTY-SEVEN

Paul's earlier contribution of two hundred thousand dollars to the Guatemalan Ministry of Archaeology had been enhanced by cash – a lot more hundred-dollar bills. Those went in the minister's pocket. MRG, the Mesoamerican Research Group headed by Dr. Mark Linebarger, was not involved in that side of things. That company merely enjoyed the fruits of Paul's labor – the concession to explore Piedras Negras.

Once they'd discovered the Hall of Records, there was no more keeping this a secret. They had to notify the authorities quickly. This project was simply too big and potentially too controversial. Word was bound to spread. One of them had to stay behind and guard the site. Mark was the logical choice to fly to Guatemala City. He was the face of MRG, the concession holder for Piedras Negras.

Thanks to Paul's contributions, the minister was delighted to grant a meeting with the famous archaeologist Mark Linebarger. The minister added another person to the meeting – the only college-educated archaeologist on his staff. Mark ran a PowerPoint showing over a hundred photographs of the glyph-covered wall and the room behind it.

Some things they'd found at Piedras Negras were omitted too. Although the pictures of the wall covered in colorful hieroglyphs spoke for themselves, Mark didn't specifically mention Olmec-Maya or Olmec-Egyptian ties. Nothing was said about Atlantis or the names "Hall of Records" and "Crypt of the Ancients." And there were no photos of the Amun-headed jar. In fact, it wasn't even in the crypt anymore – they'd removed it for safekeeping the night they found it.

At first Mark had disagreed with Paul's opinion on what to say at the meeting with them. "I'm not comfortable doing things this way. We have to be totally up front, totally transparent. This is an archaeological site under the minister's control; we have to make a full disclosure."

Paul finally convinced Mark. Even though Paul's suggestions were neither transparent nor honest, it had to be done his way. Mark would tell only part of the story.

Paul's logic made sense. "We're in a third-world country whose entire archaeological budget's almost nothing. There's only one paid archaeologist on the entire ministry staff – they're stretched paper-thin because of budgetary constraints. They spend most of their effort and resources on the well-known sites like Tikal. They physically can't act quickly when an exciting new site is discovered. The truth is, anything exciting we turn over will most likely disappear into the hands of some well-connected, willing collector."

And so they crafted a new story. Paul's part in the find was changed. Now it was Mark who had actually found the BYU archaeologist's journal. He and Paul, a wealthy investor from New York whom he'd met on the tour, joined forces afterwards under Mark's company MRG to explore Piedras Negras and look for the cave.

The minister and his archaeologist said nothing during the presentation. When Mark finished, the staff archaeologist said, "You found a wall full of hieroglyphs. Are they Egyptian?"

Mark's answer was truthful but incomplete. "I know Mesoamerican archaeology very well – I've written several books about it. What I know about Egypt I studied in undergraduate school. Do the glyphs look Egyptian to me? Yes, they do. Can I say conclusively they are? No. That'll take an expert and a lot of research to determine."

"Inside the room you found thirteen pedestals, each with a metal object on it. From the pictures, they appear in remarkably good condition. But they must be incredibly old – is that not correct? Can you speak more about those and give us your ideas on what civilization might have created them?"

"I'm a scientist. I prefer to deal in facts and things I can prove. I don't engage in speculation or theories. So my answer is, I have no idea what they are, how old they are, or where they came from. They look very sophisticated, and some have complex gears and parts. Learning more about those things will be one of our top priorities."

The minister spoke next. "I want to know more about the shelves of metal sheets covered in characters. I realize this is far from scientific, but have you heard of the fabled Hall of Records that legend says people from Atlantis built at Piedras Negras? Could these be books from an ancient civilization?"

Careful. "Atlantis? I have to say that I haven't spent much time thinking about Atlantis. I recall some story about their creating libraries for their doomed civilization's records. Wasn't one of those supposedly in Giza? Does the myth say there's one here too?"

That was an easy way to dodge the question. And his answer was completely true.

The minister replied, "As I recall, there were supposedly three Atlantean Halls of Records. One was at Giza, another in the islands around Bimini, and one here in Mesoamerica. It's a fantasy, I know," he said with a dismissive laugh. "But what if it were real?"

The minister's job was a politically appointed position. He was a friend of the president, but he had no formal training in archaeology or science. If he had, he wouldn't have brought up Atlantis for fear of ridicule. But the minister wasn't convinced Atlantis was a fable.

At this point, neither am I, Mark reflected to himself.

He gestured to the man sitting next to him. "I'm an archaeologist – a scientist like this man here. I deal in facts, evidence and proof. If I can find something to convince me Atlantis existed – if this room we've found is the Hall of Records – I'll be the first to admit it. Right now I have no idea what it is. I'm anxious to learn more about it!"

After Mark's presentation, the minister dismissed his archaeologist with a stern admonition to keep this to himself. Despite the order, Mark was certain their secret would be leaked within minutes. The archaeologist had been fascinated by the news – there was no way he'd keep it quiet.

Good thing Paul stayed behind. Hope he's got his pistol ready. I'd be surprised if he doesn't have company before I get back there tomorrow.

Mark spent the next half hour outlining his proposal for exploration and research of the cavern. Using floatplanes to move supplies back and forth to the remote site, they'd refurbish the Brigham Young archaeological shacks, create a research center and laboratory, and staff it with scientists and archaeology students.

"A noble undertaking" – the minister stopped him at last – "but sadly we have no means to fund such an enterprise."

"If you'll allow us a year's extension of our concession and approve our plan, my company will pay for everything."

He explained that the Mesoamerican Research Group was prepared to pay over a million dollars for equipment and improvements. Once their concession ended, everything would be donated to the Guatemalan Ministry of Archaeology. It was an offer the minister couldn't refuse.

As he listened to Mark's presentation, the minister realized how big this was. This could be one of the most significant discoveries in Guatemalan history and possibly the most incredible ever in Latin America. The minister and his department would no longer lack for recognition or money to operate. People would flock to Guatemala – tourists, scientists, TV crews – and he would become famous.

He accepted Mark's offer on the spot. He praised them effusively. "Thank you for your work, for keeping us informed of your progress, and for your offer to provide a laboratory to learn more about it. I look forward to working with you. Your one-year extension is approved. Representatives from the ministry and I will visit the site soon."

Mark was elated. "Give us a few weeks to get the laboratory established and you'll get the grand tour." That time would allow Paul and Mark to make sure everything was set when the authorities arrived.

As soon as his office door was closed, the minister walked to his desk and flipped off the tape recorder sitting underneath a sheaf of papers. He picked up his desk phone and dialed a number.

"Paco, I made the recording as you asked. Their discovery is more amazing than you could ever imagine." He listened to the man's response.

The minister replied, "Of course, sir. I will meet you at the usual place in thirty minutes."

He rummaged through a desk drawer, brought out a half-pint tequila bottle and took a long pull. He put the recording cassette in his pocket, walked out of his office and told his assistant he was going to lunch.

CHAPTER FORTY-EIGHT

Paul established an office in Mexico City for the Mesoamerican Research Group. Using an executive suites arrangement, he paid monthly for a fax and phone line, email account and the nonexclusive use of a secretary-cum-receptionist who would answer the phone in the company's name. There were no employees and no business, but the foundation appeared to be an established operation.

Within a few days the Minister of Archaeology mailed a formal agreement extending the Piedras Negras concession and approving the research facility. Per Mark's instructions, the office receptionist scanned it, emailed it to Paul and filed the original.

The morning he saw the email, Paul told Mark the extension had arrived and began to read it.

"What?" he exclaimed.

Mark looked up from his equipment list. "Something wrong?"

"There are a couple of things here that I bet you didn't agree to. Did you agree to allow a full-time representative from the ministry on site?"

"No way. That was never mentioned. Is that a requirement?"

"Yes. He also requires us to have the research facility up and running in thirty days. That's when our little helper will arrive."

Mark was angry. "Shit! We don't need some government hack watching our every move. We have work to do here …"

"Didn't you expect something like this? I did – I was surprised when you came back and *didn't* mention it. We're two hundred miles from Guatemala City. With lousy roads and no infrastructure, it takes twenty-four hours for someone to get out here. I can see the minister wanting a representative on site."

"What about the thirty-day requirement to be up and running? Can we do it?"

"We have to. Even with the extension, we only have twenty months. We have to move fast. It would just have been better not to have a watchman. We just have to deal with it."

They ramped up everything. With significantly increased activity, news would quickly spread about what was happening at Piedras Negras. It was imperative to keep the cavern and the research facility safe, so they increased the number of guards per shift and gave them both an automatic rifle and a pistol.

It took three thousand dollars to make what would have been a month-long project take just a week. The phone company quickly built a temporary tower at the river's edge. Now next to the ancient statue of Bird Monster there was a modern monument to current technology, providing adequate phone and Internet service.

Paul went to Tuxtla Gutierrez and bought hundreds of items on their checklist while Mark placed orders for complex scientific equipment on the Internet. All of the equipment was delivered to a freight broker at the Tuxtla airport who hired floatplanes to bring the goods to the riverbank. Some days there were three planes, others only one, depending on how much material there was to haul.

A team of laborers flew in to build a new building, hook up generators, build outdoor toilets, showers, water collecting and everything else the facility would need.

Three weeks after it all started, Paul and Mark sat in the new structure one evening, a bottle of good rum and two glasses between them.

"Cheers," Paul said, raising his glass for a clink. "Damn good job."

By now only minor pieces of equipment were still in transit. They'd installed microscopes, oscilloscopes, cameras, soil cores, metal detectors, ground-penetrating radars and dozens more pieces of equipment Mark thought they might need. They'd spent over a million dollars of Paul's virtually limitless funds so far, with more to come. And they had created a state-of-the-art laboratory.

The next morning the real work began. They started by carefully removing two items from the cavern – the astrolabe instrument and the Amun-headed jar. Mark tackled the machine and told Paul how to remove the lid of the vessel.

Paul used a swab with solvent, lightly rubbing it over and over on the black tar that sealed the lid. Mark glanced up after half an hour and saw Paul take hold of the lid as if he was going to unscrew it.

"Wait! Don't do it that way!"

"Just trying to see if it's loose yet. This is getting a little tiresome."

Mark understood Paul's desire to speed things up, but his was the scientific mind. "If this urn is eighteenth-dynasty Egyptian, it's three and a half millennia old. We have to treat it like it's an eggshell – carefully and gingerly. This solvent will wear down the tar eventually. It may take you all day; take a break now and then. When it's loose enough, you'll know it without turning it."

Mark was looking at some dials on the astrolabe instrument a few hours later when he heard Paul's exclamation.

"It's off!"

"Bring it over here," Mark instructed. They set the lid aside and directed a light into the jar. There were two things inside – one was a dark, desiccated lump about the size of a golf ball lying in the bottom. Mark probed it with a pick, saw it was loose and tipped the urn. The lump rolled out onto a cloth along with a tiny scarab – a painted beetle the size of a dime.

"What are these?" Paul asked.

"Since the urn was obviously created to resemble a canopic jar, I'd guess it was once a human organ. It's so dried up it's hard to tell. The other thing's a scarab. Not sure what it's doing in there. I'll check that out too."

The next morning Mark decided what to do with the lump from the jar. He'd dissect it, put shavings into a container and take them to Tuxtla. They'd go by FedEx to his associate in Toronto for DNA testing.

"Given that this is almost certainly an Egyptian jar, and we have a wall full of Egyptian hieroglyphs, I want to find out what this is, if it's organic and testable, and if it matches anything in the DNA of pharaohs. There's an enormous amount of DNA that's been collected from the kings of ancient Egypt. If we get a match, maybe we can learn more about how and why this jar's here. The scarab that was in the jar is a clue – it's most likely a heart scarab.

The embalmers placed scarabs in the chest cavity in place of the king's heart."

"Why?"

"Without a heart, the pharaoh wouldn't go to heaven. That's what makes this so strange. If this organ turns out to be a heart and this is a heart scarab, then someone sealed the fate of a king three thousand years ago. This could be a big deal – that's why I'm sending it to Toronto. It'd be a lot easier to use a DNA lab in Mexico City, but we can't risk it. My assistant will keep this quiet until I tell her what to do next."

Mark met the afternoon floatplane and went to Tuxtla Gutierrez. He took a taxi to the FedEx office, dropped off the package and was back at Piedras Negras by dark.

Five days later Mark got an email from the Minister of Archaeology. "Our friend's on his way. His name's Francisco Garcia. Have we bought the red carpet to welcome him?"

Paul laughed. "I know neither one of us is looking forward to having a babysitter, but it may not be as bad as you think. Maybe he'll lend a hand and help us out. Otherwise we can give him a chair and tell him to sit and watch."

He knew it was a long shot, but Paul searched online for Francisco Garcia from Guatemala. It was like searching for John Smith in the USA, and he got what he'd expected – over a hundred thousand hits. He narrowed his search, including various terms, and finally had a relatively meager eleven pages of possibilities. Of course, he had no idea if this man was from Guatemala at all or what his occupation might be.

He skimmed the results – they ranged from teachers to politicians, from drug dealers to physicians. There was nothing helpful here – the man's name was simply too common.

Two days later a longboat pulled to shore near Bird Monster's statue. The driver helped his passenger unload three suitcases. One of MRG's workmen stood waiting for him with a handcart. After an hour on the trail they arrived at the site. He met Mark and Paul, and shortly they were having a beer outside the research shack.

Mark explained his role and said Paul was his friend and backer, along to help with the project.

Then it was his turn. "So it's Francisco, right? We're wondering about your interest in all this – are you an archaeologist? Do you work for the ministry?"

The newcomer was dressed in the usual jungle gear – lightweight long pants that could zip down to shorts, a quick-drying shirt and a Panama hat. He looked to be around forty and exuded self-confidence and charm. On the surface he seemed like a decent guy.

"Call me Paco, please! I'm merely an interested bystander, and I want to say up front that I appreciate your inviting me here." He laughed and they smiled – there had been no invitation. It was the minister's requirement.

"I've been fortunate in business. I started selling computers in the nineties when the concept was totally new in Guatemala. One store evolved into ten, then a chain of megastores – and here I am today! I sold everything a couple of years ago and made a good deal of money. Now I invest it and indulge my hobby – the history of our Olmec and Mayan ancestors. I'm thirty-seven and free to move about. I've financed a dig or two for the Minister of Archaeology. When he asked me to be his representative on this project, I jumped at the chance. It sounds absolutely incredible!"

Paul stressed the confidential nature of their discovery and Paco nodded. "You're the bosses. I don't intend to get in your way. I'll lend a hand – I'll take orders – whatever you need. Tell me if you want me to do anything. Otherwise I'll stay back and observe." He explained that his intention was to be here for twelve weeks, although his business responsibilities could change that time frame.

"Did you bring a weapon?" Paul asked.

"I brought a pistol. Is that a problem?"

"No, it's good that you did. Mark and I have them too; we need to all be armed in case something happens. If people begin to hear about this place –"

"Understood," the man interrupted pleasantly, raising his hand in mock protest. "I'm decent with a gun, and you can count on me for help if you need it."

They got Paco and his gear situated in the bunkhouse, showed him around the camp, then took him to the cavern. His astonishment at seeing everything for the first time equaled theirs.

CHAPTER FORTY-NINE

Within a few days, the men had become better friends than Paul and Mark ever expected. Paco was outgoing – he enjoyed a drink, a cigar and a good story. They spent evenings conversing in Spanish about Guatemalan politics and the fervent hope of many that Chiapas state would secede from Mexico.

One evening a couple of days after Paco's arrival, the after-dinner talk turned to the rebel activity in Chiapas. Paco told them he was indifferent to the secession idea and the rebels who promoted discord in the southern states.

"In your country people who have a complaint can speak to their elected officials," he explained. "In Mexico and Guatemala, it doesn't work that way. Our people have used civil unrest as a tool for centuries. They disrupt things, they strike, picket in front of Walmart stores, block major streets during rush hour – they use these tools to bring attention to their cause. Most of them mean no harm. They merely want justice, sympathy or money for their cause."

Before now they hadn't discussed the kidnapping. Now that they knew Paco better, Mark brought it up.

"We need to tell you about our experience with the rebels."

Paco listened impassively as they recounted the hijacking, the rebel who'd called himself Rolando, and his ruthless acts.

"The moment Paul killed him was the moment we knew we all had a chance to live," Mark said gratefully.

"It's difficult to know the motives of men who are committed to a cause," Paco commented.

Paul disagreed. "Whatever Rolando's motives were, I think the only cause that bastard was committed to was taking the ransoms. Sure, he may have given a little to the secession movement, but I firmly believe the guy was a maniac whose only interest was keeping the money for himself."

Paco sat quietly for a moment, then brightened. "Shall we talk of more pleasant things?" He began to spin a tale about the beautiful women in a certain Guatemala City nightclub, their extracurricular activities, and the diseases one might contract as a result of a night of pleasure. They all laughed – Paco could tell a very entertaining story.

One morning Mark showed up for breakfast a little late, brimming with excitement. Paul was the only one in the cook shack, and he couldn't miss Mark's beaming face.

"I waited until Paco was gone so we could talk about this," Mark said. "It's about the jar!"

They hadn't mentioned the canopic jar to Paco. They'd wrapped it in cloth and hidden it for now. They'd discuss whether to tell him about it after the DNA results came back.

Paul was excited too. "What did you find out?"

"The material's not only organic, it's human, just as I expected from its being in a jar like that. And get ready for this. There's a DNA match. There's DNA already on file that matches perfectly – one hundred percent. He's

Egyptian and he's a big, big deal!" He stopped with a huge grin.

Paul didn't understand. "Wait a minute. You're saying what's in the jar matches the DNA of somebody who died a thousand years or more ago? And the DNA of that person is on file in a database somewhere? How's that possible? Who was the guy who died?"

Paco stepped inside the shack. He saw how eager they both looked and noticed Mark was holding his cell phone.

"Good news?"

Mark gave Paul a "should we tell him?" glance.

Paul replied, "Tell us, for God's sake! I want to know myself!"

"Sit down, Paco. I have something to show you. I apologize that we held back this discovery, but we wanted to wait until we had confirmation as to what it was."

He held up the jar and explained how its presence appeared to confirm that Egyptians had been here in the distant past.

"Jars that look just like this – canopic jars – were used to hold the organs of the deceased pharaohs. They were always buried in the tombs with their bodies. This is different. It's not a canopic jar although it's almost identical to one. It has the image of the chief god Amun, and there was a mummified piece of something inside. We sent a sample to a lab for DNA testing, and we just got the results!"

"Your smiles look like children on Christmas morning," Paco said. "It must be good news!"

Mark continued dramatically. "Inside a jar that was inside a cavern at Piedras Negras, Guatemala, is the heart of Tutankhamun, pharaoh of Egypt, who died around 1323

BC – thirty-five hundred years ago. Don't ask me how or why, but that's absolutely what it is!"

Paul was stunned. "My God! I knew it had to be Egyptian, but ... Why in hell is it here? Who brought it?"

"I'd hoped the glyphs might give us a clue. The Egyptians told stories in pictures, as you know, but this one is identical to one in the burial chamber of King Tut in Egypt – nothing more, nothing less except the addition of a single cartouche bearing his name. We can examine this mystery for the rest of our lives, but I'd be willing to bet we'll never learn the answer. There's never been a pharaoh whose body and possessions were more thoroughly examined than Tut's. Since they found him in 1922, one group after another has subjected his corpse to every scientific examination known to man."

He asked the men if they'd ever heard that Tut was buried without his heart. They hadn't, so he told them the story.

"In 2014, news agencies worldwide reported that new evidence showed Tutankhamun was buried with an erect penis and without a heart scarab, the amulet that was placed in every king's chest cavity to take the place of his heart. Scientists thought both of these were to make him more like the god Osiris, whose erect penis was the symbol of his prowess and whose heart was removed and hidden. Akhenaten and his son Tut were considered heretics for believing in only one god – Aten. Tut was just a boy, and his advisors succeeded in converting him back to polytheism. The 2014 theory was that Tut's erect penis and missing heart made him like the god Osiris, more pleasing to enter the afterlife than the heretic monotheist his father had made him."

"Interesting story," Paco commented. "But how does that explain the heart ending up here, a continent and an ocean away from Egypt?"

"That's the mystery. Who took the trouble – who even knew the route – to get here? And there's one more enigma that's part of all this. Do you know why every single pharaoh except Tutankhamun has been buried with a heart scarab?"

They didn't.

"Because without a heart, the embalmed king can't enter heaven. Without a heart, or the heart scarab to represent it, the pharaoh is doomed to the underworld forever."

Paul was amazed. He'd never heard any of this. "So you're saying …"

"I'm saying somebody stole Tut's heart and hid it so far away that nobody could ever take it back to Egypt. Somebody had it in for him in a big way. Without his heart, King Tut went to hell."

CHAPTER FIFTY

Mark and Paul randomly picked twenty plates. There were nearly twelve hundred in all – the rest still sat on the shelves exactly where they'd been all these centuries. Mark took detailed photos of the twenty and sent them to his colleagues in Toronto.

The researchers at the university had strict instructions to keep the project confidential. They had forty close-up photos – one for each side of the plates – showing some type of etched markings and drawings. The archaeologist gave them one more caveat – keep an open mind. Don't assume anything about the photos just because he was sending them from Guatemala.

University officials and Mark's staff knew he was back in the jungle at Piedras Negras under a concession granted by the Guatemalan government. They didn't know details of how the granting of that license happened, but they were aware he was working there. The photos almost had to have been taken at the site, but the researchers did as Mark asked. They didn't jump to conclusions. Instead, they examined the inscriptions without considering possible origins.

Given the layout of the etchings on the plates, the researchers presumed these marks were letters. If they were looking at a language, the university's computers could decipher it. They spent a week breaking apart the photos into single units, some perhaps letters and others glyph-like pictures. The forty photos yielded over a thousand single units that they uploaded into the university's computers.

The computer determined that the forty photos were in fact forty written pages, most containing both letters and pictures. As in modern languages, some letters appeared more often and others less so. The translation into English was a surprise. They read the first line:

Jfkme fjild 010101 nbd kn 00011001111010100 xhgft mkpbr 010100000100100111

The language on the plates was a highly advanced combination of binary code and words, the computer determined. The "0101" code was instantly familiar to the team's computer programmers. Nothing made sense in English, the computer determined, because the foreign words were written in a language so advanced that English was simply too basic for a translation. So the researchers asked for a comparison to every other known language.

The results were both astonishing and frustrating. It was as if a person speaking English tried to translate a book into a language that consisted only of grunts and clicks. The words on the plates were so sophisticated that there wasn't even one corresponding word in any language on Earth.

The team then turned to the glyph-like pictures interspersed among the letters. But there were no answers there either – the computer offered nothing that would explain them.

The team relayed the information back to Dr. Linebarger in the jungles of Guatemala. They had no idea the metal plates were found in a room that had been sealed shut ages ago. Whatever language was on these plates, it had to be nearly four thousand years old … if not far, far older than that.

The secrets of the ages, the knowledge an ancient civilization wanted to impart to future generations, was written in a language so highly advanced – so sophisticated – that the people of Earth weren't yet able to understand it in the twenty-first century.

There was so much more to be done here. Three months had passed in a flash, and the men working in the cavern hadn't even begun investigating the complicated instruments and machines that sat on the pedestals. That would happen over the next several months, but for now time was up for one of them. Paco was leaving soon.

CHAPTER FIFTY-ONE

Payday was at noon each Saturday; then the local workers had that afternoon and Sunday off. At midday on Saturdays a longboat arrived and took as many as wanted to go back to Frontera Corozal for a brief return to civilization. On Sunday at two they boarded the boat in town, arriving back at Bird Monster's statue around seven. That gave the men an hour to walk to the site before night fell.

On this particular Saturday there was a second longboat. This time everyone was going to town for R&R. Even the security guards needed a break – they hadn't been off-site in a month. Paco asked the minister to send five replacements for the weekend shift. They arrived on one of the boats that took everyone else back.

Paul, Mark and Paco had worked together for three months. As much as they'd dreaded the minister's watchdog showing up, Paco turned out to be both a pleasant addition to the mix and a major help. They'd taken him into their confidence, disclosing personal theories, ideas and conjecture about what Piedras Negras was all about.

Each Saturday Paco sent a weekly briefing to the minister, and he always gave Mark and Paul an advance look. The reports were complimentary of the men and their efforts to advance Guatemalan archaeology.

They had no idea that the reports were fictitious. The minister neither knew nor cared what was going on at Piedras Negras. He'd been paid a small fortune to mind his own business and he hadn't communicated with Paco in the three months since he arrived.

Today their time together would be over. "The floatplane's picking me up tomorrow at four," Paco said yesterday. That evening they'd had a going-away dinner complete with roast tapir one of the workers had killed. There was a lot of beer and a lot of stories.

Paco spent the morning packing up his gear for the trip back. At eleven the contingency of workmen and guards left the site, heading down the trail to the river. Two hours later the five replacement security men arrived.

"I'll show them around," Mark said as Paco lugged his cases out of the bunkhouse.

Finally it was time to go. Paco wanted a last look. "I suppose I'd better take a final opportunity to absorb this incredible room."

The three went down the pathway they'd traversed so many times lately, crawled through the tunnel and went through the doorway in the painted wall. They stood in the Crypt of the Ancients – a place they now were certain was one of the three Halls of Records of the Atlantean people. A bonus was the wall of glyphs and the Amun jar, providing conclusive proof that Egyptians had come to Mesoamerica too.

Each of them stood, lost in his own thoughts, until Paco said, "There are a few things I want to tell you. Do you remember the Egyptian jar you kept a secret from me until you knew more about me? Well, I have kept a secret or two of my own."

He stepped back, drew a pistol and said, "Toss your guns to me." He gathered them up and threw them back through the doorway into the other room.

"Paco! What's going on?" Mark was both surprised and afraid. He couldn't believe what was happening. "What the hell? Why are you pulling a gun on us?"

Paul said nothing; he watched the man's eyes and waited for an opportunity.

"I'm afraid I haven't been entirely truthful with you gentlemen about my motives. My name is Francisco Garcia and I am a wealthy man. That part is true. I did sell my company for many millions of dollars. Some other things about me I did not mention. I am the person behind the largest narcotics cartel in Central America. That has nothing to do with my time here in the jungle with you. It's merely background so you will understand who and what I am. The Minister of Archaeology has secrets – bad secrets. I have known them for some time, and thanks to my discretion, he keeps both his job and his reputation.

"Mark, he told me everything about your presentation, the Egyptian wall and what might be behind it. I was fascinated – I wanted to know more. I told him to appoint me as his representative for your concession and he was happy to comply. I also paid him money to forget everything he knows about Piedras Negras. He will do as I say when I am ready to show the world this discovery. The minister is a stupid man, but thanks to me, his secrets are protected.

"Oh yes, there is one more thing. I am the largest financial backer of the rebel movement in Guatemala. My little brother was also heavily involved with them. He became greedy – he struck out on his own. He forgot about the cause that had been his passion. He wanted everything for himself and he paid the ultimate price for his foolishness. Fortunately he gave me passwords, codes and bank information, just in case something happened to him, so the ransom money wouldn't be lost forever. My younger brother's name was Juan. Juan Garcia. Do you remember him, Paul? The man you knew as Rolando? The man you killed?" He fired once and Paul fell to the ground.

He turned to Mark. "You, *Señor* Archaeologist, have made an incredible discovery. It's a pity you won't be able to take credit for the wonderful things you found here in this cavern. I agree completely with you that this is the Crypt of the Ancients. Once someone interprets the metal plates, I'm certain we will begin to learn the secrets of Atlantis, because in my mind there's nothing else this could be. Someone else will discover all this once I decide it's time. It will be *my* discovery, *my* glory. And now you may join your friend. Bon voyage to hell." He fired and Mark collapsed.

Paco ducked through the doorway into the cavern. Five guards stood waiting for instructions.

"Close the door."

It took the combined efforts of all six to push the stone into place. At last it was wedged tightly back where it had originally been. They walked out, leaving two bodies behind the sealed wall.

CHAPTER FIFTY-TWO

As soon as the door began to slide back into the wall, Paul turned on his flashlight. Except for its narrow beam, the room was totally dark.

"Mark! Are you okay?"

"Yeah. I got a whack in my chest, but I'm good. I don't know what the hell happened. I thought you were dead and he missed me. I tried to lie still, hoping he wouldn't shoot me again. So how are we alive?"

"I loaded his gun with blanks. You were closer than I was, so you got a thump when he shot you. I'm glad you decided to play dead. If you hadn't, he'd have killed us with our own guns."

"How the hell did you manage the blanks?"

Paul had been cautious from the minute he learned the ministry was sending someone. When Paco arrived and Paul noticed the weapon he carried, he placed an order for blanks. A couple of days later the shells arrived in a crate of supplies on the daily floatplane.

"I was simply being careful with a guy we didn't know from Adam. One afternoon when he was taking a shower, I loaded his pistol with blanks. It was so long ago I'd almost forgotten it. When we all got to be friends, I thought about telling him, but I decided to let it go. It wouldn't hurt for just you and me to have the real ammo."

"Thank God for that. So what do we do now? How do we get out of here? The two of us can't possibly move the door."

"Let's talk this through, but first let me show you something that might ease your mind a little." He walked to the back of the room where several duffel bags were tossed into a pile. He picked one out at random. "Take a look," he said. "We have enough food and water for several days. Extra batteries and flashlights too, plus sleeping bags."

"My God," the archaeologist marveled. "You're like a magician! How in hell ..."

"That stack of duffels has been back there all along. They're full of our tools and instruments. I added provisions several weeks ago in case anybody got hurt or stranded by a cave-in or something. Remember my mentioning that if you ever got stuck in here, don't forget the packs? I even mentioned it to Paco. I guess he doesn't think we'll need rations since he's killed us."

"I'd forgotten all about that. Looks like you thought of everything."

"Maybe not. Our biggest challenge is getting through that stone door. There's no way we can do it from this side. It'd take the winch for two of us to move it."

"The longboat will bring everyone back tomorrow night from town, right?"

"That's the plan. But what about Paco and the security guards? They're obviously working for him – right?"

"Yes, but I don't know what they're going to do next. I guess they'll leave – there's a plane picking him up at four, and it can hold all six of them. If our men return and see no one here, I think they'd pull the stone out with the winch to see what happened in this room."

"And if Paco doesn't leave?"

"That makes things more complicated. There are twenty of our guys and only six of Paco's. But our men are unarmed and they won't be prepared for an ambush, so Paco could overpower them. But then ..." Paul paused, thinking through his comments.

"But if he kills them, he's got bodies all over the place. Too many people know there's something going on here. All the workmen will talk to their friends and families this weekend. They'll tell them what we've found. So Paco can't kill them and he can't take them hostage. What else can he do?"

Paul didn't mention a thought he'd had. There was something Paco could do that would effectively doom them. That one thing would be the worst scenario possible. And that was exactly what Paco had in mind.

CHAPTER FIFTY-THREE

On Sunday afternoon at two p.m., twenty men waited on the boat dock at Frontera Corozal, happy and comfortable after a weekend relaxing in town. Some had spent quality time with their families, others had hit the bars all night long, and some regaled their friends with stories of the wondrous discovery at Piedras Negras. Everyone was energized from a weekend off as they waited to return to the site.

They saw Paco walking down the concrete staircase from the parking lot high above. They were surprised he was there; he'd said he was going back to Guatemala City yesterday, his work at Piedras Negras over.

"I have some bad news," he said as the men gathered around him. "The Minister of Archaeology in Guatemala City has withdrawn the concession for Dr. Linebarger's company. Apparently there were some improprieties involving Mr. Silver's background that were not properly disclosed when the concession was issued. So you won't be going back to Piedras Negras today. Or ever again, for that matter. The site will be closed for some time until the minister can make other arrangements. Security guards will remain there to patrol the area."

The men began to talk among themselves. This was distressing news; they had made more money in the past three months than they would usually get in two years. Mesoamerican Research Group had paid the workers well.

"What about us?" one asked with concern.

"The minister has taken care of you. He was afraid the Americans might not pay everyone, so the concession requires that all workmen would receive three months' pay if they are fired through no reason of their own. There is money set aside to pay you."

Some of the men clapped at the news. "Three months' pay!" one said. "What work will we be doing to earn that money?"

"Nothing. It is called severance. It's money you will receive because you were fired from your job. The day after tomorrow I will be here with the funds to pay you in cash."

The entire story was a fabrication. The minister hadn't cancelled the concession. There was no severance clause nor any money set aside to pay the workmen. Paco would come here the day after tomorrow and pay the men three months' wages from the ransom money he'd gotten from his brother's account.

The workers would be happy that they'd been fairly treated by the minister, and they would wonder what the Americans had done to cause their concession to be cancelled. But they would not go back to Piedras Negras. There was no reason. They would move on to other work, other things, other places.

Paco's statement about the presence of security guards was true. Within two weeks he'd post sentries until he decided when and how to disclose the Crypt of the Ancients to the world. As for himself, he planned to spend the next several weeks at a luxury resort in Cabo; he'd had enough of the jungle in the past three months to last a lifetime.

Paco Garcia paid the workers and then boarded a floatplane to Tuxtla Gutierrez, where he caught an Aeromexico flight to Guatemala City. He met with the minister and handed him an envelope that bought another year of looking the other way. No one from the government would set foot in Piedras Negras until Paco Garcia said yes.

———

Paul and Mark explored every square inch of the Crypt of the Ancients and realized there was no other way out. They were stuck until someone removed the rock door from the other side. Without a winch, there was no way it could be done from where they stood.

As Paul walked the perimeter of the room, deep in thought, Mark reflected that he'd rather be trapped with this ingenious man than anyone else he knew. If someone could come up with a way out, Paul could.

Mark was an archaeologist, accustomed to dealing in facts, not hopeful speculation. He could see no solution for them. The fact was they were trapped unless someone opened the rock door. Tomorrow was Sunday, the day the workers were supposed to return from town. If that happened – if Paco hadn't scuttled those plans – they had a chance. The next twenty-four hours would give them freedom – or not.

How ironic, he thought, that his entire life had been spent in scientific pursuits and archaeological discoveries. He dealt in facts, logic and pragmatism, but today he faced a new reality. He stood in a room full of complex scientific instruments undoubtedly created by a highly-advanced culture thousands of years ago.

How about that *for scientific logic?*

Paul spoke at last. "There are two things we should do. We should try to move the shelves that hold all the metal plates. Maybe there's a tunnel or another room behind one of them. We also need to see what all these instruments do." He swept his hand around the room. "We have nothing to lose even if something goes wrong."

Mark reluctantly agreed but cautioned Paul about the devices. "What if we cause, say, a nuclear detonation using one of these things? There's no telling how sophisticated they are or what they're supposed to do."

"You have a point, but I say it's a chance we have to take. Let's look at the walls first. Maybe we won't need to try out the devices."

They removed dozens of metal plates from the nearest shelf, carefully stacking them on the dirt floor nearby. Each unit was basically a bookcase with eight perfectly rectangular horizontal shelves. They examined this one closely – there were no visible seams, pegs or nails to indicate how it was put together. It looked like one solid unit, and they had no idea what it was made of. It wasn't wood or metal. It might have been a type of lightweight stone or even an artificial material. Paul used the word "man-made" and Mark laughed. "I guess these were men. They were far, far more advanced than we are. I can almost believe they came from space before I can accept there was a civilization this advanced whose technology just disappeared in a cataclysmic event. But here we are!"

The back of the case was solidly up against the rock wall and they couldn't move it. Perhaps it was attached,

Paul mused, but it also could have been so heavy it wouldn't budge.

There was a short crowbar in one of Paul's duffels. They stuck it behind the case as best they could, then attempted to pry. No matter how much effort they gave it, the case didn't shift an inch.

They went to the other side and tried the last bookcase on that end, with exactly the same results. They called it quits for today, ate a little food, rolled out the sleeping bags, and turned off the flashlights to conserve batteries.

After a night of dreams about being caught in a trap, Mark woke and checked the luminous dial of his watch. Six o'clock on Sunday morning. Today was the day they'd learn if anyone was coming for them. He was apprehensive.

This morning they agreed to examine the thirteen complex machines. Given that these were unique, maybe the rarest things on Earth, Mark was reluctant to handle them. But now there was no alternative.

Paul took out a pad and pen to record what happened with each device they tested. He would shoot a picture of each with his phone.

"I'm glad you're optimistic," Mark commented when he saw Paul preparing to take notes. "I hope we'll need those later. Right now what we need to find is a levitation machine."

He picked up the nearest instrument, a foot-long metal wand an inch in diameter. "It'd be nice to aim this thing at that rock door and say the magic words that make the stone slide out all by itself."

On another stand Paul saw a smooth white cylinder that looked like a piece of PVC pipe. It was nearly two feet long and sealed seamlessly on both ends. There was only one protrusion on its entire surface – a small round knob.

Mark said, "We'd better do these one at a time since we have no idea what's going to happen." Paul put the cylinder back and Mark went first. He ran his hands over the smooth surface of the wand. There were no buttons to push, so he put both hands on it and turned them in opposite directions. A bright green beam shot out of one end. As he rotated the wand more, the beam got wider.

"It looks like a laser!" Paul yelled. "I can't believe it! We might have our solution in the very first try."

Mark took the device to the rock door and began to run its light along the seam. Nothing happened; the beam merely reflected off the rock surface.

"That didn't work," Mark commented as he swung the beam around the room. It hit one of the packs.

"Watch out! Look at that!"

Where the beam had hit the cloth rucksack, the material simply disappeared. It looked similar to a welding torch burning metal, but it was totally different. Where the beam hit, there was a blank space – no scorching, no searing – just an empty place where something had been before.

Mark turned off the beam. "Let's try an experiment." He took an empty can from last night's dinner, widened the beam and aimed it at the can sitting on the floor. The light engulfed the entire thing and it was gone in an instant.

"So what's the purpose of this thing?" Paul wondered out loud as Mark fiddled with the device, turned off the beam, and then worked his hands along the shaft of the wand in the opposite direction from before.

"What the …!" He jumped as another beam appeared from the wand's tip, this one bright red. He aimed the wand into a corner, turned its shaft, and watched as the empty can appeared along with the missing part of the rucksack.

"I'll be damned," Paul said. "It's a kind of teleportation device. Let's test it on the rock."

"The beam's not big enough to cover the rock. Besides, it didn't seem to work on the rock earlier anyway."

"Can we try? What do we have to lose, except our lives?"

Mark brought up the green beam on its widest setting and shone it directly on the lower corner of the huge stone. Nothing happened. He reset the wand to the red beam and aimed it at another corner. Nothing.

Disappointed, he muttered, "It doesn't work on rock. Wonder if it works on people?"

"I thought of that too," Paul replied. "Problem is, it doesn't look like it goes through rock. Presuming it didn't kill us, all we could do is move ourselves around this cavern. That doesn't get us out of here."

Despite that, Paul was heartened that one of the devices actually worked after who knew how many years in this cave. He made notes about the instrument and said, "There may be something else we can do with that one. Let's try the next."

The PVC-like cylinder sat on its pedestal. Paul slowly turned the knob on its side, but nothing happened. He picked it up, aimed it at the ceiling and tried again. Nothing.

"Maybe it's a dud," Mark said, walking to the third pedestal. He picked up something familiar – a two-foot-high candelabrum with a base and seven arms. There were no obvious buttons or knobs, so he ran his hands over every inch of its surface. He twisted and turned, but once again this device didn't respond.

"We're going to get a lot of that, I'll bet," Paul commented. "We're using today's mentality on how things turn on and off, applying that to these machines. Maybe it takes mental telepathy. We may have to *think* to make them turn on. All we can do is keep trying. At least we have one that works."

Lunch was quick because they had rationed food and water from the beginning. The supplies they had might last several days – maybe even a week or more – but they were already careful. They had no idea how much time they'd be locked in this cavern.

They examined the eighth instrument and recorded their findings – or lack of findings, to be precise. The first device was the only one so far that had done anything.

Paul moved on to the next machine, a rectangular box about two feet high and four feet long that resembled a cigar humidor. Its top was inlaid with something like glass. They peered inside and saw perplexing dials and gears.

"Looks like my grandmother's music box," Mark joked.

"It's incredibly intricate," Paul commented. "This music box must play the theme from *Star Wars*!"

Where they'd had no knobs before, this thing had a dozen of them, arranged across the bottom of the front panel. Paul turned one, then another. "Wish we had the operator's manual," he said idly. He jumped back as a wide shaft of light suddenly appeared through the glass top. It projected a pure white TV-like screen on the ceiling.

Mark suggested turning more dials. "Maybe you have to choose a channel."

The last dial made audible clicks as Paul turned it slowly. The screen didn't change at first, but as Paul kept turning, it began to glow with an azure hue. Mark moved toward the shaft of light coming out of the lid, and Paul grabbed him. "What are you doing?"

"I was going to put my hand in the shaft and see if it reflected on the screen up there," he replied, pointing to the ceiling.

"Before we practice on ourselves, let's see what that shaft does to something else." He took out a wooden pencil and stuck the end of it into the bright light.

The tip of the pencil disintegrated instantly and a faint burning smell hung in the air.

"Shit! I could have burned my hand off," Mark shouted. "Thanks for stopping me!"

Paul was deep in thought. "So what's this for? Is it a transmitter? Or a receiver? Is it like a television or a video recorder? And why is the beam so hot that it burned the pencil in a second?"

"Look!" Mark stared at the ceiling.

There was a faint, grainy picture that reminded Mark of old 35mm movies shown on a projector. They could make out what might be trees, but everything was dim and distorted.

"Let's see if we can make this thing project onto something closer than the ceiling," Mark said. "I think that's what's making it so fuzzy."

Paul put the pencil on the side of the device's lid and nothing happened. "That part's not hot. As long as we keep away from the beam and the glass top, I think we'll be okay." They slowly raised the lid; now the top was at a ninety-degree angle to the box. The beam somehow made the right-angle turn – it still projected through the lid – and now it appeared on the side of a bookshelf four feet away. The picture was vivid and sharp.

What they saw resembled a landscape painting from the 1800s. There were tall trees around a crystal blue river, nearby fields overflowing with flowers. It was an idyllic scene.

"Is this thing a visual photo album?"

"I doubt it," Paul replied, looking closely at the knobs. "I'd bet it does more, given the complexity of everything in here." He turned the click dial again and the picture disappeared. Seconds later they were astounded to see a new series of images – a video display – appear on the bookshelf.

Mark quietly said, "I'll be damned. So much for Thomas Edison inventing the motion picture camera."

The location was the same as in the single picture they'd seen before. It was a pasture filled with bright green grass; purple, blue and red flowers everywhere; and cattle in a shady spot under a tree. They watched silently for nearly two minutes as the cameraman – if that's who filmed this video – panned the area all around him. When it ended, the screen went dark.

"Looks like the Hudson Valley in upstate New York," Mark commented. "That could have been taken today, it looks so modern."

"You're right but with no frame of reference – no buildings, people, clothing, vehicles or anything else – there's no way to tell how old it is. I didn't see anything man-made, like fences or even a feeding trough for the cows. Did you?"

"No. Want to know what I think this is?"

Paul was coming up with his own ideas but wanted to hear Mark. "Shoot."

"I'll bet there are dozens, maybe hundreds of video clips on here. I'll bet there are people who are imparting information about their civilization, for the people of the future to see and understand."

"So you're convinced this came from Atlantis?"

Mark nodded. "Even more than before. This is sophisticated technology, and it still works after thousands of years. Once we get out of here, we need to watch everything –"

Paul interrupted, "Absolutely, but for now we have to keep looking. I don't see how Netflix Atlantean-style will help us get out." They moved to the tenth instrument – they had only four to go and Paul was getting discouraged, although he kept his thoughts to himself.

Mark felt the same way. "I guess it's my turn," he said as he stepped to the next pedestal. It held a shiny blue metal gun with a very large barrel. "Looks like it could shoot a flare." He picked it up with the barrel toward him and peered inside. "The barrel's got something in it – I guess this thing's loaded!"

"Could it be one of these?" Paul stood at the next pedestal, where item number eleven should be, and held up one of six four-inch-long cylinders. When he compared it to the barrel of the gun, it was exactly the correct size.

"We've got a weapon of some type –"

Paul jumped in, "Or a tool ..."

"-- and extra ammo. What do you think? Want to try it out?"

They talked for a few minutes then took a break for more food. According to Paul's watch, it was eight in the evening; they'd need to sleep soon to keep their bodies on a schedule.

"Shooting that gun could be fatal for us," Mark commented. "We have no idea what it does. What if it fills this cavern with poisonous gas? Or releases a nerve agent that paralyzes us?"

Paul had the same concern, but he looked at the reality of their predicament. He brought up the subject they'd both avoided all day.

"The workmen should be returning to Piedras Negras just about now, presuming they left town at two p.m. like they were supposed to. Within an hour or so they should notice we're missing, start looking for us and come to the cave. We have no idea if Paco sealed off the entrance some way, or if he fired our crew, or if he plans to kill them all when they come back." He held up the granola bar he was munching. "Tomorrow's the third day. If we ration food and water a lot more than we are now, we may have enough for three or four more days. Then it starts to be a big problem.

"Here's my suggestion. On the off chance that gun will kill us somehow, let's wait until tomorrow to see what kind of firepower it really has. If we're going to be rescued, it should happen by then. Tomorrow at noon – how does that sound? Either we're already out of here or we try out our new toy."

Mark added, "And tomorrow at noon we lay out all our food and water and decide how to ration everything."

"Agreed. I hope it doesn't come to that, but we need to be prepared. Tonight we sleep. Tomorrow we look at items twelve and thirteen. At noon we come back to the gun and the ammo if we're still locked in here."

Both of them slept lightly, listening throughout the night for any sound of rescue from beyond the stone door. But there was nothing. The next morning they ate breakfast and went straight to work, neither of them mentioning a word about the fate that was becoming more certain with each passing hour. No one was here. They couldn't depend on anyone but themselves now.

Device number twelve was a perfect orb possibly made of glass or maybe highly polished metal. It was a smooth sphere with no indentations or protrusions. After a close examination they set it back, unable to figure out how to make it do something.

Paul picked up the final instrument and said, "Speaking as a twenty-first-century American, I'd say this is a remote control." It was black, around six inches long, two wide and two deep. It had fourteen buttons and a tiny joystick. The back was smooth – there were no batteries for this ancient device – and it was very lightweight. "Shall I press a button?"

Mark muttered, "Why not? At this point what do we have to lose?"

Paul felt exactly the same way although he kept his thoughts to himself. "Here goes nothing." He pressed the center button and held it down firmly.

"We have liftoff!" Mark shouted. "Look at that!"

The sphere that had been on pedestal number twelve hovered an inch above the surface, pulsating in alternating hues of yellow, green and pink. Paul grasped the little joystick between two fingers and moved it. The ball rose about six feet, then slowly flew right and left as he rotated the control.

Paul took his hand off the joystick and the airborne orb paused, waiting for a command. "Wonder what else it can do?" he said. He pressed another button.

The ball shot to the right and hit the rock wall with a resounding crack. It appeared unharmed; it merely floated in the air against the wall, still changing colors every few seconds.

Mark said, "That was interesting, but I don't see that helping us out. Try another button."

Paul used the stick to position the ball in the middle of the cavern about ten feet off the ground. He pressed a button, then another. "Write down what these do!" he yelled as the ball spun wildly one time and flashed a steady bright orange the next. Paul called out the button locations on the remote as he tried each one.

When he pressed the next one, a set of long tubes popped out of the ball's left side. "Hold it!" Mark shouted. "What the hell are those?"

Paul moved the ball across the room until it was in front of the stone door. He carefully positioned it so the tubes were aimed at its seam and then pressed the next button.

A green laser beam shot from each of the tubes. Where they hit the rock, it began to crumble.

"Now we're getting somewhere!" Mark said excitedly.

Before long, they knew this device wouldn't be their salvation. It was too small to significantly affect the huge rock. Besides whatever else it did, it was obviously a laser cutter, but it wasn't strong enough. Paul pressed every button on the remote in hopes one would intensify the beams, but nothing worked. The little device chugged along, but after an hour they'd cut only a foot of seam half an inch deep. It would take months to cut through the door – if the device had enough power to operate that long – but they had only days left.

It was noon. They cut their portions in half, laid out the rest, and agreed on rations for the future. They had enough food and water for three more days. They already were growing weaker as the lack of calories began to take its toll. Neither mentioned that rescue was now unlikely, but both knew their time was running out.

Mark said, "Before we try the gun, I have a suggestion. Let's go back to square one. Let's take the first thing – that little wand that's a teleportation device – and see if we can move one of the bookshelves."

Paul liked the idea. Mark held the wand as before, and he expanded the green beam until it covered the bookshelf completely. Within seconds the shelf disappeared!

"Voila!" Mark said as he moved the wand, reversed his hands, and played the red beam out against a blank wall. The bookshelf appeared there, on the opposite side of the room.

They ran to examine the wall that had been behind the shelf. There was nothing special; it was exactly like the rest of the cavern. Over another hour they removed metal plates, used the wand to transport four more shelves, and got nowhere.

Frustrated, Paul said, "We can keep going and move every single shelf, or we can stop for now and try the gun. We're not making any progress, but one of these shelves might have a hidden passage behind it. We won't know until we move them all. On the other hand, the gun may blast us out of here. Or kill us."

"I'd just as soon die fast as slowly," Mark replied quietly.

"I think so too. Okay, Wyatt Earp. Hook on your six-gun and let's have a shootout."

"How about you shoot it?" he said to Paul. "I don't want to be the one that kills us both."

"Thanks a lot for giving me that privilege," Paul quipped, his voice happier than he felt. "Go for it. It doesn't matter who does what at this point."

Mark held the weapon in both hands, aimed it at the stone door and pulled the trigger. There was a deafening roar as the projectile shot out and struck the rock. Large chunks of the door fell into the room, but it wasn't enough – it remained in place.

"Watch out!" Paul yelled. Clumps of dirt and rock fell from the ceiling twenty feet above, knocking a couple of the ancient instruments to the floor.

They took a break. Mark said, "The ceiling's unstable because there's not much between us and the surface – maybe three or four feet of dirt and rock. What about aiming the gun at the ceiling? We might blast a hole through the top."

Paul wanted to be optimistic but couldn't find anything positive to offer. "We might, or it might cause a cave-in. We might attract bandits who'd kill us if we weren't already dead from the blast. If everything goes fine and we end up with a hole in the top, we still have to figure out how to get out. The ceiling's twenty feet above us. We don't have ladders or ropes. How's that going to happen?"

Mark snapped, "What do *you* suggest? Lie here in the dark until we starve?"

A minute passed and he said, "I'm sorry. That was uncalled for. I just want to try anything we can to save ourselves."

"We have six pieces of ammo," Paul said at last. "Given what we just saw them do to the door, I feel pretty confident one or two of the shells would open up the ceiling. How about we save a couple and use maybe three to try to break through the door? I think that's our best hope."

Eager to try anything, Mark acquiesced, and within minutes he fired the gun at the top of the door. More rocks and dirt flew into the room, but distressingly, more debris crashed down from the ceiling too. They took cover against the side walls as rocks and soil fell for several minutes in the middle.

When the dust cleared, the room was a disaster. Many of the devices were on the ground. Mark walked through the dirt, picking them up and putting them in a corner while Paul examined the door.

"We've broken through!" he yelled. "Look at this!"

There was a hole a few inches in diameter near the top of the door. Paul looked through. The cave on the other side was dark, but he knew they'd pierced all the way. He began to dig with his hands to widen the opening.

"Look in the packs and bring a pick!" he shouted.

He used the pickaxe for ten minutes, but made little progress. The door was rock solid even though part had been blown away. In Paul's weakened physical state, the exertion was draining. Mark took a turn; after half an hour they knew they had to fire the gun one more time. It would take one of the bullets to open this rock door enough to crawl through.

For the third time Mark stood in front of the door, aimed the gun and pulled the trigger.

———

Mark was the first to awaken. He didn't know where he was, only that he was covered head to toe in something very heavy. He breathed in gasps and started to move his hand up to his face. One palm was mere inches from his

287

head, but his hands wouldn't budge. As he lay there, he remembered what had happened. A second after he fired the weapon, there was a deafening roar, then blackness.

He was trapped. The ceiling must have fallen in.

He realized one of his legs was free. He could move it right and left, up and down. He tried to shake it loose, but from his hip to his head he was weighted down by dirt.

He passed out for an hour ... or maybe a day. He had no concept of anything at this point except the reality of being buried alive. He fought panic; he felt he should conserve energy, although he didn't know why. He was going to die. If it were soon, it would be better.

At some point, Mark heard a muffled sound. Maybe it was a voice. Maybe Paul's voice, maybe not. It was hard to hear, but it was unmistakably there. He listened for a few minutes then lost consciousness again.

Paul was trapped ten feet away. When the collapse happened, he was knocked to the ground and a pedestal landed partly on him. That saved him from being crushed by a stone that fell twenty feet from the ceiling and was now atop him as well. He was in a small pocket, dirt all around and his torso pinned in by the pedestal. He called out to Mark but heard nothing. He used his hands to see how much dirt was on top of him. A lot of it fell into the area where he lay and he was afraid he'd suffocate since he had no idea how far below the debris he was. He tried again. He scratched at the dirt and some fell, and then he saw daylight. There was almost no dirt covering him; it was the pedestal that trapped him.

Paul could see his watch, so he knew when a day passed, then a second one. Nobody came to check on them. Paco hadn't posted sentries at Piedras Negras yet, so nobody heard the roar when the collapse happened.

Paul lay immobile on the rough floor, his stomach rumbling. Time was running out. Now and then he still worked to free himself, and he moved an inch here, an inch there. But only an inch or so. He was so hungry, so thirsty, that he wouldn't be able to muster strength to try much longer.

Maybe it was easy to starve to death. Maybe it was as simple as falling asleep and never waking up. Was Mark still alive? If so, he must be trapped too. For Mark's sake and for his own, he hoped the end would be quick.

He lay in the dark. He was hungry, thirsty and very tired. He knew what was happening – his body was beginning to shut down. He closed his eyes.

It won't be long. I can already feel it coming. It feels like someone pulling a blanket over me. Warm.

He slept.

POSTSCRIPT

Facts about Edgar Cayce and Piedras Negras, Guatemala

The Mayan city of Piedras Negras was first explored in the 1930s by archaeologists from the University of Pennsylvania. That team determined it had been built in the Mayan Pre-classic Era, around 400–600 BC. But the highly controversial psychic Edgar Cayce said the site was much, much older. In his readings he revealed that the Atlanteans built a Hall of Records here twelve thousand years ago. The scientific community scoffed at the sensational ramblings of a mystic in a hypnotic trance. They worked with facts. They dug; explored; observed writing and art, pottery and architecture; and developed their theories rationally.

What's interesting is that both Cayce and the scientists could be right. The Hall of Records Cayce saw in his trance has never been found. He stated that the knowledge of the ages was deposited in a location near the Mexican state of Yucatan. That could be almost anywhere in hundreds of square miles. But Edgar Cayce had more to say about the Hall of Records and this information was quite specific. In one of his trances he said that the

Pennsylvania archaeologists had actually found evidence of it at Piedras Negras in the 1930s.

That would have been news to the archaeologists themselves. They were scientists, not mystics. They would have laughed at the suggestion they had discovered something linking the site to Atlantis. It's true that the diggers did unearth several ancient buildings, many dangerously unstable after so many years in the always-encroaching jungle. No one knew how old those buildings might be – some could have predated the Mayan civilization by thousands of years. If that were true, could Atlanteans have built them?

The team excavated the cores of only a few structures, but they made significant discoveries in the site as a whole, including a stone weighing almost two tons that had originally adorned the top of a temple. It was covered with hieroglyphs and ranked as one of the most significant finds in the history of that area. To date no one has translated those mysterious glyphs. Are they in a previously unknown tongue? No one knows.

In addition to the ancient buildings, there are caves around Piedras. Looters have entered some of them, and BYU archaeologists explored others. There is evidence humans were in the caves long ago, although so far no one has spent the time to determine who they were or when they were there. Some say the Olmecs visited long before the Mayans built temples at Piedras Negras. The Olmec people, whose huge carvings of African heads are puzzling to anthropologists, may have used the cave system for some purpose. Until serious archaeological efforts occur at the site, no one will know for sure.

Edgar Cayce lived for a decade after the Penn archaeology team abandoned Piedras Negras. Several of his trances during that period yielded tantalizing clues as to the possible location of the Atlantean Hall of Records, in areas the archaeologists had named the "South Group" and the "Acropolis." Referring to the records themselves, Cayce said a temple stood near their hiding place and that they were in a cave or crypt. If one believes Edgar Cayce – and many people do – it's conceivable the people from Atlantis could have created a Hall of Records that's been lost for centuries. The Maya could have found the ancient library and then erected the massive temples at Piedras Negras nearby.

Continuing this theory, it's not inconceivable that, after the Mayans also abandoned Piedras Negras, the Hall of Records once again vanished. The jungle is good at reclaiming the meager, futile efforts of men. Civilizations rose and fell, buildings disappeared into forests, and future generations forgot what the elders once had known.

The ruins at Piedras Negras sat in isolation for seventy years after the Penn archaeologists left. The jungle overtook the ancient buildings, covering trails and stone steps with vines and undergrowth until nothing was visible except huge mounds rising through the trees. In the late 1990s a team from Brigham Young University was granted a five-year concession to explore the site. Five years sounds like a long time, but a "year" – one archaeological season in the intense Guatemalan jungle – is roughly three months long. Teams can only work during the times when it's not constantly raining.

Among the more traditional goals, the BYU explorers searched for evidence of the Hall of Records as Cayce had described it. They excavated while fighting off predators of various types, including human bandits who eventually contributed to a decision to cut the expedition short and return to Utah with a plethora of materials they found. Before they left they followed Cayce's clues in an unsuccessful attempt to pinpoint the location of the Hall of Records.

In the twenty-first century Piedras Negras remains remote, inaccessible and forbidding. Many still believe it holds the knowledge of the ages – information that will prove ancient people sailed around the world, educating primitive civilizations in sophisticated techniques.

Only time will tell if the jungle gives up her secrets.

Thank you!

Thanks for reading *The Crypt of the Ancients*. I hope you enjoyed it and **I'd really appreciate a review on Amazon, Goodreads or both.** Even a line or two makes a tremendous difference so thanks in advance for your help!
Please join me on:
Facebook
http://on.fb.me/187NRRP
Twitter
@BThompsonBooks

MAY WE OFFER YOU A FREE BOOK?

Bill Thompson's award-winning first novel, *The Bethlehem Scroll*, can be yours free.

Just go to billthompsonbooks.com, enter your email address and click "Subscribe."

Once you're on the list, you'll receive advance notice of future book releases and other great offers.

Made in the USA
Middletown, DE
30 October 2019